The Game Changer

The Game Changer

J. Sterling

amazon publishing

Printed in the United States of America.

Published by Amazon Publishing
P.O. Box 400818, Las Vegas, NV 89140
ISBN-13: 9781477808665
ISBN-10: 1477808663

This book is dedicated to everyone who fell for a loveable screwup named Jack and refused to let him go. Thank you for wanting more.

ALSO BY J. STERLING

Chance Encounters
In Dreams
The Perfect Game

CONTENTS

Not a Dream

Cassie

I opened my eyes the next morning, half terrified that it had all been a dream . . . albeit a beautifully hot, sweet, romantic dream. My gaze quickly fell on Jack, sprawled on the bed next to me, looking so content as he slept. The mere sight of him made my heart beat in double time, and I resisted the urge to wake him for round two. Or was it three? All the emotions from last night jumbled within me and before I could fully process them, I realized I actually felt happy. Apparently happiness had been eluding me for months now.

My new reality flooded my brain. Jack had appeared at my door last night after six months of no communication wearing a Mets jersey and holding a dozen red roses. He looked me in the eye and told me he was sorry, that he loved me, and that he would earn my trust again. I couldn't believe he was standing there, and it took everything in me to not fall apart at the mere sight of him. I wanted to take him back into my life, but I needed to know that this time it would be forever.

And now he was lying next to me in bed. I had questions about why it took him so long to get here and why he never contacted me, but honestly, at that moment, none of it mattered.

At least, that's what I tried to tell myself.

My questions could wait, but I knew they couldn't wait for long. I didn't have it in me to let things slide without an explanation. And honestly, Jack still had a lot of explaining to do.

Slowly, I rolled out of bed, trying not to wake him. I had just put my feet on the floor when he flung his strong arms around my waist, pulling me back into bed.

"And where do you think you're going?" Jack breathed against my neck.

"Wherever I want, it's my apartment," I fired back with a laugh.

"I didn't say you could leave the bed." He sounded so determined, I couldn't help but snicker.

"I don't need your permission," I shot back, and he rolled on top of me before kissing the tip of my nose.

"You have no idea how much I've missed your feisty attitude."

"Well, I haven't missed the way you try to kill me with your body weight. Ugh, get off."

"I'm trying." His face twisted in a devilish smirk as he slid his hand up the length of my bare thigh.

I swatted his shoulder before rolling my eyes. "You're such a pig."

"Yep. But I'm your pig." He leaned down, pressing his lips against mine. Instinctively, I turned my head from him, narrowing my lips into a tight, impenetrable wall. Jack leaned away from me, rolling onto his side. "What's wrong?"

I smiled, covering my mouth with my hand. "I can't kiss you like that in the morning. I have to brush my teeth first."

He nodded his head in agreement. "You do smell like a dragon."

My jaw fell open, but I quickly snapped it closed, trying my best to breathe as little as possible. "I do not. Shut up!"

He laughed, and I lost myself in his gorgeous dimples. I'd missed those.

"I'm kidding, Kitten. You smell like roses."

"How I ever missed your annoying attitude is beyond me."

"No, it's not. This is what we do. You're a pain the ass, and I put up with you."

"Oh. My. God." I pushed myself up from the bed, throwing him my best dirty look before I scurried out the door.

"I'm teasing! You're a fucking angel for putting up with my shit."

"That's right, I am, and don't you forget it!" I shouted from the hallway.

I brushed my teeth in my tiny, one-person bathroom before returning to the bedroom. Jack hadn't moved a muscle. His blue eyes locked on mine, sending chills of anticipation shooting through my veins. It was crazy how I both loved and hated the effect he had on me. I hated the way he knew what he did to me. But I loved the way he made me feel.

I should probably seek psychiatric help.

Holding back a sigh, I sat on the edge of the bed before reclining on my side and turning to face him.

"What's the matter, Kitten?" He furrowed his brows, two lines forming between them.

"Nothing," I lied.

"I know you better than that, Cass. What is it?"

"I just wanted to ask you something."

"Anything," he said, his tone sincere.

I hesitated, unsure if I wanted to broach this subject already. He had just gotten here. I had just taken him back. But my mind was relentless. It wouldn't stop with the constant demand for answers, and I knew I'd never fully be content until I had them. "What happened after I left California to come to New York?"

"What do you mean?"

"Come on, Jack. It took you six months to get here. Six months!" My tone sounded harsher than I intended, and I watched as he shifted his gaze away from mine. He exhaled slowly and ran his hands through his dark hair.

"I'm sorry, Jack. I just need to talk about this, or I'll bury it inside me and eventually explode."

He looked at me, a small, rueful smile on his face. "No, you're right. You deserve answers."

"Do we have time? I mean, do you have to go the field today?" After all, he was a professional baseball player, and the season was in full swing.

"The team's on the road. They flew me here to get settled instead of flying me there. I have to report in tomorrow morning at ten."

"OK. So, we can talk about this now then?" My pulse raced as nerves filled my body. Jack was here, with me, in my bed. He loved me, and he'd never stopped. So, why was I so nervous?

"What happened after I left for New York?"

"Do you want a play-by-play for the entire six months? I might end up boring you back to sleep."

I rolled my eyes, and he frowned. "Just tell me the good parts."

"If this were a story filled with good parts, Kitten, I would have been here a long time ago," he teased, reaching out to caress my cheek with his thumb.

I leaned into his hand and closed my eyes, lost in the comfort his touch provided. "I meant the parts that made you take so long. Give me the CliffsNotes version," I asked softly, unsure of what words would follow.

Jack snuggled me against him, and began to tell me the story.

◇

And just like that, she was gone. But not before saying the two fucking words that plagued my nightmares. This girl always asked me to "prove it," to prove my love and devotion for her. I deserved it after everything I put her through. She didn't trust me anymore.

I wouldn't trust me either.

It's ironic though, right? That I was the one left standing all alone in a parking lot that time. I swear if my heart could have leaped out of my chest and into my hands, it would have. I imagined that for a moment . . . the blood trickling through my fingertips, splashing onto the concrete below as I watched it slowly pound out its last beats before stopping altogether.

Fuck.

My life does not make sense without this girl. And now she's gone.

Again.

How is it that I'm always losing her?

I unbuttoned my game jersey and let it fall around the top of my uniform's sliding pants. I glanced behind me toward the apartment door at the top of the stairs and slowly started to make my way there, my cleats clanging loudly on the pavement with each step. I wasn't ready to go back to the hotel with my team. Not right then. They'd be celebrating the night's win, and I needed to grieve the night's loss.

The vision of Cassie disappearing from view in that taxi played over and over again in my mind. I closed my eyes, willing the hateful image to disappear. The sound of feminine laughter and my brother's familiar voice woke me from my Cassie-filled daze.

"Oh shit. Jack?" Melissa's sympathy came through loud and clear, both in her eyes and in her tone.

I glanced up at Cassie's best friend standing on the stairs with my little brother. Dean was only a couple years younger than I was, but he'd always be little to me, even if he did almost match my height. My eyes were heavy, my head pounded, and I simply nodded.

"Come on, bro, let's get you inside." Dean wrapped an arm around my back and propelled me up the cement staircase as Melissa unlocked the front door to her apartment and stepped inside.

"Did you see her?" she asked, tossing all her crap on top of the kitchen table.

"I saw her," I responded coolly, adding my hat to the mess as I dropped into a chair at the table.

"Well, what the hell happened? What did she say?" she demanded, gesturing wildly.

"She left." I shrugged. "She's moving to New York."

"Well, of course she's moving to New York," she said, her voice turning cold.

Dean placed a hand on my shoulder, before explaining, "Melissa just means that Cassie has to start living her life for herself. She has to make decisions that have nothing to do with you."

The words hurt like hell. I jerked my head up, glaring at my little brother. "I know that. You think I don't know that?"

"Do you? Do you really, or did you think she'd just leap into your arms and you'd live happily ever after?" Dean shot back, his voice filled with accusation.

A quick huff ripped from my lips, and I smiled sheepishly. "I thought there might be some leaping," I admitted, shrugging one shoulder.

Melissa's usually sweet mouth twisted into a snarl. "That's bullshit, Jack. You expect her to give up her career because you asked her to?"

"I didn't ask her to give up her career. I just figured she'd at least talk to me. Postpone her flight. Give me a fucking chance."

"Like the way you gave her a chance before you married that skank?"

"Melissa," Dean chastised softly, touching her arm in a way that somehow managed to erase the anger from her face.

My chest tightened and my jaw clenched as Melissa's assumptions pierced me like the daggers they were. *"You think it didn't fucking kill me to leave Cassie that night? All I wanted to do was stay with her, beg for her forgiveness and—"*

"But you didn't! You didn't stay with her. You left her crying in a parking lot alone while you left with that bitch!" Melissa screamed as she released every ounce of frustration she'd built up on behalf of Cassie, her recrimination drilling into my skull and my heart.

"I know what I did!" I shouted back, my neck throbbing. *"You think I don't fucking know what I did? I have to live with it every second of every day. I fucked up, OK? We all know I fucked up!"* I slammed my palms against the table and watched as some loose change rattled and rolled onto the carpet below, bringing back memories of my first date with Cassie. My mind filled with the image of her sitting across from me in that small booth in the back of the restaurant. I remembered pulling the paper bag from my jacket and pouring the quarters out onto the tabletop, proud of my cleverness, as several rolled onto the tiled floor below. All of the memories that used to bring me joy now filled my heart with pain.

"It's not enough to just know what you did if you want to make it right. You have to know what it did to her," Melissa said, her voice starting to soften.

I glared at her, willing my temper to subside. *"Tell me."*

"Everyone knew what you'd done by the time Cassie got back from visiting you in Alabama. It was all over the newspapers that you were

getting married. And on Facebook. Did you know that the stupid school magazine she worked for had the balls to call and ask her for pictures of you? They said they only had old ones and wanted to know if she had any newer ones."

"You're kidding?" I spat out in disgust.

"I wish."

My hands balled into fists. "I'll fucking kill them, the inconsiderate little—"

She pointed an accusing finger at me, stopping me in mid-rant. "It wasn't just the newspapers, Facebook, and the magazine. It was everywhere she went. School was the worst. Cassie couldn't even walk across campus without people making comments and snide remarks. She had the most personal and painful moments of her life on display for everyone to see and judge. And trust me, everyone had an opinion about your breakup."

I cringed. Just hearing this was painful enough; I couldn't imagine my girl having to live through it. "I had no idea that was happening or I would have done something to stop it. I would have made sure no one ever said another negative word to her again."

"I'm not telling you this to make you feel bad, Jack. I'm telling you this so you'll understand the repercussions your actions had on her. You made the mistake, but she had to pay for it."

I dropped my head into my hands and pulled at my hair in frustration, my fingers twisting the strands as I fought back the tears forming in my eyes.

"You broke her, Jack." Melissa added the final blow as my stomach dropped to my feet. I'd hurt Cassie in ways I'd never imagined. Ways I'd never meant to. Ways I'd never be able to forgive myself for.

"I broke me too," I admitted, brushing away the lone tear that dared sneak down my face.

"Jack, look." Melissa sat down across from me and folded her arms on the table. *"I love you, I really do. But you have to let her go do this."*

My chest constricted with the truth of her words as I swallowed hard. *"I want her back. I need her. It's either Cassie for me or no one."*

"I'm not the one you have to convince." She reached out her hand, her fingertips brushing over my knuckles before I pulled away.

I ripped my gaze from her bright blue eyes and glanced at my brother. *"I know."*

"She still loves you," Dean said, before taking a pull from his bottle of water. My eyes narrowed and he reacted with, *"What? You don't believe that? She does."*

"It's not about whether or not Cassie loves him," Melissa said.

"It's a little bit about that, otherwise we wouldn't be having this conversation," Dean said with a smile.

"Have you even been paying attention?" she teased, her hair bouncing along her shoulders as she shook her head.

"Dean's right," I said. *"I mean, I wouldn't have a fighting chance if she didn't love me anymore."*

"So, what are you gonna do?" Melissa's expression challenged me.

"First, I'm going to get that marriage annulled. Then I'm going to hop on a plane to New York and get my girl back," I said with new-found determination.

"How?" she asked.

I ran my hand through my hair and let out a huff. *"I don't know yet."*

Uncertainty lingered in the air, awkward in its silence. Pressure gnawed at me, insisting that this time I get it right. If I was going after this girl and begging her for another chance, I'd better make sure it counted. Because if I messed this up, we'd be over for good. I knew at least that much.

"Can I use the bathroom?" I asked before standing, needing an excuse to go into Cassie's room, longing to be surrounded by any parts of her that she left.

"Of course."

"Can I use hers?" I don't know why I was asking if I could use Cassie's bathroom. What the hell was Melissa going to tell me—no? Like I'd listen to her even if she did.

"Uh, yeah," she said, with an eye roll she knew would annoy me.

I stepped into Cassie's bedroom and scanned the walls, my insides aching at the emptiness. All her photos were gone; there wasn't much left aside from her furniture. But then my eyes caught a glimpse of it, and my heart pounded out a ragged beat. I inched toward her bed, sitting down on the edge before reaching for her nightstand. The Mason jar filled with quarters sat there mocking me, almost filled to the top. The same one I'd given her, the quarters intended to "pay" her for every time I touched her. I flashed back to grabbing her arm the first time I saw her at the fraternity party that night. She ripped herself from my grip and practically shouted, "It costs fifty cents every time you touch me. Don't do it again." I wanted that sassy little mouth back in my life.

My eyes refocused on the Mason jar; the handwritten note that read "Kitten's Quarters" was still attached. She didn't take it with her. Why the fuck didn't she take it? This was a bad sign. She moved all the way across the freaking country and left a piece of us here. A very important piece.

The jar in my hands mocked me, boasting its fullness while my heart remained empty. I turned the glass with my fingers, running my thumb across its smooth surface. I thought about smashing it against the wall and watching it burst into a hundred pieces so it mirrored my fractured emotions, but knew I'd instantly regret it.

The roller coaster of my relationship with Cassie needed to stop. It's not that I wanted to get off the ride. I simply wanted it to be less like

the bone-rattling, headache-inducing, rickety wooden roller coasters of
the past, and more like the fluid smoothness of the state-of-the-art steel
coasters of modern day.

I set the jar back in its place and walked out of her room, leaving
what was left of my heart somewhere between the nightstand and the
bedroom floor.

"How come some of her stuff's still here?" I stared into Melissa's blue
eyes as I reentered the living room.

"We figured it would be easier to leave it here for now. We don't
know how long she's staying there, and I'm not moving anytime soon.
Besides, finding a fully furnished apartment in New York is easy."

"What do you mean that you don't know how long she's staying
there?" I asked, eager for every piece of information I could gather about
Cassie's future plans.

"She might hate living there. Or the job might not work out. She
just didn't know for sure, you know?"

I nodded, averting my eyes as my mind replayed memories of being
in this apartment with her. A quick vision of her in that white sundress
before I brought her home to meet my family for the first time flashed in
my head and I winced, squeezing my eyes shut against the sharp pain
that followed.

"Are you OK?" Melissa's voice forced my eyes to reopen.

Swallowing hard, I said, "Just fighting ghosts."

I needed to leave.

I needed out of that apartment where Cassie's scent and my memories of her lingered. It hurt to be there without her, and I suddenly realized what it must have been like for her when I was gone and living
with someone else. How painful it must have been to live here with the
knowledge of everything I'd done to us. How much she must have suf-
fered for my actions. She was innocent in all of this, so why had she paid
the highest price?

"I gotta get back to my hotel before they freak out and think I've gone AWOL or something." I headed for the front door, my head throbbing with each battered beat of my heart.

"You need me to drop you off?" Dean asked, his eyebrows pinching together.

"Unless you want me to take your car back to the hotel. But, you'll have to pick it up first thing tomorrow so it doesn't get towed," I noted, gently reminding him that the team was scheduled to head back to Arizona in the morning.

Dean glanced at Melissa before flashing me a smile. *"Nope. I'll take you."*

"Jack? Don't forget that I'm here too. You can call me anytime, and I'll help you if I can," Melissa said with a sympathetic smile.

"I'm gonna hold you to that." I forced a half smile in return.

"Good. Because even though you're a stupid jerk-face, you're her stupid jerk-face and you two belong together," she whispered, before wrapping her arms around my waist and squeezing me with more force than I realized her tiny frame could provide.

"You're killing me, Funsize," I choked out, and she giggled.

Dean tossed an arm around her shoulders and squeezed as he looked down at her. *"I'll see you later, OK?"*

"OK," she said, and I didn't miss the look in her eyes. Or his.

I grabbed the keys from the table, pulled my Diamondbacks hat back onto my head, and turned for the door.

We walked in silence toward the gunmetal color Mustang I'd bought for Dean, the tinted windows looking almost pitch black in the darkness. He'd complained at first, insisting he didn't need it, but I knew it was his dream car and wanted to do something nice for him when I got my signing bonus. I tossed him the keys and waited at the passenger door. He clicked the remote, two beeps filled the night air, and we both slid into the chilly leather seats.

The engine purred to life as I stared out the window, my mind racing with at least a dozen thoughts all vying for my undivided attention. I shook my head and focused on my brother. "So, what's up with you and Meli?" I asked, eager for a distraction.

He grinned as he pulled out of the parking lot, but wouldn't meet my eyes. "Nothing. Why?"

"Don't lie to me." I punched him playfully in the arm, causing him to yank the steering wheel and the car to swerve with a jerk.

"Hey! Don't do that!" He glanced at me quickly before turning his attention back on the road.

"Tell me, what's up with you two? I saw the way she was looking at you."

"What way? How was she looking at me?" Dean straightened up in the driver's seat. I clearly had his attention.

"You're kidding, right? You don't see the way she looks at you? With her eyes all hot like she wants to eat you up. Are you really that clueless?"

Dean snorted. "She doesn't want me."

"How are we even related? Dude, she wants you. Trust me on this. I know women."

The roar of the car's engine as he accelerated on the highway was the only sound in the car. Dean focused intently on the road ahead, before glancing at me and letting out a long sigh.

"I tried to kiss her once. I thought I'd read all the signs right. But she stopped me," he admitted, his voice dejected.

"Did you ask her why?"

"No. I just apologized."

I laughed. Leave it to my brother to be sorry for trying to kiss the girl he'd spent every spare moment with. "Jesus, Dean. I'd bet a thousand bucks that she wants you."

"Then why didn't she let me kiss her?" He glanced at me again.

"That's a good question. You should ask her," I said. "Time to grow a pair, little brother. How are you going to feel if she starts dating someone else?"

I watched his knuckles turn white as his grip on the steering wheel tightened. "I'm not going to be happy."

"Exactly."

Dean pulled into the hotel parking lot, and I hopped out of the car, half praying that my teammates would be in their rooms instead of the hotel bar. I walked around to the driver's side and extended my hand toward my brother, before he grabbed it and pulled me in for an awkward through-the-window hug. I pulled back, and we slapped each other on the shoulders before sharing a long look. I broke eye contact and turned to leave.

"It will all work out. You'll get her back," Dean predicted with naive confidence.

I breathed deeply before saying, "I fucking better, or I don't know what I'll do."

"I'll help you." Dean grinned up at me with a smile that looked eerily like my own.

I nodded and admitted, "I'll need it." Giving him one last pat, I said, "I'll call you later."

"Alright. Take care."

I watched as he drove off, his hand sticking out of the window in a good-bye wave. I raised my arm, waving back before he was out of view.

With a deep sigh, I headed indoors. All hopes for a quiet entrance were dashed as the sound of my last name filtered through the hotel bar and into the lobby.

"Carter! Carterrrrr! Get in here!"

I glanced to my right, noticing a few of my teammates getting comfortable with a group of good-looking women. I shook my head before walking over, making no attempt to hide the disapproval on my face.

"Where'd you run off to tonight, kid?" my teammate Costas asked, his head peering around the scantily clad woman currently sitting on his lap. I thought about his wife, staying home with their kids while he traveled with the team, and forced my judgment into quiet submission.

"I had some personal shit to take care of."

"Have a drink with us," he said and gestured for the blonde bartender. She finished drying the glass in her hands before setting it down and heading our way.

"Not tonight." I shook my head.

"More drinks for us, then." Costas winked, and my stomach turned. I wanted to lose my shit on him, just grab him by his smug face and ask if he realized what he was doing, what he was risking. How just one girl . . . one meaningless night . . . could cause his world to crumble around him. But I couldn't get pissed at Costas for my mistakes, my loss.

"See you in the morning." I turned away from the bar, their comments following behind me.

"Poor rookie, did you see his face?"

"Welcome to the big leagues, kid . . . women in every state. No offense, sweetheart."

Idiots.

They'd misread the disgust on my face as shock. Maybe if they were ever forced to lose the one person who meant everything to them, they'd understand what my face was truly saying.

I made my way into my hotel room and collapsed onto the bed. With my cell phone in hand, I stared at the screen for what seemed like hours, resisting the urge to dial Cassie's number, or send her a text message. I realized it wasn't going to be easy to stay away from her when everything in my body wanted her back.

Suddenly, I shot up from my bed and made my way toward the desk in my room. Using the hotel's complimentary stationery and pen, I did something I couldn't remember ever doing in my life.

I wrote her a letter.

Kitten,

I've realized that the only way I'll be able to stop myself from calling you, or texting you, or e-mailing you, or sending a carrier pigeon to your fucking window, is to write to you. Which sort of makes me feel like a pussy, honestly. But if I don't do this, I'm afraid I'll ruin it all before I even get the chance to fix it.

You're probably wondering what happened tonight. I know you didn't expect to see me, and I don't even know how you're feeling about the whole thing, but I hope it's the same way I feel. I never stopped loving you. I know I may have a funny way of showing it, but I'll make it up to you. You'll see.

I'm dying to get on the next flight to New York and win you back. But I can't do that until I'm free and clear from all my past attachments. I'm just trying to do the right thing by you. I realize that my idea of the right thing isn't always everyone else's, but I hope in this case you'll agree with me.

So . . . I hope you'll understand that I won't come and ask for your forgiveness while I'm still legally married to someone else.

You probably think that's stupid, right?

I'll always love you.

Jack

◇

He finished telling me about the night I left, and I blinked back the tears forming in my eyes. "You wrote me a letter?"

"I wrote you a lot of letters."

Stunned, I mumbled, "I'd like to see those someday."

Through my shock, I literally ached for a subject change. I knew I'd asked for this, but it hurt. Talking about our past shouldn't matter for our future. But that was my dumb heart talking. My heart . . . my little, keep-me-in-a-box-wrapped-in-cotton-behind-a-wall-built-with-bricks-and-stone-and-concrete-where-no-one-can-ever-hurt-me, stupid heart. My mind was at war with that beating thing. I fully believed that if my heart and my head could wage a battle within me, they would. And eventually, I'd die from it.

No, Cassie.

You need to hear this.

The only way to move forward without regret was to accept what happened. I couldn't change our past, but I could change our future. And in order for me to truly forgive him and learn to trust him again, I needed to hear what took him so long. Truthfully, I longed to begin my own internal healing.

"So, then what?" My demeanor turned serious with my tone.

"What do you mean . . . so, then what?" he asked, his expression showing he was perplexed by my question.

"That was only the night I left. Then what happened? We have six months of CliffsNotes to get through here, Carter."

"I thought I was going to get kicked off the team the next day," he admitted.

I propped myself up immediately. "Shut the hell up. What happened?"

◇

Tired and bleary-eyed, I flung the strap of my bag over my shoulder and pressed the Down button on the elevator. I fidgeted with my tie, straightening my jacket as the doors dinged before opening, and I stepped inside the empty compartment.

The lobby filled quickly with chatter as the rest of my team filtered in, dragging duffle bags, and some even dragging their kids behind them.

I checked out, tugged on my hat, and walked out toward the waiting charter bus.

"Carter, come here." Coach's voice startled me, and I dropped the bag at my side.

I walked over to him, and he tossed his arm around my shoulder. "Let's walk," he said.

Shit. Is he sending me back down to the minor leagues already?

Coach leaned in and locked his gaze with mine. "You're a good kid, Carter. I like you. But don't ever bolt out of my clubhouse again before I tell you that you can go. You understand me?" His voice was kind, but there was steel underneath it he wanted me to hear.

"Yes, sir. I'm really sorry about that—"

"Don't apologize, kid. Just don't let it happen again or I'll send your ass down to the minors so quick your head'll spin," he threatened, making sure I understood my position on the team totem pole. Message received, loud and clear.

"Yes, Coach," I answered respectfully, thankful that no one else was close enough to hear our conversation.

"Go get on the bus." He patted my shoulder with a slight shove.

◇

"I would have cried," I told him with a grimace.

"No, you wouldn't have. But I was scared shitless," he admitted with an uncomfortable laugh.

"I bet. OK, so you flew back to Arizona for the game. We both know how that went." I paused, referring to the game they lost that ended his postseason for the year. "Then what did you do?"

"I think you're enjoying this a little too much." He pulled the pillow out from under me, and my head crashed against the mattress.

"Hey!" I yelled, stretching for the pillow he held just out of reach. "Jack, really. I *need* to know."

He threw my pillow across the room and then patted the top of his invitingly. Forcing me to share his pillow, he pressed his forehead against mine.

"You want to hear how I starting stalking you as soon as I got back to Arizona?"

"Uh, absolutely," I practically squealed, and he laughed.

"I'll tell you over breakfast. I'm starving." He winked and planted a kiss on my forehead before hopping out of bed. Then he stretched his arms above him and his muscles flexed and bulged. My gaze locked onto his defined, tanned abs. "Like what you see?"

"Eh, I've seen better," I said playfully, refusing to feed the beast that is Jack Carter's ego.

"I highly doubt it." He ran a hand down the length of his well-chiseled stomach. "This is Grade-A certified goods right here. You're lucky I don't charge admission."

"To what? The gun show?" I pointed at his arms, my lips curling up in amusement.

"Exactly! The gun show," he teased, before jumping on the bed and pinning me beneath him. He held me tight as I squirmed, trying to wriggle out of his hold. "Where do you think you're going?"

"I thought we were eating," I said with attitude, cocking my head to one side.

He released a hard breath, pushing himself off the bed. "Let's go, then. You're the one who can't stop looking at me like I'm a piece of meat."

"You called yourself Grade-A! That's a meat label!" I shouted, my voice animated as I picked up a pillow and tossed it at him.

He snagged it effortlessly from the air. "Are you done playing? I thought you wanted to hear the rest of the story." He smirked before walking out of the bedroom, leaving me alone with my thoughts.

Stalker

Jack

When she finally walked into the kitchen wearing nothing but my T-shirt, I almost turned her ass around and marched her right back into the bedroom. Ignoring the throbbing in my shorts, I stared into her nearly empty refrigerator. "You have no food," I complained, closing the door.

"I eat out a lot." She shrugged. "But I have cereal. And bread."

She put four slices of bread in the toaster, and I led her by the hand to the kitchen table, pulling her chair out for her. I placed an empty bowl and spoon in front of her, followed by the milk and a box of cereal. Then I sat next to her, filling my bowl to the top with the crunchy shit.

"Can I hear about the stalking now," she pleaded as she poured milk into her bowl.

"First of all, Kitten, you have to understand that I made myself a compromise. I had to put you in the back of mind until the season was over. I knew that if I lost both baseball and you, I'd have nothing in my life. I'd never be able to survive that much loss."

I was sure she understood this, knowing me as well as she did, but it still needed to be said. The mere thought of not having baseball or my Kitten gutted me inside and left me hollow.

"I get that." Her eyes softened with understanding before narrowing devilishly. "Now get to the stalking."

Slowly I spooned a large heaping of cereal into my mouth before saying another word. My pace of storytelling was torturing her and I knew it. I liked having the upper hand in a situation where I really had no hand at all. I was lucky she didn't slam the door in my face last night. Normally not one for second chances, this girl broke all her rules for me. I'd give her anything she fucking wanted. I'd answer every question twice if she needed me too.

"You're stalling," she said, rising from her chair to grab the toast.

◇

My compromise ended the moment we lost the last home game and our postseason finished. I had two weeks to pack up my temporary apartment in Arizona and move out. I didn't have very many things there since most of my stuff still sat unattended at the house in Alabama. The house I'd shared with that bitch Chrystle. I knew I'd have to head back there to pack it all up before my life could move forward again, but I dreaded the very thought. If I could help it, I'd never step foot in that fucking state again. Thank God Alabama doesn't have a major league baseball team.

Grabbing a bottle of water, I walked into the living room and fell onto the couch. I reached for my cell, searching for my lawyer's name in my contacts. I selected his number, pressed Call, and relaxed into the cushions, pushing my head into the pillows.

"Hey, Jack, what's up?" Marc's voice rang out loudly, cutting through the noise in the background.

"Do you have a minute? I need to talk to you."

"*Of course. Hold on a sec.*" *With the slamming of a door, the previous distractions were silenced.* "*OK, I'm here. What's going on? Are you OK?*"

I nodded, forgetting for a minute that he couldn't see me through the phone. "*Yeah. I just want to talk to you about what I need to do to end the marriage.*"

"*Right,*" Marc responded quickly, and then I heard him typing. "*OK. So, obviously your two options are a divorce or an annulment.*"

I realized my jaw was clenched, and I tried to relax it. The fact that I was even having this conversation pissed me off. "*An annulment means the marriage never happened, right?*"

"*Yes, but you can only file for one under certain circumstances.*" He continued typing.

"*Chrystle lied about being pregnant,*" I said, longing to make this bullshit marriage disappear completely. I hated waiting this long to deal with everything, but I couldn't take the necessary steps during baseball season. If I needed to be in court to testify or make a statement, I wouldn't be available while we were in play-offs. My personal life outside of my baseball had to wait.

"*I know.*" The rapid tapping continued as I waited. "*OK, here's the deal. We'll file the dissolution of marriage under the fraud category, and the burden of proof is on us, if necessary. I'll file the paperwork first thing tomorrow morning. It should be a no-brainer.*"

I sucked in a deep breath. "*Awesome. Thank you, Marc.*"

"*You're welcome.*"

"*So, is there anything else I have to do? How long does it take?*"

"*You don't need to do anything yet. I'll find out if you have to make a legal statement in front of a judge or not. As soon as Chrystle signs it, we submit the paperwork, and it should only take a few weeks to finalize.*"

"*Shit. Seriously? Only a few weeks?*" My mouth dropped open before transforming into a huge grin.

"Yeah. It's just a process, but it's not a long one. I'll be in touch."

"Alright. Thanks again, Marc. Talk to you later." I pressed End before tossing my phone onto the coffee table and reaching for my laptop.

Only a few weeks. Fuck, yes!

I opened my Internet browser and typed a name in the online search engine: "Cassie Andrews."

When a ridiculous amount of options appeared, I narrowed down my search: "Cassie Andrews photographer."

Her name came up first with a link to her new position in New York. I clicked it and found myself on a page filled with her contact information. I scrambled for a pen and something to write on, as if I didn't get it down on paper immediately, it would disappear forever and I'd never get it back. I jotted down her work number, followed by her work e-mail address just in case.

Just in case what?

You cannot call her until you have your shit together. Until Chrystle is out of your life for good. No calling or e-mailing Cassie until you're rid of all your baggage.

I glanced at the clock on my DVD player. Eight p.m. That made it eleven in New York.

I thought we just covered this?

Desperation coursed through me at the very idea of hearing how she sounded. I suddenly needed to hear Cassie's voice. Convinced there was no way she'd still be in the office, I dialed her work number, my heart thundering in my chest with each ring.

"You've reached the desk of Cassie Andrews, junior photographer."

My abs contracted as the sound of her voice coursed into my ear.

"I'm sorry I missed your call, but please leave me a detailed message and I'll return it as soon as possible. If this is urgent, please press zero to return to reception. Thank you."

A beep played, and I quickly pressed the End button on my cell, my breathing ragged. She sounded happy . . . cheerful, even. My heart pinched with pain at the realization that she could be just fine without me. I longed for her happiness, but in all honesty, I wanted to be a part of it. She had become a permanent fixture within me. I struggled to remember what it felt like before she burrowed herself into my soul. I couldn't remember existing without her. Every part of me had become tied to her. It was in that very moment I realized how fucking desperate I was for her to feel the same way about me, and how I honestly had no idea if she still did.

◇

"You called my work phone and hung up? I love it." She leaned her head against my shoulder before pressing her soft lips against my cheek.

"I did that a lot."

"How much is a lot?"

"Almost every night," I admitted, reaching my hand through the open space in the chair and resting it on the small of her back. I hoped she'd think my actions were cute instead of creepy.

"You called my work voice mail almost every night, but you never called the real me?"

Shit.

"Not while I was still . . ." I paused, not wanting to say the word "married." I shuddered.

"You're so stubborn sometimes," she chastised.

"I know. But I swear my heart's in the right place." As if I hadn't asked her to understand enough already, I longed for her to understand this part as well.

"Your heart and I are going to have a chat later. Get on the same page."

"I look forward to it." I raised my eyebrows, and she swatted my shoulder.

"So, once your season was over, did you move back home with Gran and Gramps in California? I think I remember Melissa telling me that you were back there."

I pushed my chair back from the table, grabbed both of our bowls, and placed them in the sink. I'd wash them later. And for the record, I do not do dishes. But for Cassie I'd do the whole city's dishes if she asked. "Yeah. I flew back to stay with Gran and Gramps right after the season ended. I really missed them."

"I bet they missed you too." Her green eyes twinkled with her words. I love how they do that sometimes when she's excited or reminiscing.

"It was nice being home, you know? Surrounded by people who actually give a shit about you and your future."

I wiped my hands on a dish towel before leading her toward the living-room couch. I pulled her head onto my chest and sighed as she wrapped her arm around me, her fingers gripping my skin.

"Is it weird that I miss your grandparents more than I miss my own parents?" She giggled against my chest.

"Nah, your parents sorta suck."

"So do yours," she shot back defensively, her body tensing.

"No shit."

"Well, aren't we a pair?" She relaxed her shoulders and my nerves eased.

"I think so." I kissed the top of her head, breathing in her shampoo. She always smelled so damn good.

"Were Gran and Gramps freaking out about everything?"

My stomach tightened at the memories currently flooding my mind. "They were really sad, mostly. I think Gran took it the hardest. It hurt her knowing something was happening to me that she couldn't fix or make better."

Cassie's head nodded into my chest. "Poor Gran."

"Yeah. It sucked. I felt fucking horrible. I still do." My breath hitched.

She arched her neck, pulling back her head to look at me as cold air filled the now empty space on my chest. "Don't do that to yourself, Jack. It's over now." Her mouth formed into a smile, and I tried to smile back but failed.

"Do they know you're here? With me?" she asked, her voice trembling. What the hell would Cassie have to be nervous about when it comes to my grandparents? They adore her. She had to know that.

"They know. They're over-fucking-joyed about it."

"Really? Were they scared at all that I wouldn't take you back?" Her eyes focused on mine with intent.

I grinned. "Not really."

Her jaw dropped slightly. "What do you mean, *not really?*"

"Gran said she knew real love when she saw it. She was convinced that you'd forgive me. That it might not be easy, but eventually you'd come around."

Cassie's lips formed a closed-mouth smirk. "Gran's smart."

My fingers twisted through long blonde strands of her hair as my mind drifted for a moment, convinced this was only a dream. I'd waited to be right here, holding this girl in my arms, for so long now I almost couldn't believe it was really happening.

"Back to the story." Her words cut through my thoughts.

◇

"I've missed you!" Gran squeezed me before looking me up and down. "You look healthy, so that's good." The smile expanded across her whole face until her eyes were scrunched into half moons.

"I missed you too, Gran." I leaned down to plant a kiss on her well-aged cheek.

"You look bigger," Gramps said with a nod of approval, and I laughed, hugging him tight.

"I've been working out. I have to at this level."

"You always worked out," Dean said as he walked out of his bedroom and into the living room. Since I left home to play ball, I don't think Dean ever planned to move out. I couldn't blame him really. Gran and Gramps were the best.

I reached for him and pulled him into a tight bear hug before he choked out an unrecognizable sound.

I laughed. "Not like this. Not to this level, this many days or hours. It's literally a whole new ballgame being in the majors."

"Is it harder?" Dean asked.

"Way harder. They can hit my ninety-four-mile-per-hour fastball. And they can hit it far."

"That sucks."

I opened my mouth to respond. "How's the kitten?" Gramps interrupted with a cheeky grin, and my smile fell.

Gran tapped her foot against the carpet. "Let Jack put his things in his room. We can talk about all of this over dinner."

I shot Gran a look that screamed "thank you" before walking down the hallway to my old room. I looked around at my things, untouched since I'd been gone. A framed picture of Cass and me sat on my nightstand. I reached for it, running my finger across the curves of her face. Overcome with the desire to call her, I grabbed some loose paper and started writing. I'd only do this sort of bullshit for her. No one else. Ever.

Kitten,

The postseason is officially over. I was going to move out of my apartment in Arizona and fly straight to Alabama to pack my stuff, but I missed Gran and Gramps. So I'm sitting in my bedroom at home, thinking about the last time we were all here together. I miss you almost as much as Gramps does. Ha!

I forgot how much being home makes me feel secure. Maybe it's just nice to be surrounded by people who genuinely love and care about you, instead of people trying to take advantage of you. Who would have thought I'd be so easy to manipulate?

I talked to Marc the other day about the annulment and he got the paperwork started. Hopefully it will all be over soon, and I'll be there before you know it, begging for your forgiveness and praying you'll take me back.

Please don't give up on us.

I'll always love you.

Jack

P.S. I saw your photographs online today. They're really beautiful, Cass. I'm so proud of you.

Heading into the kitchen, Dean and Gramps were already sitting while Gran finished up at the stove.

"Can I help you, Gran?" I asked before reaching my seat.

"No, dear. You sit down and start talking."

I laughed. "Talking? About what?"

"Oh, you know what! What's going on with everything? When will your divorce from that awful woman be finalized?" The spoon in Gran's hand shook with her anger as she mumbled something under her breath.

"Marc filed the paperwork for an annulment. We're just waiting for her to sign it." I shrugged, feeling the weight of Dean's and Gramps's stares on my shoulders.

"She will sign it, right?" Dean asked, his tone concerned.

The weight of my little brother's question was something that hadn't occurred to me until he asked. *"I don't know why she wouldn't,"* I said, looking around the small kitchen I'd spent most of my life in before locking eyes with Gran.

Dean choked back a laugh. *"I do. Have you met her? She's a total bitch."*

"Dean! Language!" Gran's forehead furrowed as she waved her wooden spoon in his direction.

"Sorry, Gran." Dean slumped lower into his chair.

I leaned forward, placing my elbows on the table before adding, *"But it's so over between us. She signed a prenup before we were married, so she doesn't gain anything by not signing."*

"Except control," Dean remarked.

My temper flared. *"What the fuck are you talking about?"*

"How many times do I need to remind you both to watch your mouths?" Gramps interrupted before giving Gran a nod.

I huffed out a long sigh, willing my temper to calm. *"Sorry, Gran."*

"I just meant that she'd have control over you if she didn't sign the papers. She knows how badly you want out of this marriage, so it wouldn't surprise me if she pulled a bunch of sh—" Dean paused before continuing, *"stuff just to mess with you."*

I considered my brother's words carefully as Gran appeared, placing dishes filled with steaming food in front of each of us.

"He's right, Jack. She's been so evil from the very start. What's to stop her from being difficult now?" Gran asked, her voice shaky.

I reached out my hand, placing it on Gran's shoulder. *"I don't know. I guess I'm just hoping that she knows this is over and there's no point in delaying the inevitable."*

"I hope you're right," she said with a sympathetic smile.

"How's the kitten doing? Have you talked to her since she moved to New York?" I watched as Gramps's face lit up like a kid at Christmas.

"Gramps, if I didn't know better, I'd think you had a thing for my girl," I joked.

"Your girl?" Gramps teased back.

My fork clanged against the side of the plate. "Uh-huh. My girl."

Dean laughed. "Maybe I'll make her my girl. Keep her in the family."

I glared at him, the heat instantly spreading across my cheeks. "And I'll disown you before I kick your—"

"Boys, that's enough."

Dean shoved a spoonful of rice into his mouth as he grinned at me. "You're lucky she's like a sister to me."

"Yeah? I'd say you're the lucky one. 'Cause I'd kill you if you touched her and you know it."

"I'm your only brother and this is how you treat me?"

I tried to stop the smile from spreading across my face as Gramps interjected, "You're trying to take the man's kitten, Dean."

Gran laughed and my smile widened.

"Worry about your own nonexistent girlfriend, little brother, and leave my girl alone."

"Do you have a girlfriend?" Gran's focus shot to Dean as her eyes widened.

Dean shot me a warning look through narrowed eyes. "No. Jack's just talking about Melissa."

"She's Cassie's best friend, right?" Gran asked.

"Yeah."

"Did you talk to her yet?" I asked, putting him on the spot for once. He shrugged one shoulder. "No."

"I told you to talk to her," I reminded him.

"I told you she's not into me," he snapped back.

"That's crap and you know it. She is definitely into you."

"Then what's the problem?" Gramps dropped his chin into his hand, his gaze shifting back and forth between me and Dean.

"I don't know. She says she doesn't want a boyfriend, but I think she just doesn't want me as a boyfriend. Can we talk about something else now?" Dean fidgeted in his chair as he filled his mouth with more food.

"Who wouldn't want you as a boyfriend? Rubbish," our ever-loyal Gran said with a huff.

"Can we please talk about something else? Anything else," Dean pleaded.

Taking pity on my poor, uncomfortable brother, I changed the subject. "I found some of Cassie's photographs online today."

Silence filled the air as everyone stopped chewing their food, directing their stares at me. "What?" I asked nervously.

"How did you find them?" Gramps asked, blotting the corner of his mouth with a napkin.

"I went to her magazine's website. They had a feature online about moving to New York, and all the photographs in the article were hers." My chest swelled with pride as I talked about her.

"That's fantastic news! I want you to show me after dinner." Gramps's eyes lit up with enthusiasm as he slapped his hand against the table.

"Wait." Dean tilted his head as a smirk appeared. "You follow her magazine online?"

I squared my gaze, meeting his directly. "You're goddamned right I do. I want to know what she's doing every second she's not with me. And if there's a photograph she takes for that magazine, I want to see it."

"I think that's sweet," Gran said.

"I think it's psycho," Dean countered.

I changed the topic of conversation for him and this is how he repays me? "Really, Dean? After everything Cassie and I have been through, you think my following her work online is psycho?"

"It's a little weird, don't you think? You won't even talk to her in real life, but you'll follow her online?"

The chair scraped against the floor as I shoved back, jumping to my feet. My breathing hitched as my defenses rose. No one talked about me and Cassie like that. Not even my brother.

"Jack, sit down!" Gran said sternly. "And Dean, stop calling your brother names! You two are acting like little boys."

I inhaled a sharp breath before sliding the chair back toward the table and sitting down. "I can't talk to her until I'm not married anymore, OK? So until then, yeah, I will follow everything she does online. And if that magazine can give me a glimpse into how she's seeing the world, I'll take it. Because until I'm back in her life, that's the only Cassie I get. And if that makes me psycho, then I don't give a fuck. Sorry, Gran," I offered before she swatted my shoulder.

"I'm going to ground you! I don't care how old you are," she threatened with a slight chuckle.

"He started it," I said, nodding my head toward my brother. "Let's talk about Melissa some more."

Dean waved his arms in the air in defeat. "I'm sorry. Truce?"

Before I could respond, Gran asked, "How long are you planning to stay home?"

Gramps looked up from his plate and directly into my eyes. "Your whole off-season?"

I swallowed my last bite of food. "I don't know. I figured I'd wait for Marc to call me about the annulment, and then I'd go to Alabama to sign the papers and pack up the house at the same time."

"And then what?" Dean asked.

"I'll have to bring my stuff back here, but I want to get to New York as soon as possible to make things right with Cass," I admitted. "I only have a few months before I have to be back in Arizona for spring training, and I still need to find a place to rent."

"That's not much time." Gramps sounded worried.

"I know."

"What are you planning on saying to Cassie?" Gran tilted her head toward me. "How are you going to win her back?"

"I don't know yet. But it will be something along the lines of how much I suck and how much she doesn't."

Gramps laughed at my words, and I smiled.

"Very romantic." Dean sarcastically popped two thumbs up in the air.

"Shut up, Dean. No one likes you."

"You know you'll have to give her more than just some nice words, dear," Gran said as she eyed me meaningfully.

"Trust me, Gran. I know."

◇

Cassie's face relaxed as she leaned up to kiss my cheek. "I like that you followed me online. I followed you too."

My adrenaline started racing as I adjusted my position on the couch. "You did?"

"Of course I did. I still loved you, Jack. I cared about you. I wanted to see how you were. It was a big deal that you'd made it into the major leagues. I wasn't going to miss it," she explained, her shoulders shrugging like she had no choice in the matter.

"So you don't think I'm psycho?"

"I didn't say that," she teased playfully.

I pounced on her before she could get away, pinning her body beneath mine and against the couch cushions. Her chest moved heavily up and down, and it took everything in me to not rip her shirt off and lose myself in her body. My shorts tightened as I leaned down to kiss her, brushing my tongue along her bottom lip. She moaned slightly as she arched her head back, her lips parting. I

pressed my mouth against hers, my tongue and hers touching eroti-
cally in a playful tease of push and pull.

I wanted to tear her clothes off and devour her inch by inch.
I sucked on her neck, the taste of her skin almost sending me into
a frenzy. She ran her hands down the length of my back as she
pulled my shirt up. She pressed her fingers into my skin as I kissed
and licked her ear and neck before working my way back to her
mouth. Jesus, I wanted this girl. She fired me up like no one else.
Trying to maintain some semblance of self-control, I pulled back
from the kiss, and her hands tightened around my neck. I chuckled
and asked, "Don't you want to hear more?"

Her grip tightened as she pulled my face to hers. "In a minute,"
she said, as she grazed her tongue across my lips.

My hands explored the length of her body, stopping at the top
of her thigh. "I want you so fucking bad. You make me crazy."

"Then take me." She sucked her bottom lip into her mouth,
and I longed to put something of mine in there instead.

I grabbed the bottom of her top and lifted it over her head, unable to get it off fast enough. She reached for my shirt, tugging and
pulling before I sat up and tore it off myself. My insides flared as she
ran her hands down my bare chest, stopping at the button of my
shorts. When her fingertips gently grazed over my hardness, I shuddered. Just that single touch from her and I almost came unglued.

It's twisted how much she owns me. She always fucking has,
but still.

I kicked my shorts off, silently giving myself a pat on the back
when I noticed where Cassie's eyes were locked. Half tempted to
make some smartass remark about how much she loves looking at
my dick, I stopped myself. I hadn't even been back in her life for
twenty-four hours; no need to screw it up already.

My gaze moved from her eyes down to her naked body. "You're so fucking sexy." I meant the words, but they came out in a lusty growl and she bit her bottom lip again. I dropped my mouth to hers, sucking that lip between my teeth, my body falling to meet hers.

Heat shot through me as we touched. The feeling of her skin pressed against mine caused my lust to hungrily take over. I curled my fingers in her hair, forcefully tugging her head back so I could kiss her throat and jaw.

"Oh God, Jack. I want you inside me. Please. Stop teasing."

I pressed my hardness against her, and when she howled with pleasure, I pulled it away. "Goddammit, Jack. Stop fucking around." Her fingers dug into my backside as she forcefully guided me to her.

Without another word I pushed inside, my body shivering as the warmth of her completely enveloped me. "Jesus Christ, Cassie. Why do you always feel so amazing?" My breath was labored as I worked in and out of her. The sight of her nipple drew me, so I traced a finger gently around it before I sucked it into my mouth, my tongue flicking around it.

Cassie moaned, her body arching beneath me as she clawed her fingernails down the length of my back.

"You better stop that," I breathed out.

"Or what?" she teased, running her fingers along my back once more.

"Or I'll be done before you are," I admitted.

She shook her head. "We can't have that."

"Then behave," I demanded, grabbing her arms and pinning them above her head, as my thrusting continued. She laughed beneath me, and I swept my tongue across her lips before pushing it into her hot mouth. She mumbled something unintelligible against me, and I kissed her harder.

"Jack," she whispered, her breathing quickening as her hips rose up and down to meet mine. "Oh."

She moaned again as her body shuddered against mine.

Thank fucking God.

I rocked into her one last time before exploding. My thrusting slowed as I collapsed on top of her, my weight pushing her body further into the couch.

"Why do you enjoy suffocating me?" she said, swatting my shoulders.

"I like lying with you this way."

She cocked her head. "What way? With me dead?"

A quick laugh ripped from my throat. "No. I like being inside of you."

"Well, get out." She smirked. "I need to pee."

I pulled out slowly and she scooted out from under me, hurrying to the bathroom.

Stay

Cassie

I walked back into the living room wearing a new thong and nothing else. Jack was sitting on the couch, his shorts pulled up but still unbuttoned, his shirt pooled on the floor next to the one I had been wearing. I reached for the crumpled shirt, slipping it back over my head before plopping down next to him.

"That was a nice distraction," I said, leaning my body into his waiting arms.

His fingers combed through my messy strands of hair before tucking them behind my ear. "More stories or more distractions?" he asked with a mischievous tone.

My cell phone beeped in the background, and I eyed him, contemplating whether I should see who was texting me. "I'm gonna see who that is."

He nodded and smacked my ass as I ran into the bedroom. I settled back into his arms before tapping the screen on my phone. "Oooh, it's from Melissa." I turned, looking into his deep brown eyes. "Does she know you're here?"

Jack shrugged. "The trade would be reported by now, so she might be wondering."

Another sound beeped and this time, Jack reached for his phone before laughing. "Text message from Dean."

"They're so predictable."

Pressing the buttons, I read the message from Melissa:

OH MY GOD! CASSIE! JACK GOT TRADED TO THE METS!!!! DID YOU KNOW THAT? IS HE THERE? IF HE'S NOT, HE PROBABLY WILL BE SOON SO HEADS UP! AND CALL ME ASAP!!!!!!!!

I chuckled out loud.

"What'd she say?" Jack asked, his eyebrows raised.

"Well, she used all caps so this is a very serious message." I smiled, handing my phone to him so he could read it.

"Oh, she's yelling at you. Isn't that what all caps means?"

"Yeah, but I think that's her way of showing me she's freaking out. Or excited. Or yelling," I agreed with a smile.

"Heads up. I might be on my way over." Jack pressed his lips against my forehead, and I closed my eyes with his touch. So much had happened between us. So much more than any one couple should ever go through, but there we were. Together.

"I should probably text her back or she won't ever stop." I quickly typed out a response.

He's here. We're talking. Working through things. Call you from the office Monday.

I lowered the volume button on my phone before it beeped again.

MONDAY?!?! Like hell you're making me wait that long!

I laughed and typed out one last message before turning my phone to silent.

You'll survive. I can't talk now. Talk later. Love you.

"What did Dean say?"

He scanned the phone screen before smiling and handing it to me.

Dude, you got traded to the Mets and didn't tell me? Is this because of Cassie? Of course it's because of Cassie. How the hell did you get them to let you do it? Good luck. Call me after you see her.

"How can you not love Dean?" I handed him back his phone, smiling.

He straightened his back and pushed away from me slightly. "Good question. Speaking of Dean, why doesn't Melissa love him?"

"What?" My tone came out more surprised than I meant.

"No, really. What's her deal? Dean's totally into her, but she's not having it. I don't get it."

Jack's demeanor and tone gave away the fact that this situation bothered him. I found it sweet, if you wanted to know the truth. He cared about his little brother, and since I didn't have any siblings to care about me, I found it inspiring. "She's always been like that." I knew I'd answered his question unsatisfactorily, but it's all I had when it came to her.

He shook his head, not accepting my answer. "You've known her forever, Kitten. Hasn't she ever had a boyfriend?"

I scratched my head, contemplating his question and forming my response. "Not really. I mean, she's always hooked up with guys, but she's never really had a serious boyfriend."

"Why not?" he asked, apparently determined to get to the bottom of this mystery.

"I don't know."

"How can you, of all people, not know? You're her best friend. You're chicks. Chicks talk about this kind of shit all the time."

My body prickled with heat as my defenses quickly rose. "First of all, calm down. Second of all, I don't fucking know. I've never really thought about it before. Guys have always liked Melissa, and she makes out with them or whatever, but she's never really said anything to me about liking them back. I never questioned it because I just accepted it. That's the way she is. I don't know why. I don't know when it will change. And I don't know why the fuck she doesn't fall head over heels in love with Dean. Maybe you should ask her instead of sitting here grilling me."

I started to get off the couch, but he grabbed my arm and pulled me right back down. He reached for my face, turning it, forcing me to look at him. "I'm sorry, Kitten. I didn't mean to get so fired up about it. I just don't get it. My brother's a good guy. And I know he likes her. It just makes no sense to me why she doesn't like him back."

He loosened his hold on my face, but I refused to turn away from him. "I can't answer that." I shrugged, my annoyance fading.

"I'm sorry. I didn't mean to yell." Jack's lips twisted into a smile, forcing his dimples to appear.

I am such a sucker for those dimples.

"Let's get back to *our* story," he suggested. With his emphasis on the word our, my anger quickly disappeared.

"OK. But now I'm too pissed off to remember where we were," I admitted.

He wrapped his arms around me, and I allowed him to pull me close. "We were talking about Gran and Gramps. Don't be mad at me."

My breath hitched. "Fine," I relented, feeling my annoyance fade with his nearness. I hated how he affected me sometimes. "So, how long did you stay there with them?"

He inhaled a long breath before releasing it against the top of my head, causing strands of my hair to fall in front of my eyes. I pushed them away as I waited for his response. "A lot longer than I intended. My plan was to stay there for a couple weeks before heading back to Alabama to pack up my stuff and finalize the annulment. I honestly figured two to three weeks was enough time.

That the bitch would sign it and I'd be on my way here before Christmas."

"Good thing I didn't hold my breath."

He huffed. "Yeah. The past six months has been nothing but drama, Kitten. I'm not sorry for leaving you out of it, but I am sorry for letting it go on for so long."

I leaned away from the warmth of his body and into the cold cushions, squaring my shoulders toward him. "Why did it take so long? How could she fight the annulment, anyway?"

◇

My cell phone rang, waking me from a deep sleep and forcing my eyes to pop open. Anticipation rushed through me as Marc's name appeared on the screen. "Hey, Marc," I said, my voice groggy.

"Jack, we have a problem."

"What kind of problem?" I asked, scooting my back up against the wall.

"She won't sign."

"Huh? Who won't?" I stopped short before continuing. "What do you mean, she won't sign? I thought this was a done deal? An easy fix?" My heart slammed itself against my rib cage.

"Her lawyer's stating your claims are ridiculous. That no fraud was committed and therefore his client won't sign under those terms."

"Are you fucking kidding me? What terms will she sign under?" I fought to keep my anger under control.

"She won't sign an annulment. But she'll consider signing divorce papers, although his client would rather work things out."

"Work things out? Are you fucking joking?"

"I wish."

"You have to fix this, Marc. She faked a pregnancy to force me to marry her. How is that not fraud?" I threw the magazine sitting next to me against the wall and watched it fall to the ground.

"It is. But the burden of proof is on us."

"So, let's prove it then," I insisted.

"We're going to have a hard time doing that since she has plenty of documentation supporting her claims," he sighed.

"What kind of documentation?"

"Well, doctor's reports, for starters."

Fuck.

I'd forgotten about the fact that Chrystle had doctor's prescriptions, appointments, and paperwork.

"Can't we sue the doctor for malpractice or something?"

"We would have to prove that he lied as well, which would be extremely difficult given the circumstances."

When people allege that anger has the ability to shoot through them with such force that they see red . . . well, it's true. I saw red. Literally.

"This is so fucked up. What can I do?"

"Nothing, Jack. Right now I want you to stay where you are and let me handle this," he said, his tone calm and professional.

I gripped the edge of the mattress, my fingers digging into it. "All my stuff's still in Alabama."

"Don't step foot in that state until I tell you it's OK. You hear me?"

I cringed as he told me what to do. "We'll see."

"Jack, it's my job to look out for you. For once, let me do that. Please." His voice sounded strained, and I sighed.

"OK."

"I'll call you soon."

I pressed the End button on my cell phone and threw it against the wall. Why the fuck was this girl so hell-bent on ruining my life? I can't move past this one mistake if I can't put it in the past. Why couldn't she be a decent human being and sign the damn papers?

Knuckles rapped on my bedroom door. "Can I come in?"

"Yeah."

Dean walked in and glanced at the phone on the floor before closing the door behind him. "What's going on? I heard you yelling."

I looked him straight in the eyes. "You were right. She won't sign the papers."

He moved toward my bed, sitting down at the opposite end. "Shit, Jack. I'm sorry. So, what does that mean?"

I closed my eyes, pinching the skin at the bridge of my nose to relieve the stress. "I don't know. Marc's working on it."

"Do you want to go out or something? Get out of the house for a bit?"

"I need to be alone right now."

Dean stood up from my bed without another word and left my room. I grabbed the notebook sitting on my dresser and flipped it open to a blank page. How quickly this whole letter-writing thing turned into habit. It helped to put my thoughts somewhere when all I wanted to do was pick up the phone and dial Cassie's number.

$$\diamond$$

"Oh my God. That bitch! She had a doctor give her falsified pregnancy paperwork?" My eyes widened as the shock and anger sunk into my bones.

"Yep," was all he managed in response.

"No wonder you believed her," I said, shaking my head

"What do you mean?" His body tensed and his jaw tightened.

"Well, I never really understood why you believed that she was pregnant in the first place. Without checking or making sure, I mean," I tried to explain.

Jack cracked his neck as tension visibly poured from his body and rolled onto mine. "You thought I just stupidly accepted her at her word? Married her without any proof? Why didn't you just ask me?"

His bitter tone shocked me, causing my defenses to rise. "I don't know. Maybe because I was too caught up in my own heartbreak to ask you when I had the chance. And it's not like we were really talking at the time."

He reached a hand out to touch me, laying it on my leg. That one single movement shattered my defenses and I wanted to take back everything I'd just accused him of. "I'm sorry, Jack. It's just . . ."

"Don't. I'm sorry." His hand raised in a defeated gesture in the space between us. "You weren't there. You didn't know what was going on. I'm sure it looked shady as hell from the outside."

A shudder ripped through me. I never again wanted to be on the "outside" of anything when it came to Jack Carter. "But I shouldn't have just assumed."

"You didn't know."

"So, she had doctor visits and stuff?" My mind still raced to wrap around the elaborate plotting and lies. How could one girl be so malicious?

"Appointments, paperwork, vitamins, baby books, charts, schedules—she had it all." He exhaled, and I grabbed his hand in mine, our fingers intertwining as I leaned back into him.

"Can I ask you something else?" My voice sounded muffled against his chest.

He kissed the top of my head. "Anything."

"Did you ever think the baby wasn't yours? I mean, I get that you thought she was pregnant, but did you ever think it was someone else's?"

"She was a very convincing liar. She agreed with no reservations to do a DNA test after the baby was born. I honestly thought that if she were lying, she would have been nervous, or at least fighting me on the whole thing, but she encouraged it."

And then he took me back to when his world first started crashing down around him. When he was living in Alabama and playing on the Triple A team for the Diamondbacks. The night after he pitched his perfect game when Chrystle came on to him at the bar where he was celebrating with his teammates and he finally stopped resisting her. He gave in to her advances that night, and my life as I knew it would never be the same. I shuddered as I remembered the way my world started to spin around me and my heart felt like it was shattering inside of my chest when Jack called that afternoon to deliver the news. Not only had he cheated on me, but also the girl he had slept with was pregnant.

◇

I ignored the knock at the apartment door, assuming that one of my roommates would answer, and continued folding my clothes. When I heard the sound of Chrystle's voice filtering through the entryway and into my room, my whole body tightened. So we'd had a drunken one-night stand, and I threw her out when I came to my senses. What was she doing here?

She tapped on my bedroom door before walking in and closing it behind her.

"What are you doing? Get out of my room," I snapped, refusing to give her the time of day.

"I need to talk to you." Her voice shook as she spoke.

I exhaled through my nose, my impatience clear. "What is it?"

"I'm pregnant," she whispered, tears falling down her cheeks.

"So? How is that my problem?" I asked before the realization punched me square in the gut.

"Because it's yours," she said before sitting on my bed.

I sucked in a breath, my mind refusing to believe her. "Bullshit," I shot back.

"Bullshit nothing, Jack! I haven't been with anyone else since you. Ask anyone if they've seen me around. Or if they've hooked up with me. I haven't."

"I will ask. I'll fucking ask right now." I stormed out of my bedroom and into the living room, where three of my teammates were eating lunch and watching TV. When I asked them if Chrystle had been with any of them, they all shook their heads and threw their hands up in the air in denial. I asked if they'd seen her with anyone lately, and once again, they all answered no. And then they proceeded to inform me that come to think of it, they hadn't seen her around at all the past few weeks.

Shit.

My legs trembled as I stepped back into my room. My world spun around me as I willed my stomach to stop twisting. I didn't want this. Not with her. Not now. Not ever.

"It's yours, Jack. I'm sorry. I'm so sorry. I never wanted this to happen." She buried her head in her hands, her body shaking with each sob.

I lacked the desire to comfort her, so I finished folding my clothes. "What are you going to do?" I asked, my tone cold.

"What do you mean?" She peered up at me, her face red and wet.

"I mean, are you planning on keeping it?"

I watched as her jaw dropped open. "Of course you'd ask me that."

"We don't even know each other. Why the hell would you want to keep it?" My temper flared in a vain attempt to drown out the fact that I was scared shitless.

"Because it's a baby, Jack! It's a life, and I'll love it even if you won't!"

"I need you to leave."

This cannot be fucking happening. Please don't let this be happening.

She stood up, wiping her eyes with her hand before saying, "Way to be a man about this."

The heat flooded my body as I stepped toward her, my fists clenched in anger. "Oh, I'll be a man about it, alright. I'll drive you to the clinic. I'll pay for it. And then I'll even drive you home. What do you say?"

"I'd say you're an asshole." She tried to push me aside, but I refused to budge.

"I am an asshole. An asshole who doesn't want to have a baby with a complete stranger."

"Well, it's a little late for that, don't you think?"

My room circled around me as the life that existed five minutes prior disappeared from view. Terror consumed me. "Don't do this, Chrystle. Please don't do this. Don't ruin both our lives over a drunken mistake."

I watched as she winced, pulling back her head with disgust. "I'm not ruining anything."

"You're ruining everything." My voice rose barely above a whisper as thoughts of Cassie filled my head. Cassie was my girl, my world, and I knew she'd never trust me again. There was no way she'd ever forgive me for this. I'd never forgive myself. I didn't deserve her, and she deserved a hell of a lot better than a screwup like me. I couldn't believe I tossed away the best thing to ever happen to me for a piece of ass. I should *never have gotten that drunk. It wasn't an excuse, but my defenses were down, and I gave in. And I fucking hated myself for it.*

"I'm sorry you see it that way. Hopefully you'll change your mind. Maybe after the shock wears off. I'll be in touch, Jack," she said as she walked out the door.

Fuck.

If Chrystle kept the baby, there was no way she'd move away from her family. I would have to live here, in Alabama. Or at least have a place here if I wanted to see my own kid. I could kiss California good-bye for good. I'd have to spend all of the off-season here. My body sank to the carpet, my back firm against the bed, as my world crashed down around me. I wouldn't be like my father. I wouldn't leave my child the same way he left me and Dean. I'd experienced firsthand how a parent willingly leaving can royally fuck up a person. I'm a prime example. I wouldn't do that to my own flesh and blood. I wouldn't follow in my father's footsteps, leaving personal damage in my wake. I would be better than he ever was.

I couldn't believe this was happening. I wished harder than I ever wished for anything that it was all a nightmare. That I'd wake up any second and my body would flood with relief at it being all in my mind. But no matter what I did, I couldn't make it stop being real.

◇

"This story sucks." I sucked in a breath before frowning.

"I told you it wasn't happy," he said, his hand running down my side, giving me chills.

"Are we almost to last night yet?" I gazed up at him, my expression hopeful.

"Not quite."

"I think I need another break."

"What do you have in mind?" He winked suggestively.

My lips formed a pretend snarl as I narrowed my eyes to glare at him. "Jack, really. We *just* did that."

Reliving our time apart was honestly a lot to take in. I longed for all this information, but to say it didn't cause my breath to catch every few minutes would be a lie. It also scared me. If one small-town girl could be so vicious, what were big-city women capable of?

"Do you want to get out of the house for a bit? Maybe go grab a slice?" I used my newly acquired New Yorker lingo for a piece of pizza.

"I could eat," he answered with a large grin, and I leaned in to kiss each dimple.

I pulled away slowly, the rich chocolate color of his eyes mesmerizing me, as a thought hit me. "Wait. Where are you staying? Do you have an apartment or a hotel that you need to check in to?"

Nerves raced through me as I anticipated his answer. I knew I should have been more reserved or cautious or careful, but the truth was that I wanted him to stay with me and never leave again.

"I didn't book anything yet. I came straight here."

Yet. He planned to live somewhere else, and I was just the first stop. "Oh. Well, did you want to do that first?" I tried to hide my disappointment, but my tone betrayed me.

His thumb traced along my jawline before resting beneath my chin. "Not really. Anything that involves leaving you I'd rather put off until later."

Relief washed over me. My lips pressed into a tight smile as I closed my eyes. "Then don't leave," I whispered.

"I don't ever want to leave you again," he admitted, as the warmth of his lips brushed across mine.

"You could live here." The words spilled out before I consciously thought them.

Jack's face relaxed, a peaceful calm spreading across it. "Yeah? You want to live together?"

His questioning inflection contradicted the happy look on his face, causing me to silently curse myself for being so vulnerable. "It was just an offer. Don't get all full of yourself over it."

He choked back a laugh. "Nothing would make me happier, Kitten, than to know my home is where you are."

My heart jumped and thumped against my chest with such force I was surprised I didn't topple over. "Really?"

"Really." His grin widened. "I wasn't going to leave, anyway."

"Oh yeah?"

"I didn't move all the way across the country to live alone. I moved here to be with you. And that's what I'm going to do. Be. With. You." He stared into my eyes with conviction.

My insides trembled with desire, heat spreading between my thighs at his confident demeanor. "What if I told you no?" I teased.

He pressed his forehead to mine, his eyes piercing right through me. "But you didn't. You want me here just as much as I want to be here, and I know it. I'm not leaving and you won't make me."

"You're so fucking arrogant."

"Is it really arrogance when you're right?" His lip curled up on one side before crushing his mouth against mine. He swept his tongue teasingly across my bottom lip before he pulled away.

After all the heartache he'd put me through, nothing could compare to the way I lived in Jack's presence. The cracks and chips in my heart slowly dragged themselves together whenever he was around. My soul pretended the past damage didn't matter, as it tugged and pulled itself whole again. I had been shattered and broken, but my body insisted on mending itself for him.

For Jack.

Because being with him, no matter how illogical it seemed considering he was responsible for my internal carnage, completed me. We made sense together. Melissa couldn't have been more right when she described us as "the perfect mess." I realized her assessment held more truth now than it ever had before.

"Pizza?" I suggested again, longing for a change of location.

"Will you at least put on some clothes?"

I rolled my eyes, knowing it would piss him off. "You first."

Best Friends

Jack

I grabbed Cassie's hand in mine, locking our fingers together as we walked outside. I glanced around the city, noting the buildings and how different they were from everything back in Southern California. New York looked as old as it was. But it was cool as shit. Even in the chilly air, the city buzzed with an energy I'd never experienced before. New York had swagger. I liked it here already.

"There it is," Cassie said with a smile, pointing toward a small green awning up ahead.

That was quick.

"Cool." It looked small as hell. I hustled in front of Cass, pulling the door open before ushering her inside, my hand firmly placed on her ass.

The smell of fresh bread, cheese, and sauces overwhelmed my senses. My stomach growled as I perused the menu on the wall, the old man behind the counter studying me. I'd gotten used to being stared at, but I convinced myself this guy couldn't possibly know who I was already. Sure, the trade was reported in the papers and online, but I hadn't started playing with the team yet.

"What are you getting, babe?" I asked my girl, mesmerized by the long blonde hair that spilled down her back.

She's so fucking hot. I just want to tie that hair in a knot to my bedpost.

"I'm gonna get a couple of slices."

"Want to just get a whole pizza and then we can bring the rest home for later?"

She nodded enthusiastically. "Yes! Great idea! You're so smart," she said, before rising to her toes to kiss my cheek.

"Smart and starving. You have no food at your place. You'll kill me, woman."

"I know who you are!" The man's expression turned joyful as he waved a fat finger in the air. "You're our new pitcher! Jack . . ." he paused, his eyes squinting, " . . . Carter, right?"

Cassie's mouth dropped open as she looked in shock between me and the man behind the counter. "Yes, sir," I replied with a quick nod. His hand reached across the cold steel counter for mine before he extended his hand toward Cass.

"I'm Sal, sweetheart," he grinned widely, taking her in.

See, Kitten, even old men think you're hot.

"I'm Cassie. It's nice to meet you. How'd you know who he was?" Cassie asked, her voice slightly stressed.

He released her hand. "I'm a huge Mets fan. I follow everything about the team. We're all really excited to have you here. Welcome to New York!"

His voice boomed with such sincere enthusiasm that it soaked straight through my skin and into my bones. "Thank you. I'm *really* happy to be here." I looked directly at Cassie, saying the last words.

"How come you aren't with the team in Chicago?" His gray eyes fixed on me quizzically.

"They did me a favor and didn't put me on rotation until Monday night. I flew straight here to get settled."

"That's wonderful. You two living in the Lower East?"

My eyes met Cassie's quickly before responding, "We are for now."

"Well, I'm Sal. Anything you want is on the house."

"Oh no, Sal, you don't have to do that. Thank you, though," Cassie answered sweetly before I could respond. That was one of the things about being well-known, or famous, or whatever you wanted to call it that never made any sense to me. People enjoyed giving you free things when you could clearly afford them. The irony of giving free things to people with plenty of money wasn't lost on me.

"It's nice to meet you, Sal. And really, we're more than happy to support your business, since I assume you'll be supporting mine." I smirked, noting the Mets banners and framed posters hanging on the walls.

"So, what can I get for you two?"

Cassie glanced toward me. "I just want pepperoni."

"Can we get two large pepperoni pizzas?"

"Sure thing, Jack." Sal turned toward the kitchen behind him and shouted, "Two large pepperoni pies."

Pies?

As if reading my mind, Cassie leaned into my ear and whispered, "They call them pies here. And if you want a piece of pizza, they call it a slice."

I smiled, thankful for my first lesson in New York slang. I kissed the top of her head, taking in the tiny restaurant. Two small tables huddled with old green chairs next to the oversized window. "You wanna sit?"

She nodded, choosing a table and then sitting down. I almost pinched myself to ensure this was really happening. Having Cass back in my life renewed me. I felt like a new fucking man . . . like I could do anything simply because this girl was with me.

I placed my hand on the table before Cass reached hers out, laying it on top of mine. Her fingers moved across my skin, and I was instantly aroused.

Get it together.

"I'm still blown away that she fought the annulment. And had all that fake paperwork and stuff. It's crazy to me," she said as she shook her head.

"It's insane is what it is."

"And vindictive. And malicious. And horrible."

I released a quick breath. "Yeah. It's all those things."

"So, when did you finally go to Alabama?"

I pulled away from her grip, leaning back and linking my hands behind my head as I stared into her green eyes. "I was just sitting there, waiting. A whole month had gone by and she still hadn't signed the papers. I felt like I had no control in my own life, and I was getting pretty pissed off."

◇

"Hey, Dean. Question: How long is your winter break?" I asked my kid brother over dinner.

"Uh, we go back at like the end of January, why? What's up?" He cocked his head and continued chewing his food.

"You wanna fly out to Alabama and help me move my shit back here?" I lifted my chin at him.

"Jack! Language." Gran swatted my arm.

"Sorry, Gran." I pressed my lips together as Gramps laughed at my discomfort.

"Don't encourage him." Gran tossed an evil look in Gramps's direction, and he quickly choked back another chuckle.

"Of course I'll go," Dean said, ignoring everyone else. "When?"

"After Christmas, we'll head back. I want to get out of that state as soon as possible," I said, my voice filled with disgust.

Gran reached out and squeezed my arm. "Did she sign the papers yet, dear?"

I averted my eyes and shook my head. "She's still fighting it. Says I can't prove that there was fraud involved."

"But she faked her pregnancy! She tricked you." Gran's voice rose as her cheeks reddened with indignation.

"I know, but she has records that confirm she was pregnant." I sighed, shoveling a fork full of Gran's delicious cooking into my mouth.

"How can she even do that?" Gramps looked up from his plate, his eyes heavy with worry, and guilt rushed through me at the thought of causing him or Gran any unpleasantness.

I swallowed before responding. "I have no idea. Maybe the doctor was an old family friend? Her family goes back generations in that town so they're pretty well respected."

Gran let out a disgusted grunt. "They don't even know the meaning of the word!"

"So, wait." Dean wiped at his mouth with a napkin before placing it back in his lap. "Are you saying that there's nothing you can do to fight it?"

"I'm just saying that the burden of proof is on me. And how do I prove all that?"

"That's one messed-up bi—" Dean stopped short as Gran jerked her head, glaring at him. "girl. I was gonna say, that's one messed-up girl."

I realized my teeth were clenched. "You're telling me."

"I'm worried, Jack. This is taking so long. The longer it takes, the more you have to lose," Gran added.

I knew what her underlying concern was. Gran was worried about me and Cassie. I'll admit I was worried too, but I'd be damned if I'd *let that little bitch win.* "I'll fix it, Gran. Don't worry. She'll sign the papers."

"Don't do anything foolish now," she warned.

◇

"Jack, your pies will be up in a minute, OK?" Sal's gravelly voice echoed throughout the small restaurant, shaking me free from my memories.

"Sounds good, Sal. Thanks."

"What did Marc say about going to Alabama?"

"I didn't tell him."

She laughed, running her fingers through her hair, and I wanted to reach out and touch every fucking part of her. "Of course you didn't."

"Well, come on! He would have *advised* me not to go. I was still paying rent on a house I wasn't living in. I needed to get my stuff before spring training started in February, and that was only a little more than a month away."

"Were you freaking out?" Her forehead creased with worry, and I wanted so badly to take it all away, but remembering Cassie's relationship deal-breaker rules, I refused to lie.

Rule number one: Don't lie.

I closed my eyes before opening them again. "I was definitely freaking out. You see, Kitten, aside from all the bullshit going on . . . my stuff still being in Alabama . . . Chrystle not signing the annulment . . . it was always about you. All I cared about was getting back to you. And I am sorry that time slipped away from me so fast, but—"

"Don't do that to yourself," she interrupted. "I understand better now."

I shoved my hand into my hair, tugging at the strands like I tended to do around her. "I know that I probably should have called you. But while it was all going on, I was so caught up in fixing everything. I was obsessed with every detail being in perfect order before I came here. There were no exceptions."

"But you're here now. And that's all that matters." Her gorgeous eyes glistened, and I knew I'd lose my shit right here in front of Sal if she cried. Her tears could absolutely fucking gut me.

"To go, right?" Sal shouted toward us, and I coughed my emotions in check.

I glanced at Cass, who nodded her agreement. "To go, Sal. Thanks," I answered.

I pushed my chair back and walked toward the small counter. "Do you have a car, Jack?" Sal tilted his head in my direction, his eyes narrowed.

Initially confused by his odd question, I leaned back and thought for a moment. "No," I said haltingly, wondering why a stranger was asking if I had a car.

"I only ask because my little cousin Matteo is a driver. You don't want to take the train to the stadium every day, and forget trying to take a taxi. I'll write down the number of his car company and you ask for him directly. He'll take care of you." Sal scribbled Matteo's name and number on the back of a business card before shoving it toward me.

Relief washed over me. Sal wasn't some creepy stalker; he was just a nice guy. "Thank you. I hadn't even thought about that," I said with a smile, tucking the card into my back pocket and making a mental note to call the number later.

"Don't mention it. You two just make sure you come back in here and visit me every once in a while, OK?" He slid the two large boxes in my direction.

"Sure thing." I reached out my hand, and he gripped it firmly.

"We'll see you soon. Thank you." Cassie smiled before holding the door open for me and our large pies.

See? I catch on quick.

We walked back toward our apartment as Cassie started laughing. "I can't believe he knew who you were."

"That was crazy, right?"

"Yes!"

I shrugged my shoulders while balancing the pizzas. "I've always heard New Yorkers are intense."

Cassie stopped briefly, her eyebrows raised. "Oh. You have no idea."

Her tone made me smile. "Guess I'll learn soon enough."

"You just better win your games, mister," she warned, her tone sounding half-teasing, half-nervous.

We walked into the apartment building where the elevator doors waited in the open position. Cassie pressed the button and as the doors drew closed, I found myself wanting to drop the boxes to the ground and pin her against the elevator wall. My pants tightened as my thoughts took off on their own. In my mind, I'd leaned over and pressed my lips to her neck, licking and nibbling my way up her jaw as moans escaped from her lips. I thought about pressing my mouth against hers, silencing her sweet little cries as our tongues played a game of hide and seek. She cleared her throat, and I looked up to see her holding the elevator doors open.

"Do you and the elevator need some time alone?" she asked, her eyes flicking to the bulge in my pants.

"I was just thinking about all the things I'd like to do to you in here." I winked and bit my bottom lip, hoping for a reaction from her.

She cocked her head to one side, her lips puckering in that cute little way that always turns me on. "Oh, really? Elevators are nasty. You're gross." She turned her back to me and jangled her keys toward the door as I let out a slight laugh.

Once inside, I placed the hot-as-hell pizza boxes on the kitchen table and shook the heat from my hands. "As soon as you sit down, I'll tell you the best parts," I shouted at her retreating back.

"Oooh, really?" She looked back at me from the bathroom doorway with a smile. "Just let me wash my hands."

After a quick search, I grabbed two plates from the cupboard and placed them on the counter before pouring two glasses of water.

Note to self: get some beer.

Cassie walked into the kitchen, her face all smiles. "I'm ready," she said, grabbing both of the waters as she practically skipped to the kitchen table.

$\diamond$

"Who are you talking to?" Dean was sitting on the couch, and I punched him on the arm as I walked past.

"Melissa," he answered, raising his eyebrows with her name. "Meli, hold on a sec." Dean covered his cell phone with his hand and lowered it toward his thigh. "She wants to come with us." I eyed him, my face clearly confused. "To Alabama," he added.

"Why?" I asked, not understanding why she would possibly want to take that trip.

"She said she's bored at home without Cassie. And she wants to help. Personally, I think she just misses me." He laughed.

I thought for a second before realizing that the idea of Melissa coming with us didn't annoy me. "She can come."

"Really?" Dean broke out in a big smile.

"Yeah, I don't care," I said quickly. It would be fun with her there. And she'd probably be really helpful. She was a girl, after all, and girls like to organize, clean, and take care of shit. Right?

◇

"She did not go with you to Alabama," Cassie said, her jaw dropping wide open.

"Yes, she did. She even met Chrystle," I told her with a large grin before stuffing a slice in my mouth.

"What?" Her shoulders dropped. "She didn't tell me a thing!"

I reached across the table for her, cupping her cheek in my hand. "I told her not to. I made her promise she wouldn't tell you anything until I could come get you."

"But she's *my* best friend," she whined. "And she knew how much I was hurting. If she would have just told me what was going on, I wouldn't have had to go through all of that. The waiting, the not knowing . . ."

"Trust me, Cass, she fought with me a lot about it. She wanted to tell you every day, and every day I had to make her promise she wouldn't. I threatened to stop filling her in on things and she said if I did, she'd call you that second and tell you everything." I half smiled to hide my discomfort. "So basically, we had an understanding. As long as I kept her in the loop, she kept her mouth shut." It didn't feel wrong when I asked Melissa to keep all this from Cassie at the time, but sitting here now, saying it all out loud, the fact that I had been a complete dick overwhelmed me.

"*Hmph.*" Cassie crossed her arms across her chest and pouted. My eyes followed her arms but stopped abruptly on her chest. Just one look and my manhood started to wake up. I forced myself to look away and think about anything other than the woman I loved sitting across from me, her breasts heaving up and down with each disgruntled breath.

"I'm sorry. I just couldn't have her tell you what was going on until it was all over. I had asked you to understand so much already. I refused to ask you to understand that too."

"But I would have. I would have understood." She uncrossed her arms before continuing. "Or I would have at least tried to."

She's right. She's so fucking right. But it's too late. I can't change the past. What's done is done.

"I know that, but it didn't seem fair." I reached across the table and stroked her cheek with my thumb. "I was trying to be honorable. And I felt that coming to your door while I was still carrying Chrystle-sized baggage was not the honorable thing to do."

"You and all your *right-thing-to-do* ideas. You sorta suck at doing the right thing."

"I hear that a lot."

◇

"Jeez Jack, this house is really nice," Melissa said, running her hand across the granite countertop in the kitchen of my rented house.

I nodded. "The rent is really cheap here," I paused before adding, "And I thought I was staying awhile."

"Well thank God you're not! Can we go out tonight? Please? Somewhere fun?" she begged, her bottom lip jutting out.

I smirked at her suggestion before glancing at Dean. "Sure." I shrugged, taking a swig from my lukewarm bottle of beer. There were only two bars in this small Alabama town, and after that hellish night when I met Chrystle, I'd sworn I'd never step foot in that particular bar again. So that only left the other one, and I had no idea what it was like.

"Yes!" Melissa practically shouted before disappearing upstairs to the guest bathroom. "I get to shower first!"

I eyed my brother. "What's the latest with you two?"

"She likes to kiss me." Dean smiled like a lovesick idiot. "A lot."

"Are you in junior high? What the fuck does that even mean?"

Dean's face dropped, and I genuinely ached for him. My brother was pretty much the polar opposite of me. He got attached to girls willingly. Whereas I cut every cord possible that tied me down to anyone—until Cassie that is—he fastened triple knots to the people he cared about. When Dean fell for a girl, he fell hard. I half wondered if he did it just to spite me. Just to prove how unlike me he really was.

"It just means that anytime that girl will let me kiss her, I'm going to take it. I like her, alright. I just don't think she really likes me."

I punched him in the arm. "Kiss her better then, jackass."

"I kiss her just fine, fuck you very much."

"Obviously not," I teased. Sensing his defenses on the rise, I backed off. I loved to torment my little brother, but I didn't enjoy actually hurting him.

"You want me to talk to her for you?" I offered, wondering what Melissa's deal was.

Dean's back straightened as his shoulders tensed. "Definitely not. The last thing I want is for you to talk to her."

"Just tryin' to help, little brother." I took another sip before pouring the rest of the bottle down the sink. Warm beer tasted like piss. The shower turned off and Dean glanced up the stairs. "Go up there, already. What you should have done was hopped in the shower with her," I suggested with a laugh.

"You're such a dick," he shot back as he headed toward the bathroom.

"But I'm right," I shouted as he flipped me off over his shoulder.

◇

We sat around the small circular oak table, drinking and laughing. Melissa pounded her tiny fist against the tabletop before shouting over the music, "Jack, I forgot to tell you that I sent Cassie the jar of quarters the other day!"

My mind drifted back to the night she left, standing alone in her old room while I stared at the jar she'd left behind. "Why?"

"She asked for it. And she made me promise to wrap it in like a thousand layers of bubble wrap so it wouldn't break."

I raised my eyebrows and offered a cocky grin, happy to hear this revelation when my eye caught sight of the last possible person in the world I'd ever want to see, with her maid of honor trailing behind her. My jaw tensed as I cracked my neck.

"Oh, look who it is, Vanessa. My husband." Chrystle's grating voice rang in my ears, and I suddenly wished I were deaf. "And if it isn't his delicious brother too. Vanessa, you remember Dean, don't you? From the weddin'?" She looked toward Vanessa, who shifted uncomfortably but didn't respond. "Hi, Dean. How you doing, sweetie?" Chrystle cooed in her syrupy accent as she continued to invade our space.

I glanced at Melissa, who was making fists with her hands, her eyes narrowed into tiny slits, and her mouth snarling. "Jesus, Jack, I guess it's true what they say about beer goggles," Melissa sniped, giving Chrystle the once-over with pure disgust in her eyes.

Chrystle's jaw dropped slightly and her eyes got huge. "What did you say?"

"I said you're as ugly on the outside as you are on the inside," Melissa spat out. For a tiny thing, she sure was ballsy. I fucking loved it. Melissa said everything to Chrystle that I couldn't say without it potentially being used against me in court.

"*And just who the hell are you?*" Chrystle braced herself and tried to sound tough but failed, and I noticed Vanessa fighting to hide a grin.

"*None of your fucking business,*" Melissa shot back before taking a drink from her glass.

"*But it is my business. See, you're sitting with my husband and my brother-in-law.*" Chrystle ran her fingertips down Dean's arm, and he tensed before swatting her hand away.

"*Oh, great.*" Melissa rolled her eyes. "*You touched her, Dean. She's probably pregnant now.*"

With that comment, I couldn't hold back any longer. Thunderous laughter ripped from my lungs and spilled out into the air.

"*Now, why don't you take your ugly skank ass away from our table so we can enjoy the rest of our night?*" Melissa turned to eye me. "*Seriously, Jack. How drunk were you to fuck that?*" Her tone filled with contempt.

Struggling for a comeback, Chrystle scurried away from our table, almost tripping on an out-of-place chair as Vanessa quickly trailed behind her.

"*Holy shit, Funsize. That was awesome.*" I reached out to high five her from across the table.

"*The easiest way to get under any girl's skin is to call her ugly. Especially when she's not,*" she said matter-of-factly.

"*Good to know.*" Dean nodded.

"*Don't get any ideas, buster. You pull that shit with me, and I'll never speak to you again,*" Melissa said, with a sassy neck gyration that made me want to laugh.

"*Yes, ma'am,*" he responded, placing the bottle to his lips and chugging.

Pussy.

◇

"Holy shit, that story is amazing!" Cassie's eyes squinted as she howled with laughter.

"It was pretty hilarious." I laughed along with her, thankful for the upswing in her mood.

"How did Melissa keep that from me? That's the best story ever!"

"She's probably dying to tell you," I admitted, feeling guilty that I'd asked her best friend to keep so much from her.

"Did the evil troll sign the papers after that?"

The smile fell from my face as I remembered what came next. "No."

◇

The three of us walked toward the exit of the bar as Chrystle jumped in front of me, grabbing me by the arm. I freed myself from her wretched touch before shouting, "Don't fucking touch me, you crazy bitch."

"I just want to talk to you, Jack." She batted her eyelashes and tilted her head in some bullshit attempt to appear sweet.

"How about we talk after you sign the papers?"

Instantly, her mouth pursed together in frustration. "I'm not signing those. You can't prove anything and you know it."

"You keep telling yourself that," I lied, hoping she'd buy it.

"You're lying."

Fuck.

"Just remember how many friends you have before I subpoena them all and make them testify against you. If you get them to lie on the stand, I'll make sure they go to jail."

"You wouldn't dare!" she spat.

"*The fuck I wouldn't.*" *I leaned in close to her face, my words laced with anger and hate.*

"*It won't work anyway. I've covered all my bases, so to speak.*" *She grinned wickedly, and I wondered what the hell I did in a past life to deserve this.*

"*Just sign the fucking papers, Chrystle.*"

"*No.*"

"*Why the hell not?*"

"*Because I refuse to make it easy for you to get rid of me.*" *She smirked, and I wanted to smack the ever-loving shit out of her.*

"*Is this a fucking game to you?*" *I asked through clenched teeth, my temper rising to a boil.*

"*I want to stay married, so I won't sign anything if I can avoid it.*"

Her smugness radiated from her with such force that I had to fight the urge to scream and shout like a lunatic in the middle of the bar.

Keep your cool, Carter. Do not let this crazy bitch push you over the edge.

"*Avoid it? You think you can avoid this?*"

"*Actually, yes I do.*" *Her voice, thick with deceit and confidence, made me want to gag.*

"*You're just a bad person.*" *I threw my hands up into the air in my frustration.*

"*So are you!*" *she fired back.*

"*No. I'm an asshole. There's a difference.*"

This girl pushed every goddamned button I had. And not in a good way. I half wished Melissa would walk past me and deck her. Lord knows I couldn't. If it were socially acceptable to punch a girl, this might have been the time I'd actually consider doing it. If she were a guy, I'd knock her teeth down her fucking throat.

"*I will do whatever I have to do to be rid of you. You hear me? Whatever I have to do.*"

"Are you threatening me?" she asked, her voice overtly raised.

"If I were threatening you, you'd know it. Sign the damn papers." I turned away from her, punching the bar door open with my fist.

◇

"I didn't think it was possible to hate her more." Cassie exhaled as she shook her head in disbelief. "Who does stuff like that?"

"Crazy bitches. I swear I'm never talking to another girl who isn't you again."

That actually isn't a half-bad idea. If I never talk to another female fan, I'll never get in trouble with Cass and she'll trust me again.

"Gran might get sad." Cassie's sweet voice interrupted my new plan.

"Right. You and Gran," I amended before continuing. "So, Chrystle filed a restraining order against all three of us the next day."

"Shut the fuck up! Against you, Dean, and Melissa?"

I nodded. "She said we threatened her life and she feared for her safety."

"Are you joking? That bitch better hope I never run into her or she will fear for her safety." Her fingers tapped the top of her plate, making a loud ping with each touch.

I laughed out loud. "I like it when you get all protective over me, Kitten. It's cute."

"You should have had her locked up in an asylum or something when you had the chance." Her voice filled with anger, and I found myself amazed at the amount of craziness in my life over the past year.

"I still can't believe Meli didn't tell me any of this. I mean, after I saw you at your game that night, I called her right away. She told me to get over you. She said I needed closure, but she knew everything that you were doing the whole time."

I grabbed the back of my neck in discomfort at the memory of seeing Cassie with some other guy at my baseball game and also how irritated Melissa had become. "Yeah. She was pretty pissed at me by that point."

"Why?"

I tugged my neck to the left, cracking it before exhaling loudly. "She told me that I had a deadline. Either I told you by a certain date, or she would."

"When was the deadline?"

I looked away from her eyes, the truth still a painful reminder. "Before I left for spring training this season."

I watched as her mind worked, the pieces clicking together like a puzzle that only fit together in one particular way. She was making the connection between Melissa's demands of me months ago and their conversation after seeing me at the game a few weeks ago. "But she never told me. I mean, she never said anything. And obviously, neither did you." She stopped, her forehead wrinkling with her continued confusion as she realized that Melissa threatened to confess everything to her, but never followed through. "Why didn't she tell me? She knew how hurt I was."

I nodded. "I know. She said that you were finally happy here. That you were giving people a chance and you loved everything you were experiencing. And she was afraid if she told you everything that you'd go back to being sad and close yourself off. She figured telling you would only make you take steps back, instead of forward."

I watched as her forehead softened, releasing the tension. "Because of Joey?" she asked softly.

"Yeah. She said that even though it wasn't the same, she could hear the subtle excitement in your voice whenever you talked about him." I forced a smile while my stomach churned and twisted with jealousy.

"So that's why she pushed me so hard to go out with him." She stopped picking at her nail polish and looked at me. "You knew about him, right? I mean, before that night at the field?"

"Mm-hmm" was all I trusted myself to say in response. I had no right to be angry, but the thought of someone else with my girl made me want to punch holes in the wall. Or his face.

"From Dean?" she asked, her voice curious.

"Mostly. After Melissa got pissed at me, I think she enjoyed telling me you had someone else in your life. She blasted me one night after Chrystle had finally signed the papers, but I still hadn't called you. I told her I was trying to figure things out, but she fucking flipped out on me, yelling and screaming into the phone."

I shuddered at the memory of making Melissa angrier than I'd ever heard her before. For a little thing, she sure was loud. "She demanded to know what the fuck it was that I still needed to figure out. Then she told me to leave you the hell alone and stay out of your life forever."

Cassie moved her hand to cover her open mouth, her eyes wide as she listened.

"By that point I was waiting to see if the trade would go through. No one knew I was trying to get traded. Not even Dean."

"I . . ." Cassie paused, exhaling, "don't even know what to say."

"I feel like someone out of a fucking Lifetime movie. Or some piece of shit from the Maury Povich show. Saying all of this out loud." I stopped to look at her green eyes.

God, she's so beautiful. How could I have ever hurt her?

"It's all so insane to me."

"It's a lot to take in," she agreed.

Subject Change

Cassie

Reliving it all, when it wasn't that far in the past to begin with, was beyond overwhelming. I had no idea all the things Jack had gone through during our time apart. Parts of it broke my heart and other parts downright pissed me off. I was half tempted to tell him to stop. That I didn't want to hear any more. That I'd heard enough. What could there possibly still be left to say?

But my mind—my ever-loving, godforsaken, pain-in-the-ass mind—wouldn't let it go. My mind would be the biggest monkey wrench in our getting back on track. I didn't want to be stupid. I'd already accepted Jack's apology and welcomed him into my home with open arms, but going forward, I didn't want to be dumb ever again. There would be no next time if he fucked up. There would be no more chances. A girl can only take so much.

"Another break," I suggested, and knew immediately what crossed Jack's mind when I saw the knowing look on his face. "Not that kind of break."

"Why not?" He licked his lips and my jaw dropped open.

"A change-of-subject break."

"And change-of-location break?" He nodded his head toward the direction of the bedroom.

I narrowed my eyes, barely able to see him through the tiny slits. "Fine. But only talking first."

Jack laughed. "Talking first. Sex after."

"Jack!" I howled, my cheeks flushing.

"Come on, I can barely move anyway, I'm so full. New York pizza is fucking good."

"I know, right?" I said. New York pizza was unlike anything we had in California. Don't get me wrong, we had plenty of "New York style" pizza places back home, but they were nothing like this. This had become, hands down, my most favorite style of pizza. Ever. "They say it's the water."

"They say what? What water?" Jack asked as he put the dirty dishes into the sink.

"The pizza. They say it's so good here because of the water. It does something to the dough. I don't know if that's true, but I to- tally buy it." Every time I shared a tidbit of information I'd learned about New York since living here, an excited chill coursed down my spine. I loved being the person teaching Jack all this stuff.

"Sounds good to me." He grabbed a towel and dried off his hands before turning to me. "Shall we?"

"If you insist," I said.

"Oh, I insist alright."

I walked into the bedroom and began stripping down, when Jack blurted out, "I thought you said we weren't—"

"I'm just getting into my pajamas!" I interrupted. "I hate lying in bed in jeans."

"Damn."

"I thought you were full?"

He licked his lips. "I am, but there's always room for K-I-T-E- N." He sang the word like the Jell-O jingle, and I laughed.

"You forgot a T," I teased.

"It wouldn't fit. You try to sing it with two t's." He patted the top of the bed before leaning his head against a pillow as the Jell-O jingle played in my head. "Get over here."

I slipped into a pair of boy shorts and a tank top before literally jumping onto the bed. When I snuggled my head against the crook of his shoulder and wrapped my arm around him, he sighed with contentment and pulled a blanket over us.

"So, what's our subject change?" he asked.

"Your new baseball team." I smiled against his shirt.

"What about it?" His chest rose and fell against my cheek.

"Tell me about it. How does it work in the big leagues? What do you have to do?"

"I have to report to the field on Monday morning. I need to be there by eight so I can fill out some paperwork. And I'll spend the day there until the game."

"But the game's at night, right?"

"Uh-huh."

"You'll be there all day long?"

"Yeah, well, I need to get checked in, get my locker, make sure my uniform fits, meet the manager, work out, take infield, have batting practice, eat lunch, attend meetings—" He stopped abruptly before continuing, "and miss my Kitten."

I laughed before sitting up to look at him. As much as I loved lying against his chiseled body, I enjoyed looking into those chocolate-brown eyes when we talked. Call me crazy.

"Should I come to the field after I get off work? Are you pitching? Do you want me there if you're not pitching?" Working in the office Monday through Friday all but assured that I'd miss plenty of Jack's games. While a part of me hated knowing how many I'd miss, other parts of me reveled in the dreams and goals I had for myself. I'd moved to New York to advance my career, not follow

Jack around the country. Still, the idea of him traveling and playing in stadiums without me filled me with sadness.

I feel like a walking contradiction.

His eyebrows pulled together. "I have no idea if I'm pitching or not. But I want you there no matter what." He reached for my hand, his thumb caressing my knuckles. "I always want you there, Kitten."

My heart skipped with his touch, his words. "Then I'll be there." I smiled softly as he raised my hand to his lips. The truth surged through me in that moment. There was a rush that happened whenever I watched Jack play. Nothing compared to sitting in a stadium, no matter how big or small, and seeing Jack on top of that mound of dirt. It was magic.

"I'll have a ticket for you at Will Call and you'll get an ID card so you can go underground after the game."

"An ID card?"

"It's mostly for the away games. That way security knows you're a player's wife—" He stumbled before quickly recanting, "or girlfriend. So they know you're with the team."

All other feelings escaped in a rush as jealousy settled into my stomach. I wondered if Chrystle possessed one of the ID cards in question. As if reading my mind, Jack added, "She never had one."

I exhaled and inhaled quickly. "I know it's stupid to think about stuff like that, but I can't help it."

Jack quickly shook his head. "It's not stupid. Those thoughts are in your head because I put them there." He leaned his mouth next to my ear, his breath warm and enticing. "I won't mess us up again. I promise." He nibbled on my earlobe before he pulled away.

I closed my eyes, drinking in his vow. Part of me cringed, acknowledging the vulnerability that coursed within me. I needed to be strong, but the reality was that Jack would be away a lot and I wouldn't be able to go with him. As much as I wanted to believe that his mistake with Chrystle was a one-time major screwup, I'd be lying to myself if I said I wasn't fearful.

I was.

And I wasn't sure I'd ever not be.

"Do you believe me?" he asked, his brow furrowed with worry.

I fought back the tears that formed in my eyes. "I want to." What I wanted to do was bottle my anxiety up and put it on a shelf where it could only come out in small doses, but I didn't know how. Right now it lived on the outside of my skin, like an extra layer I couldn't shed no matter what. My emotions had taken full control over every other part of me. I'd become victim to my own insecurities.

"I'll show you." His forehead pressed against mine as he continued. "I'll never lose you again."

"What if I want to be lost?" I teased with a half-serious tone and watched as he pulled his head from mine.

"I won't let you."

"You won't let me?" I mocked, secretly loving the way he wanted me.

Jesus, Cassie, you're a fucking nutcase right now. Pick an emotion. Pretend like you're in charge here.

"No. I won't let you. End of discussion." His mouth remained stoic.

"That wasn't really what one would consider a *discussion*."

"Because there's nothing to discuss. I'm not leaving you ever again. And you're not leaving me. No matter how pissed off I make you, or how frustrated. I fucking love you, and I'm not going anywhere."

I attempted to fight back the smile that formed. "And I love you. But really, if you ever cheat on me again, I'll cut your nuts off and hang them from the Empire State Building."

You're Bossy

Jack

And now I needed the subject change. I'd relived my mistake with Chrystle every moment since I made it, and talking about cheating with Cassie fucking wrecked me inside. "You know, there isn't much more of the story to tell If you want to quit interrupting and let me finish." I cracked a smile.

She crinkled her nose in response to my words, a slight smile spreading across her cheeks. I waited for what I was certain would be a smartass remark when she simply said, "OK. Finish."

Wrong again, buddy.

I breathed out a long, steady sigh before picking up where I left off.

◇

I leaned against the couch in my newly rented Arizona apartment. Spring training for pitchers and catchers was in full swing, and I was still a married man.

"We should really start on divorce proceedings, Jack." Marc's uneasy voice buzzed from the phone at my ear.

"Is that your professional opinion?"

"We're only dragging this out further. She's never going to sign something that makes her look as bad as the annulment does. As it is, there's a thirty-day waiting period after we've filed the divorce paperwork."

My head pounded as my rage exploded. "Thirty days? Fuck!"

"I know. Let's just get this over with for you, OK? Let me withdraw the annulment and start the divorce paperwork. Although I have to warn you, she can refuse to sign the divorce papers too."

"Jesus Christ, Marc. Just give her whatever the hell she wants and get me out of this." I jammed my finger into the End button before pitching the phone full speed against the wall of my apartment. Pieces of plastic flew into the air, leaving a hole in the wall behind it.

Shit.

The next day I opened my e-mail inbox to see a message from Chrystle's best friend, Vanessa.

Jack,

We need to talk. I can help you. Call me as soon as you get this.

Thanks,

Vanessa

I stared at the e-mail with her phone number for a good half hour before remembering I'd shattered my phone. Before practice, I picked up a new one and almost knocked the salesman out when he suggested I change my number to a local one. I'd never change my phone number to a number Cassie didn't have, and the mere suggestion almost cost that guy his pretty little face.

"Jack?" Vanessa said when she answered my call.

"What do you want?" I asked abruptly. This girl was Chrystle's best friend. She knew everything Chrystle lied about and did nothing to stop it.

"I can't let her keep doing this to you, Jack." Her voice broke, but I remained unconvinced and questioned anyone who could stay best friends with a person like Chrystle. "I didn't know she faked her *pregnancy," she whispered before continuing. "I mean, at first I didn't know."*

"Did you know at the wedding?" I asked through gritted teeth.

"No. She was still lying to everyone then."

I didn't care. "Get to the point."

"After seeing you at the bar and hearing the things she said to you, I tried to talk to some sense into her. But she won't listen. She got even crazier after that night. Like more determined or something . . ." Her voice trailed off.

Annoyed, I huffed into the phone. "Vanessa, I don't have time for this. Either get to the point or I'm hanging up."

"I'm trying to say that I'll testify on your behalf. I'll talk to your lawyer, or judge or whomever. I'll tell them that everything you wrote in those annulment papers is true. And I'll tell them everything they need to know that not even you know, Jack."

My chest heaved as disbelief and elation coursed through me. The air around me thickened as I struggled for a response. "Why would you do that?"

"Because you don't deserve what she's doing to you. It's wrong, and I don't want to be a part of it anymore."

I wanted to believe her. "If you're serious," I paused, still unsure of truth versus lies when it came to those girls, "I'd like to pass your phone number along to my lawyer and have him call you. Is that OK?"

"Yes, of course. I'm really sorry, Jack. I hope this helps."

"Thanks, Vanessa."

◇

Cassie swiveled her head back and forth in disbelief. "This story. Seriously. Crazier and crazier."

"I know, but thank fucking God Vanessa e-mailed me when she did. Marc was just about to file the divorce papers when I called him."

"Of course. Just in the nick of time, like a well-played movie." She raised her eyebrows.

"A well-played Lifetime movie," I added with a smirk.

"So, Vanessa followed through? She wasn't lying?"

I knew Cassie's mind wandered to the same places mine had originally. Was this another trick, a lie, another baited hook I was sinking my teeth into? "Not only Vanessa, but she got their friend Tressa to make a statement corroborating my claims on the annulment. Chrystle signed the papers that week."

"Wow. Wow." Her hand covered her now gaping mouth. "Just like that? That's all it took to get her to sign?"

I raised a hand in the air. "Just like that."

"Unbelievable."

With her head back on my chest, I wound my fingers in and out of her hair. "Yep. That was spring training, then the season started, and here we are."

She lifted her head back up from my chest, a wicked grin covering her face. "Uh-uh. I want to hear about you seeing me at the field with Joey the other night."

"The other night? That was weeks ago," I complained.

"It sometimes feels like the other night."

"You're a cruel girl, Cassie Andrews. Anyone ever tell you that?"

"Maybe once or twice." She leaned in, her soft lips pressed against mine.

"That's the perfect way to get me to stop telling you stories." I deepened the kiss, my tongue pushing its way into her mouth.

"Tell me first; kiss me after." She leaned away from my face, and I thought briefly about teaching her a lesson. One that included the fact that I'd kiss her whenever I damn well pleased. But I was close to finishing my story and I wanted to move on.

◇

I kicked the mound of dirt at my feet, adrenaline coursing through my veins. I fought with my head to keep its focus, but it kept drifting to thoughts of Cassie. I was in New York, and she lived here.

She won't be here.

She doesn't come to your games anymore.

My stomach twisted as I faced my catcher, tossing warm-up pitches into his glove. I'd thrown no less than ten pitches when a man's voice shouting stopped me mid-pitch. I almost threw my fucking arm out stopping like that.

"Cassie! Cassie, wait!"

The air in my lungs escaped without warning, and I almost dropped onto the dirt mound at my feet. I glanced in the stands toward the sound of her name, catching sight of her long blonde hair flying as she ran. I'd know her anywhere. A guy chased after her, and my chest blazed with jealousy. I clenched my jaw, every muscle in my body tensing at the sight of her with someone else. She turned around to face the guy, and her eyes met mine for a brief moment as my temper raged like an out-of-control inferno. The guy put his arm around her, and I forced back the urge to charge him like a bull in a bullring. I wanted to break his fucking arm. No one touched my girl but me.

"Carter, let's go!"

I turned away from her, refocusing on the batter's box, and threw the ball with all my strength.

◇

"I didn't know he was taking me to the game." Her eyebrows creased as her expression turned remorseful.

"That . . ." I paused, reliving the feeling of seeing him toss his arm around her shoulders again, "made me almost come unglued."

"Well, I'm glad you didn't. I'm so sorry you saw me there with someone else."

"It's in the past now. Ready to hear how nervous I was when I got here last night?" I played with her hair again.

She moved to straddle me, sweeping her legs on either side of my waist. "I'd like to hear about that in a minute." She leaned down, sucking my bottom lip into her mouth, her hips grinding into my waist.

She thinks she's in control.

In one quick movement, I flipped her onto her back. Pinning her beneath me, I pressed my hard-on against her shorts. "Is this what you want instead of story time?" My mouth plunged toward her neck, nipping gently before licking and kissing up to her ear. "This what you want, Kitten?" I breathed against her.

"Mm-hmm," she moaned softly, her back arching.

"Say it." My hands wandered up her thighs before finding the sweet spot between her legs. "You're burning up down there," I said. Knowing how hot she was for me fueled my hard-on even more.

She moaned my name, and I covered her mouth with mine. "Say it," I demanded, breathing into her.

Her eyes opened, her chest rising and falling. "I want you instead of story time. Now, stop fucking around." Her hands wrapped around the nape of my neck, tugging and pulling my hair. I leaned away from her, enjoying the control.

I pulled her clothes off, tossing them over my shoulder before adding mine to the pile. Bringing my fingers and body back to hers, her back arched and writhed as she begged, "Jack, please."

"You need to learn some patience."

"Fuck patience. Get in me!" she practically screamed, her hand wrapping around me. I bucked against her gently before peeling her hand away. I tried to be strong, but who was I fooling? I wanted her just as badly as she wanted me.

Maybe more.

I placed my arms on each side of her gorgeous naked body before guiding myself inside her. "So wet, Kitten," I said, instinct and need taking over.

Her eyes closed as her fingertips pressed hard against my shoulders, working their way down my back and settling on my ass. I moved in and out of her, slowly at first. The feeling of her tightness surrounded me. Coupled with my feelings for her, I knew I wouldn't last long.

This girl is ruining my ability to last in the sack.

"Jack. Faster." Her voice was breathy and filled with need.

Goddamn, she'll be the death of me.

I quickened my pace as she pushed and pulled against me, her breathing accelerating. I drove myself into her with more force, fighting the urge to explode right then. I leaned into her mouth, gliding my tongue along her bottom lip before pushing it inside her mouth. We breathed into each other, tongues desperate and needing, as her body started to quiver.

There is a God.

I refused to stop, pushing deeper as pleasure-filled screams tore from her lips and filled the air between us. Her body trembled as I grew harder, the blood draining from the rest of my body and pooling in one central location.

Her eyes focused on me just as I closed mine. A growl escaped as I called her name. I released myself inside her, my hips slowing before finally stopping. I collapsed on top of her with a laugh.

"Seriously? Get. Off," she demanded, gasping as she exaggerated her inability to breathe.

"I thought I just did."

Cassie rolled her eyes, shoving me with all her strength. "OK, OK. I'll move." I wrapped my hands around her shoulders and rolled us both over. I pulled her naked body against mine, refusing to let her go.

"Now I'm hungry again." She kissed the top of my nose. "And ready for the rest of the story."

"You're bossy."

"You like it."

I'll Never Leave You Again

Jack

I waited for Cassie on the couch in the tiny living room. Looking around, I surveyed the small apartment and thought to myself that we'd need a bigger place soon. And I needed a gym. But we could deal with that later. She walked out in her pajamas, grabbed one of the boxes of pizza, and tossed it on the coffee table near our legs.

"I'm ready now."

◇

I walked into the lobby of Cassie's apartment building and was immediately greeted by an older gentleman in a dark gray suit and black bow tie. The doorman's kind face almost set my rattled nerves at ease. Almost.

"Good evening, sir. May I help you?" he asked, eyeing the packages in my arms curiously.

"Yes." I forced a smile before asking, "I was wondering if you could help me out?" I moved toward him and placed the packages carefully on the tiled floor. His eyes raced between my now revealed Mets jersey and the boxes at my feet. I could sense he was nervous, or maybe it was caution I picked up on, but I immediately wanted to put him at ease.

"These are for Cassie Andrews. She lives here."

A large grin covered his face, replacing the uncertainty. "I know Miss Andrews. Lovely girl. Talented, too."

I knew that tone. It was pride, and even the doorman in Cassie's apartment building felt it for her. "Yes, she is."

I extended my hand toward him. "I'm Jack."

"Fred. How can I help you, Jack?" he asked, gripping my hand with more strength than I expected.

I sat for a moment wondering just how much to tell this stranger and how. "Long story short, Cassie was my girl. But I fucked everything up and lost her." I eyed him apologetically after swearing. If Gran heard me talk like that to an older person, she'd smack me upside the head. "Sorry for the f-word."

"It's fine. Go on." Fred leaned against the reception desk, his eyes sparkling with interest.

"I'm here to get her back. Each one of these packages is a different gift. I need to get them to her, but I can't be the one to do it." My voice shook as I tried to explain. "Am I making any sense?"

"Yes." He smiled again. "Do they all go at once?"

I threw my hands in the air, thankful for his question. "No!" I shouted a little too aggressively. "Sorry. They go separately. There's an order to them."

"Do you know which gift goes first?"

I looked down at my feet. "Yeah. It's really heavy, though."

"That's OK. Here, let's hide the rest behind the desk. Just in case she wants to come down and get the first one."

"OK, so what's the plan?" I stared at the man I now found myself depending on.

"I'll call her and let her know that a package arrived. She can decide if she wants to come down to get it or if I should bring it up. We'll go from there."

"Sounds good," I said, before cracking my knuckles and pacing nervously.

Fred pressed a button and began speaking. "Miss Andrews, there's a package down here for you. Do you want me to bring it up, or would you like to come get it?" His eyes met mine as we both waited for her response.

The speaker crackled and her voice filled the otherwise empty lobby. "Can you bring it up, Fred? I'd really appreciate it."

I literally had to brace myself against the wall at the sound of her voice. That voice filled my dreams at night. That voice belonged to the girl who belonged to me. That was my voice, and I wanted it back.

"Unless you're busy, then I can come down. Whatever is more convenient for you, Fred. Thanks."

That's my kitten. So considerate of others all the time. I took a deep breath as my chest relaxed. "OK, Miss Andrews. I'll be up soon," Fred responded politely.

"Ready?" Fred asked me with a smirk.

I nodded, bending down to lift the weightiest box first. "It's really heavy," I warned him before dropping it into his arms.

"Jesus, what's in this?" Fred remarked, his voice strained.

"Quarters. A hell of a lot of quarters," I said with a smile, and rushed over to press the elevator button for him.

When the elevator doors opened with a ding, I watched him walk inside, press a button and cock his head at me. "Wish me luck," he added with a smile.

"Hell, wish ME luck!" I shouted back as the doors closed.

Fuck. What if she gets pissed off? What if she hates me? Why did I let so many months pass by without talking to her? I smacked the side of my head with my palm and reminded myself that I was a fucking idiot. No girl in her right mind would take someone like me back. I suddenly *found myself praying that Cass was crazy. Or at least half crazy. That way I'd have a shot.*

A few moments later, the elevator doors dinged back to life and Fred stepped out, a smile on his face. "One down."

"What'd she say? Anything?"

"She thinks someone is sending her weights." He chuckled.

I laughed loudly just imagining her saying that, and it echoed through the small lobby. "OK, here's the next one." I watched as his body braced and tensed at the anticipation of the second box. "Don't worry, it's not heavy," I said and watched as Fred exhaled in relief. "But it is fragile. There's a bunch of picture frames in there."

"Be right back." Fred's smile was contagious, and I found myself smiling just as broadly as he was.

I paced the tile floor, waiting for his return. This had to work. This was my girl we were talking about. If wasn't going to be Cassie by my side, then it would be no one. I'd never love anyone the way I love this girl. There's no way we went through all of this bullshit for nothing.

The elevator ding interrupted my thoughts. Fred stepped out, his face still scrunched up from the force of his smile.

"What'd she say this time?" I searched his eyes for answers.

"Nothing. She wondered if this package arrived with the first one. I told her no." He shrugged. "What's next?"

"You're enjoying this, aren't you?"

"Actually, yes."

"Well, here you go," I said, dropping another light box into his waiting arms.

That delivery was filled with Cassie's rules and all the ways in which I'd broken them. And all the ways in which I'd never break them again. I made promises to her in that box and by the grace of God, or whatever higher power exists in this world, I hoped she'd give me the chance to make good on those promises.

Another ding and Fred emerged. "She's confused," he admitted. "She doesn't know what's going on."

"Confused is good. It's better than mad. She's not mad, right?"

"She doesn't seem mad. She did want to know who was bringing the packages."

"What'd you say?" I asked as nerves shot through my body.

"I told her some kid was dropping them off one at a time."

"She bought that?" I huffed out a laugh.

"She bought it." He grinned mischievously.

"You're good, Fred. Thank you. Here's the next one." I handed him a manila envelope as he entered the waiting elevator.

This was the next-to-last gift I had, the gag about eye-rolling and all the ways in which it was bad for you. There was only one more small box to go before I stood outside of her apartment door and hoped she'd open it. I looked down at my Mets jersey and ran my hands over it, making sure I looked presentable.

"She's crying," Fred said, the moment he exited the elevator.

"Shit," I exclaimed as my heart fell into the pit of my stomach.

"She said they were good tears, though, so I think you're in the clear," he added, patting my shoulder.

I looked up at the ceiling and swallowed hard. "Whew. OK. This is the last one, Fred, but I have to come up with you. Is there anywhere for me to wait without her seeing me while you deliver this last package?"

"You can wait in the hallway, around the corner. She won't see you there," he suggested.

"Sounds good. You ready to see if I get my heart back?" I asked, clutching a dozen red roses.

"I have a good feeling," he said, glancing at the flowers.

We stepped out of the elevator together and into the illuminated hallway. Fred pointed at the door marked #323, and I nodded, hurrying around the opposite corner. The knock on the door was soft, but the *sound carried. I heard Cassie tease Fred about how she should just leave her door open all night.*

Fred informed her that this would be the last package. Was that disappointment I heard in her voice as she thanked him? Her door closed softly, and Fred cleared his throat. I peered around the corner, and he waved me over. "Good luck, Jack." He reached out his hand.

"Thank you so much for all your help. I couldn't have done this without you."

"Yeah, you could have," he said with a grin before stepping into the elevator and disappearing.

The last package simply contained a letter from me and a small note asking her to open her front door. I hurried to Cassie's apartment door and waited with the roses clutched in my sweaty hands, right in front of the Mets logo on my jersey. It was in this exact moment that I realized I'd left my confidence somewhere between my old life in Arizona and my new one here. I was nervous as hell. What if . . . so many what-ifs plagued my mind as the door flew open.

"Oh my God," she said, as her voice rang out into the hallway.

She looked beautiful. I wanted to grab her, throw her against the wall, tell her how sorry I was for everything, and make up for each moment that had been lost between us. I lowered my arms, allowing the lettering on my jersey to show.

◇

"I'm enjoying this," Cassie's face scrunched up with her broad grin.

"Enjoying what exactly?" I teased through my vulnerability. It was tough reliving the parts we'd just lived through. I had no idea if Cassie would ever forgive me or take me back. There was a good chance she wouldn't. Last night was a huge risk for me, but I'd do it all again for her.

"Hearing all of this from your point of view. I want to see the rest of last night through your eyes."

I inhaled deeply, knowing that I'd give her anything she asked for, and then I continued.

◇

"Why are you wearing a Mets jersey?" she asked, her voice carrying a mixture of excitement and confusion.

"I got traded."

"They traded you?" She sounded surprised. No, she sounded offended.

"Well, technically," I couldn't stop the smile from taking over my face, "I asked."

"You asked what?" Her green eyes narrowed.

"I asked to be traded to the Mets." I shrugged and looked down at the floor, wondering how long she was going to keep me outside.

Her eyes grew wide. "So, you live in New York now?"

"Just got here. Can I come in?"

"Of course. Yes." She stumbled as she moved aside for me to enter, and I stifled a laugh. Was she nervous too?

"These are for you." I pushed the long-stem roses toward her.

"Thank you. They're beautiful." She leaned in to smell them, and I watched her eyes close as she breathed in their fragrance.

She walked into her tiny kitchen, and I looked around her apartment, my eyes falling on the couch. "I see you got my gifts."

"Mm-hmm," she mumbled, and I wanted to silence her and make her moan all at the same time.

"Cassie." I said her name as I inched my body close to hers. I tried to resist touching her, but being that close . . . a man only has so much willpower. I don't know what it was exactly about her hair, but I was tempted to reach out and run my fingers through it. Instead, I found

myself tucking strands behind her ear as she touched my face. I swear I turned into putty with her touch.

"Do you still love me?" I asked, as desperation and uncertainty coursed within me.

"I never stopped."

That's all I needed to hear. "Me either." I grabbed the back of her neck, unable to wait a single solitary second longer. My mouth was instantly on hers, the heat between us radiating. My tongue reached out to meet hers before I pulled away. I needed to apologize before I tossed her fucking clothes to the ground along with my pride.

"I'm sorry for lying to you that morning. I'm sorry for cheating on you that night. I'm sorry for not being the person you knew I could be."

Her lips pursed and I was desperate to kiss them, so I leaned in, kissing her bottom lip lightly. "And I don't know if you can ever forgive me, but I'd never forgive myself if I didn't at least ask you to try."

Please fucking forgive me.

"And I'm sorry it took me so long to get here. She was fighting the annulment and it took months to get it processed and finalized. I refused to fight for you while I was still carrying all that baggage. But it took a lot longer than I had expected. I should have called you. And I'm so sorry I didn't."

Please don't let it be too late.

"I thought you hated me," she whispered, her eyes avoiding mine, and I swear my fucking heart split into pieces.

She thought I hated her.

I'm such a dick.

Instinctively I reached for her chin, tilting her head up toward mine. "I could never hate you. I thought I was going to have to come before the annulment was complete when I'd heard about you and the guy from your work." I forced my clenched stomach muscles to loosen their grip on me.

"How'd you know who he was?"

"Dean. I kept tabs on you, Kitten. Not in a creepy way, I swear. Just in a making-sure-I-wasn't-going-to-lose-you-all-over-again way. See, you've always been able to see past the front I put up. I never thought I'd be able to find someone who would know the real me and still want to stick around. And then I saw you at that frat party and my life was never the same." I spilled my guts to her, hoping that something I told her would click and she wouldn't kick my ass to the curb.

A single tear ran down her cheek as I continued. "I know I don't deserve you, but I need you." I reached for her face, wiping the tear from her gorgeous face, finding myself lost in the green of her eyes.

"I need you too. I hate feeling vulnerable, and I want to pretend like I don't, but it would be a lie."

"Then don't pretend. Tell me you'll try to forgive me so we can move on from our past."

Please forgive me.

"I already have," she said, and I was torn between collapsing at her feet on the floor and jumping into the air like a pussy.

I leaned my head against hers, "I'll earn your trust again. I promise." I emphasized the word trust, hoping she knew just how much I meant everything I was saying to her.

With her face buried into my shoulder, I breathed in the smell of her shampoo, her soap, her skin. Her arms wrapped around my waist and her breath was hot against my neck as she inched closer toward my face. I was already turned on and excited from her nearness. "Prove it," she whispered suggestively into my ear.

"Oh, I plan to," I answered confidently, before giving her a chance to change her mind, or even think at all.

I lifted her into my arms, my hands firmly cupping her ass. She wrapped her legs around my waist, and I pressed her back to the wall, rubbing my growing hardness against her. She moaned, and I grew even *harder as my tongue traced the curves of her neck, her salty skin familiar and enticing. I licked and nipped my way toward her jawline, where her mouth waited, slightly parted.*

Another breathy sound from her, and I thrust my tongue into her mouth. The feel of her tongue against mine caused my body to shudder uncontrollably. I pulled my mouth away, burying my head into her neck once more. I licked and sucked at her, her hips pressing against me as I continued grinding her into the wall.

"I've missed you," I whispered into her ear.

"I've missed you too." Her voice hitched, causing me to hesitate.

Against my better judgment, I pulled my head away from hers and looked into her eyes. "Do you want to stop? Is it too soon?" I considered momentarily that having sex might not be the best idea. No matter how badly my body craved it.

"I could lie and tell you I think we should wait. But honestly, I've waited long enough. I've been without you for too long already. I want you, Jack," she insisted, her fingers digging into the muscles in my back.

"I'm so sorry for everything, Kitten."

"I know. No more apologies. Tomorrow you can start again, but not right now." She touched the side of my face, and I half wondered if it was all a dream.

Cupping her ass, I walked us into her bedroom, her tongue running along my bottom lip before entering my mouth with ravenous intent. I wove my fingers into her hair, pulling lightly as she released a quick gasp.

"If you don't stop making those fucking sexy noises, I'm going to lose it right here."

She smirked, clearly enjoying the power she had over me. She leaned into my ear, her tongue sucking and nibbling on it before breathing a heavy, long, drawn-out sigh.

"Oh, that's it. You're gonna get it," I teased, before throwing her on top of the bed. I pulled off my Mets jersey and threw it to the floor, quickly followed by my white undershirt.

"God, I've missed your body," she exclaimed while biting on her bottom lip, her eyes eating me up.

"I'm not man candy, Kitten," I said with mock offense.

"Yeah, you are," she insisted with a mischievous grin.

A smirk took over my face before I leaned toward her, my hands grabbing at her pajama bottoms. She lifted her hips and I pulled them down past her feet and discarded them. Then I straddled her, pressing my hardness against her mound. I wrapped one arm around her back and lifted her up toward me. Her arms instinctively wrapped around my shoulders, her nails digging into my back. I pulled at her tank top and she lifted her arms into the air before pressing her exposed breasts against my chest.

I'd been waiting so long to have her—thinking for months about the moment she would be mine again, hoping I'd get this chance—and the mere feel of her skin against me nearly sent me over the edge.

When my knees hit the edge of the mattress, I lowered her to the bed and inched slightly lower. She rested her head on top of a pillow, and I kissed her breasts, my tongue swirling, and my mouth sucking. She moaned as she reached for my head, her hands keeping me firmly in place. I sucked some more, my mouth hungry for every inch of her. My hands slid down her stomach to the front of her thong, my fingers rubbing against the material. I slipped my hand underneath the elastic, exploring, before entering. I moved my fingers in and out of her as she squirmed and tossed her head back.

My tongue traced a path between her breasts, up her neck, and into her hot mouth. She briefly pressed her tongue against mine before pulling away. "No more teasing. I want you, Jack."

The sound of my name being spoken breathlessly from her mouth caused my breath to catch. My fingers slid out from inside her as I sat up again. I yanked my boxers to the floor before pulling her thong down and watching her kick it off with her feet. Her legs parted, making room for me, welcoming me home. "I love you, Kitten," I said, as I slid inside her.

She fucking felt amazing as I rocked in and out of her. "Goddamn..." My voice trailed off as she moved her hips with mine, her breathing growing louder with each push. I thrust myself deeper until I could go no further, her moans growing in intensity and her breath quickening.

"Harder, Jack," she demanded, and I pushed myself into her with more force. Each movement deep and hard, I knew I wouldn't last much longer.

"Oh God," she breathed out. "Don't stop."

And I prayed she'd come before I did. Her body rocked against me as sounds of pleasure escaped her lips. My pace quickened, and her body trembled as she tightened on me, her movements jerking lightly. I continued thrusting until I could take no more. My dick throbbed, and I released myself inside of her, a deep groan escaping my lips.

My breathing uneven, I stared into her eyes before pressing my mouth to hers. "I love you," I said, my thumb caressing her cheek.

"I love you too." She smiled, her hand weaving through my hair.

"I'll never leave you again," I promised, my heart finally feeling whole.

"If you do, I'll fucking kill you," she threatened through a smile. "Deal."

I watched as she untangled her body from mine, slipping out from the bed and into the bathroom.

Welcome to the Big Leagues

Cassie

And here we are." I wiped the tears falling down my cheeks.
"Here we are." Jack reached out his hand, brushing his
thumb along my jaw.

"I can't believe that was all last night. How is it possible that it feels like so long ago?" I asked, feeling like a freaking lunatic.

He sighed before responding. "Because today has been like six months all rolled into one single day. I'm fucking exhausted."

"Me too." I laughed.

Scanning his muscular body with my eyes, I was momentarily distracted when he asked, "Do you think I should call Sal's cousin tomorrow? I mean, do you think setting up a driver is a good idea?"

I nodded my head before answering. "I do, actually. I think it's a great idea. You should see if you can hire him exclusively."

"So he wouldn't drive anyone else around?"

"No. Not like that," I tried to explain, my brain literally pinging with fatigue. "Just see if having the same driver all the time is an option. I think it would be beneficial if we only had one person taking us places."

"Us?" He raised his eyebrows, taunting me.

"Fine. I'll hire my own driver," I shot back.

Jack lunged, pinning me beneath him as he planted a kiss on my nose. "Like hell you will. He'll be *our* driver. If I like him, that is."

"Fine."

"Fine? You're not gonna give me some sort of smartass comment, like 'What if I like him and you don't?' Just, *fine*?"

"Sorry. I'm too tired to pretend argue." I yawned, unable to hide my fatigue any longer.

"Bed?" he asked, his eyebrows wiggling.

"Yes. But for sleeping."

"OK, Kitten. For sleeping."

◇

Monday afternoon, the phone at my desk rang incessantly, begging me to pick it up. The words Front Lobby displayed across the small screen and I reached to grab it before it stopped.

"This is Cassie"

"Hi, Cassie. Your driver is here."

My what?

Oh, right. Sal's cousin.

"OK, thank you. Can you tell him I'll be right down?"

"Of course. See you soon."

I hung up the phone without saying good-bye and shoved into my purse the camera Jack had bought me after my original one was stolen the night I was mugged at Fullton State. I rushed to file my last-minute photos into their corresponding online folders before speed walking to the elevator.

"Have fun tonight, Cassie." Joey's broad Boston accent filled the air, and I turned quickly toward him.

An uncomfortable blush crept over my cheeks. "Thanks, Joey," I said with a tight smile. "See you tomorrow." I pressed the elevator button, wishing it would hurry up and retrieve me. Working with Joey now that Jack was back in my life wasn't necessarily the most relaxed of situations. I should have added a rule number five to my list after that night: *Never date someone you work with.* Because when it ends badly, it's awkward for everyone. And there's no escape.

The elevator dinged, and I stepped inside the crowded space. Squeezing my way in, I sandwiched myself between two men who thankfully didn't smell terrible. Each time the elevator stopped and the doors opened, the people waiting on the other side realized it was too crowded for them to enter. They would step away as I offered a sympathetic smile, the doors closing. This happened repeatedly for twenty floors until we reached the lobby.

Finally free from playing sardine, I bolted into the lobby, looking for a driver who resembled Sal, complete with overstuffed belly and kind eyes. I scanned the room before stopping on a tall, striking man dressed in a black suit and tie. A pair of black sunglasses rested on top of his spiky dark hair, and even through his suit, I could make out the muscular body lurking underneath.

Good Lord, that is one good-looking man.

The security guard caught the man's attention and then pointed at me as a wide grin spread across his face. The tall drink of water looked in my direction and asked, "Miss Andrews?" I stepped closer to him, my insides trembling.

You've got to be kidding me.

"Please, call me Cassie." I smiled, trying my best not to look him up and down.

"I'm Matteo. Mr. Carter sent me to bring you to the game. Are you ready?"

"Yep," I squeaked out when I noticed the hint of a tattoo peeking out from under his collar.

Jack sent a model to pick me up. A tattooed, freaking hot-as-fuck model.

Matteo opened the rear passenger door, and I settled inside. Suddenly feeling like an entitled snob, I fought the urge to climb over the seat and sit up front with my new driver. Unless I was in a taxicab, sitting alone in the backseat while someone else drove always struck me as odd. I reached for my phone, checking my personal e-mails as the car lurched forward. I glanced up briefly during the quiet drive to find Matteo's blue eyes watching me in the rearview mirror. I darted my gaze from his and returned to my phone, fiddling with it to look busy.

Putting my phone down, I looked outside the window as the city flew by. I constantly found myself in awe of this place, with its massive buildings and old architecture. It was the ideal setting for the photographer in me.

"So, you're Sal's cousin, huh?" I asked, breaking the uncomfortable silence between us.

"Yeah. You see the resemblance?" He angled his head toward the backseat for a moment, and I caught sight of the smile spread across his tanned skin.

I smiled in return, my lips firmly pressed together as I imagined Sal's oversized belly and receding hairline. "Definitely. You could pass for twins."

He laughed out loud.

"How'd you like Jack?" I asked, attempting to bring my boyfriend into the conversation.

Boyfriend.

Still weird.

"Mr. Carter is great. He's a really cool guy, if you don't mind me saying so," he offered politely, and I wondered what thoughts were racing in his head.

"Why would I mind you saying so?"

He huffed out a quick breath. "Because it's not very professional of me to use the word 'cool.' And I probably shouldn't give my personal opinion on clients."

Now I huffed out the loud breath. "Jack is cool, so I get it. And I asked. You were simply answering my question." I wondered how Jack liked Matteo and if we'd be hiring him as our regular driver. Until I had those answers, I refused to get too chummy with Matteo. Chrystle proved that strangers can't be trusted. At least, not in this business.

"It's cool that he plays baseball for a living. You must love it, huh?" he asked sincerely.

My heart lodged in my throat. I struggled to formulate a response to his seemingly simple question as every emotion possible coursed through me in record time. "Yeah. It's pretty great," I lied.

We pulled up to Citi Field and Matteo parked the car in front of the Will Call window and hopped out. He opened my door and offered me a hand. I declined, pushing myself up from the plush leather seat.

"Your ticket is at the booth. I'll be parked right here after the game ends, but Mr. Carter warned me that it may take awhile," he added with a smile.

I flashed back to the many times I'd waited for Jack after his games ended. "Yeah, it takes a little bit to get back out here once the game's over. Sorry about that."

"It's not a problem. I'll see you around eleven."

"Thank you so much. It was nice to meet you." I smiled before walking away.

◇

With my ticket clutched firmly in my hand, I struggled through the crowds toward the section of seats reserved for the wives and families of the players. The smell of popcorn and hot dogs wafted through the air. I looked at the number printed in black ink and walked slowly down the stairs, observing the row number with each step. Almost walking right past it, I stopped abruptly. I glanced at the group of heavily made-up women in my section, watching my every move. Their eyes scanned the length of my body from the top of my natural hairstyle down to my inexpensive shoes. I hurried to my assigned seat before sitting down and stuffing my black purse between the side of my leg and the armrest.

I turned toward the women, who still stared at me, their faces devoid of any emotion. "Hi. I'm Cassie," I said loud enough for the occupants of all three rows of seats to hear. The women simply continued to eyeball me, offering literally nothing in return. Not a smirk, not a sound. I started to wonder if I had something on my face.

I turned to speak to the women in the row behind me before thinking better of it. I sized up each of them instead, taking mental notes of their expensive clothing, brand-name accessories, perfectly styled hair, and overly made-up faces. One woman with an obvious spray tan and dyed blonde hair glanced at me before raising her eyebrows in disgust and shaking her head with an audible huff.

"Did you see her purse? What is that, Target brand?" I heard a voice whisper before a chorus of laughter followed.

What the hell?

I fought back the urge to defend myself. From what exactly, I wasn't sure. But I suddenly wanted to shield my body from the exposed and raw feelings that took over. It hadn't even occurred to me that these women would be rude or unkind. It was one thing I hadn't overthought. Hell, I hadn't thought about it at all.

Why didn't Jack warn me?

He must not know. How could he?

Shoving my vulnerability into my gut where it rested like a giant boulder, my eyes fell on the enormous rock sparkling from Miss Spray Tan's finger. It was the biggest, most ridiculous diamond I'd ever seen, and I'm from LA.

Wonder what her husband's overcompensating for?

My gaze quickly darted to the left hands of all the other women, realizing that each sported their own hefty-sized rocks. Feeling like I was surrounded by a new kind of sorority girl, I turned my scrutiny from them and stared down at the field. Clearly I wouldn't be making any friends tonight.

I thought I left this kind of bitch behind in college.

I craned my head in the direction of the bullpen at the end of the field, forgetting all about the rude women surrounding me when my eyes fell on Jack's powerfully built frame. Heat flooded through my body and seeped into my veins with one look at him as he jogged toward the pitcher's mound. The muscles in his legs flexed each time his foot crushed against the ground, and a smile crept across my cheeks.

God, I've missed watching him play.

His Mets uniform reminded me so much of the one he wore in college that I couldn't stop the memories from replaying. I clearly envisioned the first time I saw him pitching. It had been a truly beautiful experience, although I never admitted it at the time. His transformation into a completely different person once he stepped on top of that mound of dirt at Fullton State was unlike anything I'd ever witnessed before. Watching Jack play baseball was almost like a having a spiritual awakening. Through all my heartache and heartbreak, I'd forgotten this part.

How my pride soared as I watched him play baseball, knowing how much of his heart it held. And how it literally warmed me from head to toe being the person he loved more than it. I relished the moment, reaching into my purse for my camera.

I looked through the viewfinder and grunted audibly. My seat was great for viewing the game, but not photographing it. I was simply too far away, and I didn't have my larger zoom lens with me. I snapped one picture anyway, just to remember the night by, before shoving the camera back into my non-designer purse.

In my dazed state, I barely noticed that the seat to my right was newly occupied. Convinced it was another horrible wife, I hesitated to acknowledge this person. I second-guessed myself, suddenly feeling no better than those other women, when a warm voice with a British accent interrupted my thoughts. "Hi. You're new."

I turned toward her and stopped my jaw from falling wide open. This woman was stunning. She had an exotic look that I assumed brought guys to their knees. Her long straight brown hair looked like satin. That combined with her naturally tan skin made the green flecks in her hazel eyes stand out even more. I didn't think she had a stitch of makeup on, and I was convinced she was the prettiest woman in this stadium.

I offered a small smile. "Yeah. I'm Cassie."

She reached out her hand. "Hi, Cassie. I'm Trina." A wide smile appeared, and she grew even more gorgeous.

"It's nice to meet you," I told her, my voice genuine. After what I'd just witnessed, the fact that she was willing to talk to me at all eased my nerves.

"You too. So, who do you belong to?" She nudged my shoulder with hers.

"Jack Carter." I tilted my chin toward the field. "He's pitching tonight. And you?"

"The second baseman, Kyle." She lifted her hand, pointing him out on the field, and I glanced at her ring finger. My shoulders relaxed when I noticed the absence of rings.

"Where are you from? I love your accent," I said before suddenly feeling stupid.

"London. I like yours too." She grinned.

"I don't have an accent!" I laughed.

"You do. It's like a totally Californian accent, dude," she said, trying to mimic the way I sounded to her.

"Well, that's awesome," I attempted to say with an English accent, but failed miserably. "So, how long has your boyfriend been on the team?" I asked, desperate for her friendliness to continue.

"This is our second season. He got traded last year."

"What's with them?" I tipped my head subtly in the direction of the mean girls.

Trina's face instantly filled with irritation, her perfectly shaped brows pulling together with distaste. "They're bitches. They won't talk to you until Jack has," her manicured fingers shot into the air and did the symbol for air quotes, "paid his dues."

"Until Jack has what?" I asked, with an expression that I'm sure reflected the confusion my brain was experiencing.

"He has to earn the respect of his teammates. Once he does that, then you'll earn the respect of the Bratz dolls over there."

"Seriously?" I reached for my head, massaging my temples as she continued filling me in.

"There is a class system among the wives. And well, you and I already have one strike against us because we're not wives. We're only girlfriends."

"Uh, didn't they start off as girlfriends?"

"I like you." Trina laughed. "Of course they did, but that doesn't matter. We're nothing to them. The only way they'll talk to you is if you do something wrong or get in their way. It's ridiculous."

My head ached as I tried to wrap my thoughts around the insanity that came with the baseball wives. Thankfully, the crack of the bat grabbed our attention and we watched as Kyle fielded the hard-hit grounder effortlessly. Trina released a breath, and a broad smile stretched across her cheekbones. My smile followed, thankful for the out. I wanted Jack to have a great first game.

I couldn't keep from staring at Trina's perfect features. "I'm sorry, but you're ridiculously gorgeous. You look like a model." The words escaped my lips before I could be embarrassed by them.

Trina let out a giggle. "Thank you, Cassie. I actually am." She paused. "A model, that is. Not gorgeous. Oh, gosh."

I laughed. "A nice model? Who woulda thought?"

"Not most people, that's for sure."

As I focused on Jack again, his fluid movements caused sensations in me I couldn't hide. My cheeks warmed as he leaned his body forward, focusing on the catcher's glove. Even from where I sat, I could sense the intensity in Jack's eyes. A battle waged between the hitter and the pitcher, and Jack hated to lose. A quick nod and one deep breath later, Jack's arm hurled the ball past the batter, who swung his bat mightily, but missed.

"And definitely not them," she said, directing her displeasure back toward the mean girls.

"They're just jealous because you don't have to bleach your hair some fake color or spray tan yourself orange to look good."

She continued to smile at me. "Do you work, Cassie?"

I nodded. "I work for a magazine."

"Strike two." She arched her eyebrows, and I crinkled mine. "Didn't you know it was our duty to quit working as soon as we started dating them?"

"Apparently I didn't get that memo."

"They hate girlfriends. And they hate anyone who works." She shrugged. "You would think that we'd all support each other and be friends since we're forced to spend so much time together. But that's not how it works. You should have seen me last season, trying to talk to them at every game. Someone finally had to tell me that they would speak to me when I was worthy. That's the word she actually used. Worthy," she said, emphasizing it slowly, almost in a whisper, and I couldn't hide my disgust. "But she's not here anymore. Her husband got traded."

"Wow. I did not sign up for this," I said, the realization hitting me that these women would now be part of my life whether I wanted them to or not.

Trina brushed some loose hair from her eyes before continuing. "The worst one is Kymber."

"Kymber? Even her name screams bitch," I said with a quick laugh.

Trina's eyes darted to Kymber before returning to mine. "She's the queen bee here. That's how she refers to herself. The Queen Bee. Who says that?"

Cheers erupted into the air, causing both Trina and me to look at the field as our team jogged off, disappearing into the dugout. I'd made it through half an inning. Only eight and a half more to go.

"Her husband has been playing the longest and makes the most money. That's why she's the queen. And all the rest of the wives bow down to her."

A disgruntled sound ripped from my chest. "I've never been really good at bowing down to anyone. It's not really in my nature."

"Don't worry, Cassie. She won't make your life a living hell or anything. She'll just act like you're invisible. Like you don't exist. And if that kind of thing doesn't bug you, then you'll be fine."

I pondered her words, trying to figure out exactly how the situation made me feel. Was it better to be a verbal punching bag or to not exist at all?

◇

When the game finally ended, I followed Trina down a long staircase. Her shoes clicked and clacked down the last set of public stairs before she headed through a private door, guarded by security. Once inside, I shivered as the air of the cold brick tunnels coursed through me. The tunnels ran the length of the stadium, and I quickly thanked Trina for taking me under her wing.

"No problem. I had no idea where the clubhouse was after my first game, and no one showed me. By the time I got down here Kyle was waiting for me, wondering what took me so long."

A burly security guard stood between two metal guardrails. He smiled as Trina approached, giving her a quick hug before staring at me, the wrinkles around his eyes deepening.

"Carl, this is Cassie. She's Jack Carter's girlfriend."

He reached out his massive hand, and I gripped it. "Nice to meet you, Carl."

"You too, Cassie. Hell of a game tonight for your boy. Make sure you tell him I said good job, OK?"

"Absolutely."

"I'm sure I'll be seeing you around."

"Honestly? I'll probably get lost."

Trina giggled. "Isn't she funny, Carl? We're going to be good friends."

We followed the white bricks as they curved gently around a long corridor. Once around the corner, a Mets sign protruded from the wall, announcing the location of the player's locker room. I smiled when we reached the double mahogany doors with a sign that read New York Mets Clubhouse above them. I curbed my desire to whip out my camera and photograph the doors and sign.

"And now we just wait?" I asked Trina quietly.

"Yep."

I Insist

Jack

I walked out of the clubhouse, eager to see Kitten. It was my first outing as a New York Met, and I'd been credited with the win. I pitched six innings and gave up three hits, no walks, and one run. I scanned the crowd of waiting women and children, searching for the one who owned my heart.

There's my girl.

I smiled as soon as our eyes met, the pure fucking joy it brought me to see her made me feel like the biggest pussy on earth. I noticed the hot chick standing next to her, but I didn't give a shit. My heart belonged to my Kitten, and I'd never fuck that up again. I hustled over to her, scooping her up in my arms before I planted a long, dramatic kiss on her waiting mouth. My tongue begged for her lips to part and once she finally opened them, I had to remind myself where we were. I pulled back from her slowly, holding her face in my hand. "I missed you," I whispered, mentally patting myself on the back as her cheeks turned pink.

"Uh, babe. This is Trina. She's Kyle's girlfriend." Cassie's voice stuttered, and I stopped myself from announcing it to the entire tunnel.

Jack Carter makes his girlfriend lose her composure with just one kiss! Oh yeah, he's THAT good.

I extended my hand to Trina, shaking hers firmly. "Nice to meet you."

Way to go, Peters.

"Thanks for hanging out with Kitten."

Trina's forehead creased as she shot Cassie a confused look. "Kitten?"

"Oh my gosh, don't listen to him." Cassie swatted my arm. "Don't call me that to other people like it's my name," she demanded, which made me want to pull her aside and show her who was boss.

She was.

"It was nice to meet you, Trina. I've gotta take this one home now." I winked as I interlocked my fingers with Cassie's, pulling her away from the crowd.

We exited the stadium where waiting fans lingered for autographs, pictures, and whatever else they could get from us players. Cameras flashed as Cassie and I walked past, and I pretended not to notice when two women screamed my name. Cassie jumped at the sound of their voices. "It's OK, Kitten." My fingertips brushed against her shoulder. Even with Cassie by my side, women still behaved like lunatics.

"Jack! Will you sign my son's ball?" A man's voice echoed into the night air.

I glanced at Cass, and she smiled, slowing her pace to a stop. "Sure." The rest of the fans quickly gathered around, and I scanned the group, only signing balls and posing for pictures with kids or guys.

"Can I get a picture, Jack?" I looked up to see a pencil-thin, busty blonde batting her eyelashes at me. I wanted to fucking puke.

I looked at Cass sympathetically as she nodded, letting me know she didn't mind. With a terse "Not tonight," I barely looked in the woman's direction before throwing my arm around Cass and walking toward the car. The woman mumbled "asshole" under her breath, and Cassie's shoulders tensed.

Anxious to get going, I scanned our surroundings, not wanting to be surprised by anything or anybody as we walked toward our waiting car. I spotted a large, muscular silhouette in the distance. "How do you like Matteo?"

Cassie stopped abruptly, turning to face me. "Can you believe he's Sal's cousin?"

I laughed because I'd thought the exact same thing when he picked me up earlier. "No! I almost died when I fucking saw this guy. He's good-looking, right?"

The guy looked like someone you'd see on a billboard or a shopping bag at the mall. I hired a fucking model to drive my smoking hot and incredibly kind girlfriend around town.

I'm an idiot.

"Yeah, he's pretty good-looking," she responded matter-of-factly.

I could always fire him.

Or hit him.

"You don't get to leave me for some driver." My body tensed as jealous insecurity raged through me.

Her face contorted; I could see that my words were settling for her. "Uh, you're insane."

"I might be insane, but I mean it. You can't ever leave me for someone else." The very fucking idea of Kitten leaving me for another guy made me want to rip someone's head off. I'd die before I let that happen. This girl is my world.

"Jack, where is all this coming from?"

"I don't know. Maybe I think since I fucked up so badly, the only way for us to be even is for you do the same thing." I shrugged and watched as her face changed from concern to anger.

She placed her hand firmly against her hip as she lit into me. "First of all, you don't get to tell me what to do. You also don't get to be the one to dictate what makes us even when it comes to your colossal fuckup. Do you understand?"

I knew she didn't really want an answer, so I remained quiet as she continued her tirade. "The biggest thing you don't get to do is turn this around on me. I'm not the one who did anything wrong. I'm not the one who cheated, got someone fake pregnant, and then got married. So you do not get to make this an issue where you're the one feeling bad and I'm supposed to feel guilty over something I had no control over. That's bullshit, Jack, and you know it."

Chills surged down my neck, causing the hairs to stand on end with her demands. She was hot as fuck when she was angry. I wanted to rip her clothes off and take her right here, while our model driver watched. "You're right. You're totally right. I'm sorry."

Her breathing still erratic, she reached for my hand, pulling me toward the giant waiting shadow. "Don't be like that. It's not fair to me. I'm the one who gets to be upset and have insecurities, and figure out how to trust you again. Not the other way around." Her voice turned to a whisper as we neared Matteo.

"Good evening, Mr. Carter, Miss Andrews," Matteo's voice rang out as he pulled open the rear door.

"Seriously, Matteo, call me Jack. Or Carter, even. Just drop the mister. Please."

"Are you sure?" he asked one last time.

"I'm fucking positive," I answered with a laugh, hoping that the f-word would break the ice even further.

"OK, boss. If you insist."

That's right. I'm your boss, model boy. And I do insist.

"How about you, Miss Andrews?"

Cassie leaned her head to the side, her lips puckering. "How about me, what?"

Is she flirting with him?

"What do you prefer I call you?" His eyes locked on to hers, and I wanted to introduce my fist to his jaw. Or piss all over Cassie in an effort to claim her as mine.

Get it together, Carter.

"Just Cassie would be great. No Miss Andrews. It's sorta weird and creepy."

"You're weird and creepy." I leaned into her ear, whispering.

She whipped her head around to face me, and I grabbed the back of her neck, pulling her mouth to mine. Her tongue parted my lips, and I deepened the kiss, my hands roaming down her back to her ass. I squeezed and she moaned into me. My lower body willing and able, I suddenly wished for privacy glass so I could take her in the back of this car.

Matteo cleared his throat as he eased the car forward. "Sorry. I just wanted to make sure we were heading home and not stopping anywhere first."

"We have to stop somewhere. I'm starving," I said. "But no pizza. I need meat."

The sound of Cass's cell phone beeping distracted me from my starving stomach as I wondered who was texting her this late. As if sensing my question, she said, "It's Melissa. She wants to know if we're fighting already." She scratched the side of her head, her hair dangling around her fingers.

"What the hell does that mean?"

"I don't know. I'm asking her." She barely responded as her fingers raced across the cell phone screen.

"I keep forgetting it's three hours earlier there, you know?"

"I know, right? Me too," she said, still typing.

I watched as the Manhattan skyline grew closer with each passing moment, marveling at the unmatched character of this city. I'd never seen so many tall buildings in such a small space before. I knew that seemed stupid, but there was nothing like this in Southern California. I fucking loved it here already. Cassie's phone beeped again. And then again, as I turned to her.

"Oh my God."

"What is it?" I focused as she covered her mouth with her hand. "Cass?"

She waved a finger in the air. "There are pictures of us online already. From when we were just talking a few minutes ago. They look bad."

Cassie shoved her cell phone in front of my face, and I stared at the three attached photos, all showing Cassie looking upset and angry while I stood there like a jackass. The Internet caption on the photo read: "Jack Hits a Home Run on the Field, but Strikes Out at Home!"

"What do you want me to do?" she asked, her voice shaking.

I tossed my arm around her shoulder, pulling her body against me. "There's nothing you can do. We should probably be more aware from now on when we're out in public." Anger worked through me as I digested the simple fact that nowhere was safe from prying eyes. It was the one part of being a professional athlete that I loathed. I hated having no control over which pictures were posted of my personal life and when. I honestly couldn't give a shit what they posted about me, but posting things about Cassie crossed the line.

"I'm so sorry, Jack. I didn't even think about who might be watching." Her breath warmed my chest.

"It's not your fault." I planted a kiss on the top of her head. "We didn't have to deal with this kind of stuff before."

"I look like such a bitch in those pictures."

"It doesn't matter." I tried to reassure her but ended up pissing her off instead.

She pushed away from my chest, squaring her shoulders to me as her breath quickened. "What do you mean, it doesn't matter?"

I leaned forward, cupping her cheek in my hand. "I'm just saying that people are going to think whatever they want to think, no matter what we look like in some online photo."

Her eyes closed as her breathing evened out. "But I don't want people to think you have some crazy mean girlfriend who yells at you after your games."

"They won't," I told her. I couldn't promise her that people wouldn't think badly of her, but I'd do my fucking best to try. I'd fight the press for her. I'd do anything to keep her feeling safe, happy, and loved. She didn't deserve to be vilified online for any reason. Hell, if the public knew anything about our relationship, they'd be hunting me down daily with pitchforks and chanting. "But you have to promise me something, Cass."

Her brow furrowed. "What?" she pouted, looking up at me with those big green eyes.

"You can't let them get to you. The press will write and post whatever they think will sell ads or get them attention. They say things all the time that aren't true, and you just have to remember what is and what isn't. OK?"

I'd experienced how rabid the press can get when it comes to players. I'd escaped the scrutiny somehow in regard to everything that happened between Chrystle and me. I always wondered if Marc had something to do with that, but I'd never asked him. I watched my teammates' relationships crumble under the pressure and never once blamed them or their girlfriends for not being able to handle it. But I knew I couldn't let that happen to Cassie and me. I'd make sure of it.

"Cass? Just try not to read anything if you can help it. Tell Melissa to filter what she sends you," I suggested.

"Like only send me something if it's good?" She shrugged.

"Yeah, Kitten." I pressed my lips against her forehead. "Tell her to only send the good stuff."

When Life Gives You Lemons

Cassie

Not wanting to wake up Jack, I grabbed my things for work as quietly as possible and headed out our front door. Once outside the apartment building, I rushed toward the subway station, noting the time. If I missed my train, I'd have to grab a cab. And grabbing a cab would take forever at this time of the morning.

I passed by a local newsstand as a headline caught my eye: "WELCOME TO THE BIG APPLE, JACK CARTER! GRAB A SEAT AND STAY AWHILE!" Jack had a love-hate relationship with the press. He told me once that the press only likes you when you're winning. But the second you lose, you're the first one they blame. It didn't serve any purpose for him to read the things written about him by strangers, so he never did. He always said that he knew what he needed to improve upon, and he didn't need it shoved down his throat by some reporter who had no idea what it was like to stand on that mound.

Plus, the bad articles really pissed him off, and he almost punched out a reporter once. One long-winded talk in the manager's office with the media director present, and Jack vowed to never read any more press about the team again.

Even still, seeing this paper caused my heart to swell in size. His first win for the Mets was printed in black ink, and I wanted to cherish the memory, even if he didn't. I figured since the article was positive, maybe Jack wouldn't mind. So, I purchased one copy to read and another to keep.

I ran down the dank subway stairs, my papers clutched firmly in my hand as my train pulled in. The brakes squealed as it came to a complete stop before the doors opened. I hustled through the crowd and into the packed subway car. Not wanting to stand the whole way, I silently thanked God for the empty seat I spotted. Once sitting, I flipped open the paper to the sports section, immediately scanning the article on Jack. After skimming the highlights, I mistakenly decided to flip to the Entertainment & Arts section.

My pride-filled heart suddenly exploded inside my chest, and I almost choked on the air around me when I caught glimpse of a familiar photo. I stared at the larger-than-life picture of me pointing my finger at Jack, my face clearly twisted in anger. I looked furious as Jack simply stood there, dejection written all over his face. My eyes fell to the photo caption where my first name was posted as clear as day. "Mets new golden boy gets reamed by girlfriend Cassie off the field."

Shit. How'd they already figure out who I am?

I snapped the paper closed and looked at the people sitting around me. I prayed they hadn't seen the picture or noticed I was the one in it.

Shit. Shit. Shit.

That stupid picture showed up online last night and now it was printed in the newspaper for everyone to see. I reminded myself that no one actually read printed papers anymore before I realized that the online version would probably include the same articles. Shaking the embarrassment off, I fidgeted in my seat until my stop.

Walking into the office, I tossed my things down on top of my cluttered desk before heading into the small corporate kitchen. The magazine's senior editor, Nora, flipped through the pages of a newspaper before glancing up at me.

"Morning, Cassie. I see you had quite the night last night." Her gray eyes softened as she held the paper up for me to see.

I released a tense breath. "Yeah. It's not what it looks like." I attempted to defend myself, dunking a bag of chai tea into my cup of hot water.

She smiled, her short brown hair perfectly curled. "It never is." Her voice soothed my fraying nerves.

"It looks bad though, right? Like I'm crazy angry?"

She glanced back down at the photo. "You look pretty pissed off." Her gaze returned to me as I winced. "Don't worry about it. It's just one photo and no one will think anything of it." She waved a hand in the air, and I wanted to believe her.

"Thanks, Nora." I smiled, appreciative for her kind words. I turned to walk out when she called my name.

"Sit with me for a minute." She pointed at the chair across from her.

Uh-oh.

My legs started to tremble as anxiety consumed me. That picture could be bad for the magazine, and I doubted they wanted to be associated with any negative publicity. What if she fired me over this?

"Stop looking at me like I stole your cab and sit down. You're not in trouble." I relaxed into the cold chair, still clutching the hot teacup in my hand. "I just wanted to hear about your first Mets game as a player's girlfriend."

A small breath escaped from my lips as I relaxed even further. Nora had been kind to me since the day I started in the office. She complimented my work, encouraged me to learn, and challenged me to grow on a daily basis. I respected her, and I wanted to earn her respect in return.

"So, how was it?" She cocked her head to the side, her eyes locked on to mine.

"It was," I hesitated, "different than I expected."

"Different how?" she asked, before sipping her coffee.

I glanced up at the white ceiling tiles, attempting to formulate my words into cohesive thoughts before answering. "It was amazing watching Jack play again. Nothing in the world compares to how that feels." My heart squeezed inside my chest. "But the wives on the team are really mean. Like, none of them would even speak to me, mean."

She let out a loud guffaw, her head tilting back. "You're joking."

I shook my head. "I wish I were."

"So they wouldn't talk to you?"

"No. They just stared at me at first and then they refused to acknowledge me at all. It's like I wasn't even there." I rolled my eyes, annoyed at the fact that I'd be seeing these women again later.

"That's awful. And so unnecessary. Why do we women treat one another with such disrespect?" she asked as my coworkers milled in and out of the small kitchen, casting curious glances in our direction.

"I don't know." I suddenly remembered the one bright spot in the evening. "Oh, yeah! One woman did talk to me. She was really nice. Her name was Trina. She's a model. Freaking gorgeous." I bit at my bottom lip.

"Trina Delacoy? Beautiful brown hair, bright hazel eyes?"

"Yeah. How do you know her?" I asked in surprise.

"She's worked with us before, very nice girl. Who is she dating on the team?" she asked, bringing the ceramic mug back to her lips.

"The second baseman, Kyle Peters."

"Make sure you tell her I said hello." The lines around her eyes deepened with her grin.

"I will."

"So, Cassie, now that your gorgeous super jock is back in your life, you're not going to quit the magazine, are you?" She smirked at me knowingly as I pinched my eyebrows together.

"No. Why on earth would I quit?" The last thing I wanted to do was leave this job. While the very idea of Jack being back in my life caused my soul to beam with love, I still had career goals I wanted to achieve. I moved across the country to work for this magazine, and Jack didn't affect my feelings about that.

"I was just making sure. I'd hate to lose you and all that beautiful potential you have."

"As long as you'll have me, I'm yours," I said with a nervous grin.

"Good. I assume you'll be traveling with the team some, won't you?"

My breathing hitched as the question echoed in my ears. "I don't know. I hadn't even thought about it, to be honest. Work is my priority, so I guess I'll go to some of the away games on the weekends if I'm not busy."

Jack's schedule hadn't even entered my mind. I'd been so overjoyed at simply having him back in my life, it never occurred to me. I had no idea how long he'd be in town before he turned around and left again. I made a mental note to talk about his travel schedule that night, after the game.

"Maybe we can schedule some magazine work in with your boy's away games. Kill two birds with one stone?" she offered with a wink.

I fought back against the burn of tears forming in my eyes. I would not cry, no matter how kind and amazing this woman was to me. "If that would work out and it makes sense for the magazine, it would be amazing. But you don't have to do that."

"I know I don't. And I'm not making any promises. Just bring me a copy of Jack's schedule, and I'll have my assistant look into it." Her eyes wandered, glazing over as she tapped a finger against her lips. "Maybe we can work in an online feature where we travel with you, highlighting some local human-interest stories from wherever you are. Or we can highlight the team and the charities they visit when they travel?" She hummed lightly. "So many possibilities. Although I'm not sure how they will work since the teams are usually in and out of towns rather quickly. But something to consider nonetheless."

I listened to the thoughts and ideas that spilled from my boss's mind, quietly waiting for her to dismiss me as my own excitement grew. The idea of being able to possibly work and travel with Jack at the same time thrilled me, but I refused to get my hopes up for something that might not be feasible.

"Go." She waved me away. "We'll talk about this later."

I scurried out of the kitchen before flipping on my computer and scanning last night's e-mails. I smiled when I saw Melissa's name in my inbox.

Cass,

Just remember one thing . . . when life gives you lemons, cut 'em open and squeeze the juice in life's face!!!!! That'll teach life to mess with you! HA!

Hang in there. The photo will blow over. You can always call Mom and talk to her if the shit hits the fan. In the meantime, I'll monitor all the websites you guys show up on and see if I can run interference. You know, post things anonymously to try to help. I've already favorited the local NY gossip sites so I've got you covered, GF!

Love you. Miss you.

Melissa's mom owned a successful boutique publicity firm in Los Angeles. She maintained an exclusive group of big-name clientele, but always made sure to keep that small business feel. Inadvertently I'd learned a lot from her over the years just by overhearing her business meetings and phone calls. This sort of thing was right up her alley, and I knew she'd be more than happy to help me if it got to that point.

Please, dear God, don't let it get to that point.

I hit the Reply button and quickly typed out a response before handling my daily duties.

Meli,

That picture was in the paper this morning. The actual PRINTED version! And they printed my name, but just my first name, thank God. I'm so freaking embarrassed, but what can I do, right?! Ugh. I will definitely call Mom if things get out of control, but I'm going to work on being more aware of my surroundings from now on. Hopefully they won't have anything to print of me going forward, unless it's my face wearing a big-ass, shit-eating grin. :) Call you soon.

xoxo

My cell phone vibrated as I searched online for upcoming events our readers might be interested in seeing. The magazine printed human-interest stories, with the inclusion of local politics, news, and happenings around the five boroughs. When I started, I mostly handled the research for future issues, but once a week I was assigned a general event to cover and photograph. My bosses never promised me that my photographs would be used, but since I started working here six months ago, they always have.

I glanced at my phone, noting one new text message from Jack on the screen. My body trembled at simply seeing his name. I pressed the button, displaying the message:

Matteo will pick you up at 6. You need to go to the sales office and pick up your ID card. See you after the game. Love you.

Without responding, I set my phone aside. As I completed my work assignments, my thoughts kept drifting to my conversation with Nora from earlier, hope filling my mind.

◇

Matteo pulled up outside the Will Call booth again, and I averted my eyes from the hint of a tattoo that crept up from underneath his white dress shirt. I wondered what it was, but I was too embarrassed to ask. I caught sight of his blue eyes watching me in the rearview mirror and smiled. He turned to exit the car when I stopped him.

"You don't have to open the door for me. I got it. Thank you, though. I'll see you later." I scooted out of the backseat, shutting the car door behind me. Matteo waved before driving off.

I approached the booth window. "Hi. I'm Cassie Andrews, Jack Carter's girlfriend. He said I needed to pick up an ID card?"

The young girl smiled. "See that building over there?" She pointed to my right, and I nodded. "Just go inside and they'll take your picture and print your card for you."

"Thanks." Confused and unsure, I asked, "Do I still need a ticket to get in?"

"Yes, you do. The ID card is so you can get down to the locker rooms at away stadiums." She handed me an envelope with one ticket inside.

"Ah. That makes sense. Thanks so much." I turned to leave, walking toward the other building.

My freshly printed ID card in hand, I made my way to my assigned seat. It wasn't the same seat from last night's game, but it was still in the same section. Tension galloped through my body like a racehorse as I neared the seats filled with the mean girls.

"Try not to yell at your boyfriend tonight, Cassie!" A manly voice mocked me from behind and I stopped midstep.

"Bitch," another voice mumbled within earshot.

You've got to be kidding me.

Resisting the urge to look over my shoulder and confront the hecklers, I straightened my shoulders and continued toward my appointed row, my heart pounding out beats in double time against my flesh.

"If poor Jack gets cussed out when he wins, imagine what she does to him when he loses!" another voice bellowed, barely louder than the pounding that echoed in my ears.

Suddenly feeling vulnerable, I quickened my pace down the concrete steps. I shuffled into my seat, recognizing the meanest wife, Kymber, right away as she watched the situation unfolding. She laughed and whispered something into the ear of the wife sitting next to her. Both women glanced at me before directing their attention elsewhere.

So, it's really going to be like this. Awesome.

My phone vibrated, and I pulled it from my pocket. Thankful to see Melissa's name on the screen, I clicked the text message button.

Put that shit-eating grin on, babe!

That was all she wrote, followed by a picture of me walking in the stadium, an uncomfortable look plastered all over my face.

I shoved my phone into my purse, feeling nervous and extremely exposed. It was one thing to be in a stadium filled with people when no one knew who you were, but it was quite another when you were recognized. I'd become completely identifiable to the thousands of people around me, all of whom knew—thanks to the pictures popping up online and in the press—I was Jack Carter's girlfriend.

These fans had already formed their own opinions about the picture printed in the newspaper this morning. They assumed they knew me, or knew the kind of person I was. They made judgment calls about my character based on nothing but a simple photo taken completely out of context, which, as a photographer, really pissed me off. I strived to maintain my integrity when I was shooting, making sure that my photographs and edits always captured what was truly going on in the scene. I never attempted to create a false illusion with my pictures. Apparently it was too much to ask others to do the same.

If people wanted to take pictures of me without my knowledge, they absolutely could . . . and they would. If they wanted to approach me, there was nothing to stop them. I lacked any sort of self-protection, and it worried me. If the other wives weren't such raging bitches, I would have asked them how they got through it. It amazed me that none of them offered to help, or asked if I was OK. I looked around for Trina, but she was nowhere to be found. And since Jack pitched last night, he wouldn't be pitching at all tonight.

I toyed with the idea of calling Matteo and going back home, but the potential fallout cemented my ass right to my seat. I imagined pictures of me leaving the game early followed by distasteful and untrue headlines.

Nope. I wasn't moving. My pride refused to let me.

My phone vibrated again and I considered not grabbing it. One reminder pulse later, I reached into my purse, pulling it out. Another text from Melissa. Did I want to see this? Resigned to whatever fate was throwing at me tonight, I clicked the Read button.

Remember: LEMONS! In. Their. Faces.

A smile crept over my face as I stifled a laugh, hearing her voice in my head. Meli was right. I inhaled a sharp breath, suddenly filled with the determination to rise above this madness. I would not let them beat me. Not the mean-spirited fans. Not the horrible wives. Not the newspapers or online sites.

I watched this game for one reason and one reason only.

Jack. Fucking. Carter.

No one in this stadium had any idea the kind of hell Jack and I had endured in the past, and I'd be damned if anyone was going to ruin this for me after all we'd been through. I crossed my legs and leaned my back against the cold, hard seat, silently wishing Trina would show up soon.

Yes, I wanted to prove everyone wrong. I wanted to show them that they wouldn't tear me down and wreck this experience. But it sure would be nice to have a friend by my side while I stayed strong in the face of such intentional ugliness.

You'll be fine, Cass. You can do this.

And I did.

For nine long innings, without Trina by my side, I endured. I left my seat before the game officially ended in order to separate myself from the rowdy crowd as it exited. As I walked up the staircase, the sound of someone snorting and coughing briefly caught my attention. I continued up the stairs, but the sound of wetness hitting the pavement forced my attention downward. My gaze stopped on the blob of spit mere centimeters from my front foot.

"Stupid bitch," a clearly drunken voice slurred.

Without thinking, my middle finger shot up from my right hand and flashed the crowd as I exited the aisle and into the tunnels.

Shit. I probably shouldn't have done that.

◇

The next morning infamous photos of Cassie flipping the bird photos were all over the Internet. Captions read: "Jack's Sweetheart is Anything But!" and "Sassy Cassie Has Quite the Temper!" They were childish and annoying, but they affected me nonetheless. Embarrassment crept over me as I found myself thankful that Jack avoided the Internet. I quickly typed out a text to Melissa.

Make sure Dean doesn't show that shit to Jack. I don't need him worrying about me or yelling at me or being upset with me over this. Please make sure you talk to him.

If anyone could curb Dean's actions, it was Melissa. I worried about him sending Jack the same type of text messages with pictures that she had been sending me. I knew better than to let the jerks know they affected me, and now I'd have to pay for my stupid actions with the online postings, comments, and whatever else came along. The last thing I wanted was for Jack to be worried about me, or think I couldn't handle myself in the face of some stupid drunk hecklers, so I was determined to keep my behavior a secret from him.

My phone chirped.

You got it. Dean won't tell Jack anything about his crazy middle-finger-flipping girlfriend. LOL But hey, you gotta keep it together or these fans will eat you alive. You're better than that.

I sighed inwardly and typed.

You're right. I know. I lost my cool. It won't happen again.

I worked the rest of the day uninterrupted and only started to get nervous about the game when Matteo dropped me off at the stadium. If he knew about the pictures, he wasn't saying anything.

"Have a good night, Cassie. I'll see you later." His smile reached all the way to his eyes, and I shoved my nervous energy aside before smiling back.

"See you later Matteo. Thanks for the ride." I slammed the door shut, hoping no one would notice me. If the comments started already, I'd probably turn around and chase Matteo's car all the way back to Manhattan.

Attending Jack's games solo all the time might start to get old. I really needed to make some friends who liked watching baseball. I guess I wouldn't want new friends so badly if the wives had been kinder. And as much as I liked Trina, it was obvious that her modeling jobs kept her from coming to most games; that sucked for me because without her there, I felt completely alone.

A few nasty comments burrowed into my eardrums as I walked out of the tunnel and into the night air. One deep, steadying breath later and my nerves started to settle. I repeated a chant in my head as I walked toward my assigned seat: *Don't give them anything to talk about. Don't give them anything to talk about.*

I avoided looking directly into anyone's gaze for fear that they might see through my façade. I played tough on the outside, but it wouldn't take much to break me down at this point.

◇

The game ended and I started walking toward the exit, the sound of drunk men stumbling in line behind me. A quick shove forced me to slam into the guy in front of me, my hand grabbing his shoulder for balance. "I'm sorry," I quickly offered as he shook me off. Another rough shove and I started to wonder if they were accidental.

Reaching the end of the aisle, I turned to eye the person responsible for the shoving, when moisture splashed against the back of my shirt and bare neck. The smell of beer filled my nostrils as

I winced, rolling my shoulders forward away from my damp and sticky shirt.

"Oops," an oversized man said with a sarcastic gruff before heading away, laughter ripping from his lungs. I watched as his friend patted him on the back in congratulations.

I stopped moving, the crowd filing out around me as my eyes met Kymber's. She looked at my soaking back and continued walking, her eyes saying it all. She didn't care what happened to me out here. She wasn't on my side and she damn sure wasn't going to do or say anything to help me. The other wives followed behind, all of them glancing in my direction, but none of them stopping to help.

I hurried toward a concession stand, my eyes scanning for a jersey with Jack's name and number on it. I breathed out in relief when I saw it displayed against the silver fencing.

"Can I get a Carter jersey in medium please?" I asked.

After paying for my purchase, I rushed into the nearest bathroom. Tearing off my beer drenched top, I reached for the faucet. I placed my black top into the basin and allowed the warm water to drench it. I wrung my shirt out before filling it with more fresh water, repeating the cycle numerous times until I was satisfied that the beer smell had dissipated. Soaking the shirt with water one last time, I scrubbed my body with it the best I could. I tried to get the stickiness and stench off of my back, but it was hard to reach.

"Do you want me to help you?" a lady around my mom's age asked from behind me. Her brown eyes looked sorrowful as I viewed her in the mirror.

I turned on my heels to face her, thankful for the kindness. "Please?" I refused to let myself cry from the frustration, embarrassment, and sadness. "Thank you," I said, turning back toward my reflection.

I watched as she scrubbed at my exposed skin, taking extra care to not get me too wet. Once finished, she grabbed some paper towels and patted my back dry.

"There you go."

"Thank you so much," I smiled before pulling my new shirt out and slipping it over my head. I shoved my wet shirt into the bag and pulled the drawstrings tight. Glancing into the mirror, I ran my fingers through my damp hair and knew Jack would smell the beer on me if I didn't wash it out.

I twisted my head down toward the sink, allowing the warm water to penetrate the beer soaked ends of my hair. Walking over to the hand dryer, I pressed the start button. It roared to life and I placed my wet hair under the heat. Once dry, I quickly sniffed at my hair, satisfied that no one would smell the beer unless you were searching for it. I pulled out a small bottle of scented vanilla lotion and rubbed it on my arms and my neck to help mask any lingering smells.

Shoving the bag that contained my damp shirt into my purse, I headed out of the bathroom and in the direction of the locker room. I prayed Jack wouldn't be able to tell that anything happened and that I'd be able to hold it all in. I knew keeping this from him was probably wrong, but I convinced myself that it was in Jack's best interest. He needed to keep his mind on the field and his head in the game at all times. He wouldn't be able to do that if he knew this kind of shit occurred. And I'd never be able to forgive myself if anything happened to his career because of me.

A Lot of the Guys Cheat

Jack

After the game and the team meeting, I changed, took a quick shower, and headed out of the navy blue locker room doors. I burst through, looking around for her face. The minute I locked on her tired green eyes, I knew something was off.

"What's wrong?" I asked, as my protective instincts flared.

Her lips formed a tight smile and I eyed the Mets shirt that hugged the curves of her body. "Nothing's wrong. Like my new shirt?"

She turned around, lifting her hair to proudly display my last name and jersey number written on the back of the shirt, Carter 23.

"Like it? I fucking love it," I answered and her face softened, but the worry lines between her eyes remained.

My mind instantly flashed back to the night she was mugged at Fullton State. She was with a group of my teammates heading toward campus to meet up with me when a guy high on drugs and alcohol assaulted them and claimed to have a gun. I was scheduled to throw out the first pitch for the softball team that night, but I left the second I heard whispers about what happened, running into Dean and Brett along the way. I remember sprinting across the parking lot as quick as my legs would move me, toward the street searching for any signs of her. When I saw her silhouette, being helped up by my buddy Cole as they walked, I nearly crumpled with pain. It was my job to protect her and keep her safe, and I failed.

Seeing her beautiful face bruised and beaten in my mind caused my blood to start boiling. I promised her that night that I'd never let anyone hurt her again, and I meant it. The thought alone could make me come completely unglued. No one could fuck with my Kitten like that ever again.

"You going to tell me what's wrong?" I pressed again and she avoided my eyes.

"Really it's nothing. I just want to go home. I'm exhausted."

I leaned my head toward her, my lips grazing over her ear as I whispered, "I know you're lying. Tell me in the car." I kissed her ear before pulling my lips away and throwing my arm around her shoulder.

I relaxed the moment she pulled her body into mine and confessed, "I love you. I'm so fucking happy that you're here. That we're here together. You know that, right?" She smiled as the words left her lips.

God I loved that smile. I loved everything about this woman.

"I am too. I love you."

I refused to stop for any fan autographs or pictures, instead walking straight to the car, my arm around my girl. Cassie's body tensed as small flashes of light exploded around us. I was used to this, but she wasn't. I squeezed her tighter, longing to reassure whatever bothered her.

"Hey, Matteo."

"Hi, Jack. Cassie." His smile quickly faded when he said her name. He sensed it too. Something was wrong.

Once in the privacy of our car, I reached for Cassie's hand, stroking the top with my thumb. "Tell me what's wrong, Kitten."

The car sped forward and Matteo glanced at us in the rearview.

"I'm just really tired, Jack. It's a long day when I come straight here after work, you know?"

She had a point. Cass was gone in the mornings before I woke up, and we didn't get home until well after eleven.

"You don't have to come to all the games." I offered her a way out. Did I want her there? Of course I did. I wanted that girl everywhere I was. But maybe I was being unreasonable by asking her to come to the games when I don't even play.

Her eyes softened, and I had to touch her. I cupped her chin in my palm, her eyes closing. "I want to be at your games, Jack. I'll miss plenty of them because of work. I want to watch every one that I can."

I sighed.

Actually fucking sighed.

Matteo was probably thinking about what a giant pussy I was. Hell, I was thinking about what a giant pussy I was.

I changed the subject. She was avoiding my question for a reason, and I refused to push her about it in the car. I'd ask her again once we were home...and alone. I handed her a manila envelope filled with paperwork.

"What is this?" She scrunched up her nose, and it was so goddamned cute that I instantly hardened.

"It's my travel schedule for the next three weeks."

Her eyes widened, "Oh! I meant to ask you about that the other night, but I completely forgot."

"Well here it is." I slid my hand up her thigh. "Part of it anyway," I added before she swatted my hand away.

"Stop it," she whispered, her cheeks turning pink.

I loved the way I affected her. It made me even harder, and I adjusted my jeans, attempting to relieve the pressure. She flipped through the papers, pausing to read some pages more thoroughly than others. I leaned into her neck, the smell of her skin over-whelming my senses. I kissed her softly, allowing my tongue to glide up her neck as she released a slight gasp.

"I'm going to fuck you in the back of this car while Matteo watches if you don't stop making those noises."

Her jaw dropped open, her eyes falling to the bulge in my pants before widening with embarrassment. "Jack!"

"Screaming my name isn't going to help you," I teased, my tongue sliding around her earlobe as I sucked it in my mouth gently.

"Oh my God," she whispered. "Stop." She adjusted her body, moving my face away with her hands. "Wait 'til we get home," she begged, casting a glance in Matteo's direction.

I moved my hand up her thigh again, stopping before I reached her spot. Want filled her eyes, even through her constant pleading for me to stop. I pulled away swiftly, putting my hands behind my head and leaning back into them. "OK. I can wait."

Her chest heaved, her breathing uneven.

Fuck. I couldn't wait, but teasing her was worth it.

She attempted to distract herself by flicking through the paper-work again, her hands shaking. "So this is all your travel informa-tion. Flight, hotel, bus, and game times?"

"Yep. It's all there." I tried to ignore the throbbing between my legs.

"I have a question."

How the hell do females just turn off the ability to be turned on? It's like they're superheroes or something. Can go from worked up to shut down in two seconds flat! Guys don't work like that.

"I have an answer," I said as evenly as possible.

"Who does all this for you guys? Someone has to book all your flights and coordinate all this. I'd freaking die if I had to do all that administrative bullshit," she admitted, shaking her head.

"We have a travel secretary. Her name's Alison, and I'll give you all her contact information in case you ever need to reach her." I tilted my head to each side, cracking my neck loudly.

"What happens when I want to go to an away game? Do I call her for my travel too?"

I laughed. "No. She only books the team's travel. All the wives, girlfriends, and kids are on their own."

"Jeez. But if I wanted to get on the same flight with you, I can, right?" she asked as two worry lines appeared above the bridge of her nose.

I shook my head. "No. We have a team plane that—"

"You have a team plane? Like a Mets plane?"

I rubbed my eyes with the back of my hand. "No. If you'd let me finish."

"Finish," she interrupted with a smirk, and I wanted to finish her.

"We have a commercial airline that we charter, so no one else can go on it. It's just the team, the manager, the coaches, the trainers, and the equipment guys. And we don't sit in the airport or anything either. We use a separate area so we don't have to deal with fans."

"I had no idea all that happened. That's pretty cool for you guys. Sorta shitty for me." Her lips formed a small faked snarl. "But whatever."

"What's with the snarl?"

She huffed, "Well Nora mentioned that I might be able to do some assignment shooting in conjunction with your road trips. But that's not firm or anything."

"You'd get to travel with me and work? I love it." The idea of having her travel with me all the time was exactly what I wanted, and I refused to hide my enthusiasm over the suggestion.

"Don't get too excited. She only mentioned it once and she also said it might not work." She cocked her head to the side before asking, "Do a lot of the wives go to the away games? I mean, what about the ones with kids?"

"Most of them don't travel with the team. I think it's just easier to stay home."

She nodded. "OK. So if I want to go to an away game, I have to book my own flight, and what else?"

"You'd have to get a rental car. The team travels by bus. And you'd have to let me know you're coming because Alison would need to change my room."

"Change your room, how?"

I shifted in my seat, uncomfortable about the information I was about to divulge. "If a wife or girlfriend comes to an away game, we get put on a different floor of the hotel than the rest of the team. Or if there's another wing to the hotel, we get moved over there."

I braced myself, wondering what was going on in that pretty little head of hers. "If a wife or girlfriend comes, you're separated from the rest of the team? I don't get it."

Oh, Jesus.

"Basically it's for your own good. There are things you don't want to see on the road, Kitten. And if we're not on the same floor as them, then you won't necessarily see it." I coughed into my hand. "Unless you go into the hotel bar. Don't ever go into the hotel bar. Don't even look in there. Do you hear me?"

She still looked lost. I needed to spell it out for her, and I really didn't fucking want to. Not with our history. Not with our painful past. I imagined the groupies and cleat-chasers that showed up in the hotel bars every night after our games. They always knew which hotel the team stayed at and didn't hesitate to make themselves available to any player who wanted them.

I'd seen things happen in those bars I wished I could erase from my memory, and I didn't want them seared into hers. I hated hurting her. I glanced toward Matteo, who clearly knew what I was about to say. He quickly shook his head, as if advising me not to tell her.

"A lot of the guys cheat on their wives, Kitten. That's why we're put on another floor if we're actually with our wives or girlfriends. And that's why you avoid the hotel bar at all costs. There are things you do not want to see in there. OK?"

Matteo's eyes narrowed in the mirror as he shifted his view from the road to Cassie and back again. She looked shocked, her face losing color. "Oh. Right."

I reached for her chin, turning her to face me as her blonde hair spilled down around my hand. "Those other guys, they can cheat all they want. But I won't. I've learned my lesson. I don't even go into the hotel bars anymore. I refuse to put myself in that position ever again. And I'll ask to be on the wives' floor every road trip if that will make you happy."

I tapped my foot against the floor mat, nervous energy running through my veins as she turned away from me. I waited for her to respond. "Cass?" Her eyes met mine. "Say something. Anything."

"I don't have anything to say."

"You always have something to say. Just say it. Please talk to me," I begged. This girl brought me to my knees, and I'd fall to the floor willingly for her every single time.

She swallowed before inhaling deeply, "I just think it sucks. Obviously management knows that cheating goes on and by putting the wives on separate floors, it's like they condone it. I just don't understand why the integrity they demand from you guys on the field isn't demanded once you're off it?"

"It's not that, babe. The cheating is going to happen no matter what anyone says. The wives eventually started asking to be put on different floors. They didn't want to see girls coming out of their friends' husbands' rooms."

The car slowed to a roll before coming to a stop altogether. In the height of the conversation, I'd almost forgotten where we were. Matteo exited the car before I could stop him, opening our door and extending a hand to Cass. He pulled her with care from the backseat, guiding her toward the building entrance by placing his hand on her shoulder.

"Thank you," she said politely.

"Thanks, man." I reached out for Matteo's hand and gripped it tight. He gripped it just as firmly in response, and I fought the urge to squeeze it until his bones popped. If this was some sort of pissing contest we were having, I'd be the one winning. "See you tomorrow?"

"Absolutely. Good night and good luck." He raised an eyebrow, and I patted his back.

"Thanks."

We walked through the lobby, saying hello to Fred before taking the elevator up to our apartment. Once through the front door I emptied the loose change from my pockets onto the table. I sorted through it, grabbing all the quarters and removing them from the pile.

"What are you doing?" she asked, peering around the refrigerator door at me.

"Taking out the quarters."

"Whyyyy?" she asked, dragging out the y sound for emphasis.

"You know why," I said with a wink.

"Humor me."

"I don't spend quarters anymore, Kitten. They all get saved and put in that box right over there." I pointed to the box filled with quarters Fred delivered that night, sitting on the shelf.

"I owe you a lot of touches, Mr. Carter."

"You're telling me. Why do you think I keep adding to the box?"

She laughed, and I watched her face light up before I took her smile away. "Now that we're alone, will you please tell me what's wrong? I know you're tired, but something else happened tonight. What was it?" She hesitated, and I sensed she didn't want to tell me. "Cass. Please. I'm starting to go a little fucking crazy here. Did someone hurt you?"

"No." She shook her head, her eyes avoiding mine. "No one hurt me."

"I know something happened. I can see it in your face. There might not be bruises this time, but I can see it just the same."

She winced at my bringing up the mugging. We barely talked about that night, partly because they caught the guy, but mostly because it made me uncontrollably pissed off. I could barely think about that night, the way she looked and the way she trembled in my arms, without wanting to break into jail and kill that asshole with my bare hands.

I searched my memory for anything I might have said or done recently to piss her off. "Why the fuck are you making me drag it out of you like this? Just talk to me!" My irritation started to build as my tone escalated.

Why wouldn't she just fucking talk to me? "Dammit, Cassie, just spit it out! Are you pissed at me? Did I do something wrong?"

My phone beeped, signaling a text message. Irritated, I grabbed it and slammed my finger against the buttons.

Cass will kill me for sending you this Jack, but you need to see it. It's from tonight's game.

Attached to my little brother's text was a picture of Cassie getting a cup of beer thrown at her back.

I Don't Need a Babysitter

Cassie

I hated that Jack instantly thought it was something he did. I didn't want to tell him about the fans. Or the wives. Or any of it, really. The last thing he needed to do was to worry about me when he was on the field. Baseball was his job, not some hobby he played for fun on the weekend. I didn't want to be the kind of girl that distracted him, and suddenly, I would do anything to avoid him seeing me as a burden. The stadium was filled with thousands of people every night. It's not like he could stop them from saying whatever they wanted to me.

Jack was growing agitated, and I needed to tell him something. I remembered the last time I kept my feelings from him back in college. That first away game episode was a complete disaster. The two cell phone pictures that girl had shown me where Jack and some brunette were walking into a hotel room looked pretty damming. I convinced myself that Jack was cheating on me while his team played in Texas, and I refused to answer his phone calls or texts until he basically lost his shit on everyone around him. Turns out the brunette from the pictures was there to see Brett, Jack's roommate for the weekend, but I'd never given him a chance to tell me any of that until he returned from the road trip completely pissed off at me. Had I learned nothing from that?

His phone beeped, and I watched his demeanor change from irritation to something else entirely. "Kitten," his voice practically whispered as his eyes burned with a mixture of rage and sadness.

As I leaned against the cold granite countertop, I didn't know what to say. I wasn't sure where to start.

"What happened tonight?" He was instantly at my side, his lips burying themselves against my neck. I sensed his restraint. He was trying desperately to keep his calm, but my hesitation in answering his question tested his resolve.

I swallowed the lump in my throat before turning to face him. "Um, your fans are mean sometimes, and the wives on the team are really bitchy." I cringed with my admission.

Jack's body tensed, his hands balling into fists. "Getting beer thrown all over you is more than mean, Cass."

"How'd you know about the beer?"

He slid his cell phone toward me. "Dean." I nodded, knowing that not even Melissa could have stopped Dean from sending Jack that picture.

"What else?" He asked through gritted teeth and I played dumb.

"What else, what?"

"What else has been happening during the games? And stop trying to protect me, or whatever twisted thing you think you're doing 'cause I'm about to fucking come undone."

"The fans heckle me sometimes."

"What do you mean, they heckle you? Heckle you how?"

"A couple guys just said some things about the pictures that have been printed is all." I looked away from his eyes as they narrowed. I tried to make my voice sound nonchalant, like it was all blown out of proportion, but Jack didn't buy it.

"What pictures?" His voice sounded bitter and confused.

It suddenly occurred to me that Jack hadn't been alerted to any of them. Of course he hadn't. It's not like he bothered reading the press, and if Dean didn't tell him, then who else would? The team's press and public relations departments stayed out of anything that didn't have to do with the team or a player directly. Anything that only regarded me wouldn't come up.

"That picture Meli texted me the other night was printed in the newspaper the next morning. And there have been a few others since then." I purposely avoided bringing up the one of my flipping off the crowd.

"Are you fucking kidding me?"

"No," I said, staring straight past him, my gaze focused on the wall.

"Anything else that you're not telling me?"

My eyes refocused on his dark irises, and then I blinked them closed before the next confession. I exhaled a slow breathe, "Someone tried to spit on me last night. But that's it."

"Oh, that's it?" He shook his head in disbelief before throwing his hands in the air. "This is not OK. This is not fucking OK." He reached for me, his body shaking with anger as he pulled me against his chest. He wrapped his arms tightly around my waist before resting his head against mine. "You can't keep this stuff from me. I can't stop it if I don't know it's happening. You have to let me in."

"I didn't want to burden you." I admitted, feeling sort of stupid once I said the words out loud.

He squeezed my body hard against his. "You are never a burden. Do you hear me?" he asked, tilting my face up to his. His eyes squeezed closed before reopening. "I can't believe this is happening to you. I'm so sorry, Kitten." He started pacing, pulling at his jet-black hair as guilt washed through me.

This is exactly what I didn't want to happen. For Jack to be so worried about me that he couldn't think straight. "Don't be sorry, Jack. It's not your fault. And I'm not unsafe. There's security everywhere. Please, don't do this to yourself. Don't worry about me. I'll be fine." I performed my best impression of an overly confident girlfriend, but inside I was choking. The truth was, I hadn't felt entirely safe, and I wasn't sure how fine I'd be.

"Don't worry about you?" He laughed and huffed at the same time. "That's like asking the Chrysler Building to not be tall!"

I loved Jack's passion for me, but I longed to calm him. I wanted to be the one person on this earth who could bring him peace and serenity, not agitation with my presence.

"Maybe Matteo should go to the games with you," he suggested slowly, before becoming more excited as the idea sunk in. "Yeah," he nodded. "That's it. Matteo will go with you to the games."

"What? That's crazy. You can't ask him to do that. He's our driver, not our babysitter."

"Why are you so stubborn? I would rather know you're safe and with someone like Matteo, than alone and vulnerable in a giant stadium where everyone knows exactly where you sit."

"No. This is ridiculous." And I didn't know why I was fighting, honestly, because it was a brilliant idea, and I already felt more settled at the very thought of someone like Matteo by my side. He was strong and intimidating, and I knew he'd fight to keep me safe. I honestly believed he'd do anything Jack asked him to do.

"It's not a fucking discussion, Kitten." He leaned in close, his breath hot on my face. "I can't be on the mound, trying to concentrate on my game, when I'm worried about what people are doing or saying to you up in the stands. Matteo will go with you, and that's the end of it." He raised both hands into the air as if I had no choice, and my defenses flared.

"That's the end of it? What am I, twelve? I don't even get a say in what happens in my own life? I'm a prisoner to your press and your fans when I'm at the stadium, and now I'm a prisoner at home too?"

"Goddammit, Cassie, just listen to me!" His voice raged and I jumped, startled by its intensity. "I'd do anything to keep you safe. Anything! But I can't protect you when I'm down on the god-damned field!"

He sucked in a short breath. "And I promised you after that night at Fullton that I'd never let anyone hurt you again. Do you remember that? Because I do. I remember every single detail about that night. You didn't see what I saw. You don't know how you looked through my eyes. I felt like my entire reason for existing was crumbling around me as the girl I loved sat there spitting up blood."

His eyes glistened at the memory. "I failed you that night, Cassie. I'll never forgive myself for not making sure you were safe and protected. That should have never happened to you. And it won't ever happen again. I promised you I'd never let anyone hurt you like that. Just let me keep my fucking promise to you," he finished, exasperated as the worry lines deepened on his face.

I choked back the emotions brought on by his words and released a small sigh. "OK, babe. I'll sit with Matteo."

He closed his eyes, and the tension lines faded from between them. "Thank you. It's my job to protect you. It's my job to keep you safe. Let me do it or I'll fucking go insane."

"I already said OK." Jack was right, and I didn't want to fight anymore.

"You already said OK?" He mimicked my voice and I glared at him. "That's right, you said OK." He took two steps toward me, and my insides quivered as he neared.

Without warning my back was pinned against the wall, his mouth hot and wet all over my neck. "I love you," he breathed against my flesh, my legs nearly giving out. "Don't argue with me about your safety again," he demanded, and I moaned in response.

"Goddammit, Cassie. What did I tell you about those sounds?" His tongue made its way toward my mouth, where I parted my lips in anticipation of him.

We were ravenous. So hungry for each other, it was if we couldn't stop from eating this meal if we wanted to.

I don't want to.

He sucked at my bottom lip, bringing it into his mouth before nibbling and grabbing hold of it with his teeth. I couldn't control the sounds escaping from my lips as my tongue licked and explored the inside of his mouth before he pulled back slightly.

"Tell me you love me." His voice was hot, commanding me to obey.

And obey I did. "Of course I love you."

He forced my arms up with one of his hands and with his other, he pulled my shirt off and dropped it on the floor. His dark chocolate eyes took me in before his head dropped and he buried his face between my breasts. His fingers unclasped my bra, and the material between his lips and my skin fell away, baring me to him.

I tangled my hands in his hair as his hardness pressed against me. He grabbed my ass and lifted up. Instinctively, I wrapped my legs around his waist, grinding into him with each step he took as he walked me toward the bedroom.

"Jesus, Kitten. I'm going to fuck you on this floor if you don't stop doing that."

I laughed, his tongue entering my mouth with new determination. He placed me on the bed before positioning himself on top of me. My hands groped his back, fingers digging into his muscles as I lifted my hips to meet his.

I traced the lines of his muscles down his arms before working my hand between our hips. I fumbled with the button on his jeans until he gently lifted up, making sure not to put all of his weight on me. I unfastened the button, unzipped the zipper, and worked his jeans down over his hard ass.

He pushed himself from the bed, standing to remove the rest of his clothing. Then he looked at me, a deep grin appearing. I lurched forward, desperate to plant kisses on each dimple when he forced me back down. He removed my pants and underwear, and I lay on top of the bed, completely exposed.

"You're so beautiful. I love everything about you." He planted a kiss on top of my foot. "Even when you're stubborn . . ." His tongue glided up my shin as excitement beelined throughout every fiber of my body. "And bossy." His lips kissed my thigh, his tongue continuing its assault. "And a pain in my ass." His breath warmed the skin near my hip.

He slipped a finger inside me, and I moaned with pleasure. I rocked against him, his tongue licking my lower stomach before working its way up toward my breasts. He sucked and nibbled as my back arched with pleasure. "You like that?" He moaned against my skin.

"Mm-hmm," I hummed, tangling my fingers in his hair again. "Get in me," I said, and he moved his hardness toward me before pulling it away. "Get in," I repeated, and he inserted the tip of himself inside of me.

I gasped and shuddered at the feeling of him entering me as I pulled on him to move deeper. He gave in, and my legs spread further apart, welcoming him. He rocked in and out of me as my hips ground against him, creating that familiar building of sensation. He pushed inside me with intensity, his tongue licking, his mouth sucking wildly from my breasts to my neck and back down again. I moaned and his mouth crushed against mine, silencing my pleasure. He rocked harder, faster as I moved against him, heading toward climax.

"You feel so good. You always feel so fucking good," he breathed against me, his arms flexing above me.

My hands followed the lines of his back until they landed on his ass. I squeezed, pulling him forcefully into me. "Oh, Jack. Just like that." I worked against him, pulling, grinding, building. He quickened his pace, our bodies moving in unison as we barreled down the same ecstasy-ridden path.

"Fuck. Yes, Jack. Oh my God." I gasped as my body shook and trembled with excitement. The heat rushed all through me, my body throbbing as Jack worked himself into a frenzy.

"Fuck, Cassie. You're so fucking hot." His mouth sucked at my breasts, taking them into his mouth between his teeth. I grabbed his hair, pulling at it lightly as I moved my body with his. He hardened even more inside me, still working in and out as he pushed in deep one last time. Grunting loudly, he exploded inside of me, pulsating with each small thrust.

He pulled out slowly before collapsing next to me. "Go pee. I know you have to." I swatted his shoulder before hustling from the bed into our bathroom.

A moment later, I joined him back in bed, pressing my head against his chest as he wrapped an arm around me. "While we're on the subject of safety . . ."

"We're not on the subject of safety," I teased before continuing, "anymore."

His chest rose up and down sharply, my head moving with it. "I think we should look into getting a new place. Not that this isn't great, but I think we can afford something a little bigger with a full-time doorman."

I couldn't fight the fact that I'd been thinking the exact same thing. And I would feel much more secure having a full-time doorman instead of a part-time one only at night. "I've thought about that too."

"We could look somewhere closer to Central Park if you wanted." My insides fluttered to life at his suggestion. I adored Central Park and wanted to live near it initially, but couldn't afford a place on my own. At least not where I looked. Before I answered, he added, "I know it's farther from your office . . ."

"It's not that much farther," I interrupted, lifting my head from his chest. "I mean, it is, but I don't care. I love Central Park, especially the area near the Plaza Hotel. How'd you know that?"

He grinned like a mischievous Cheshire cat. "Your pictures online for the magazine."

I remembered the photos I'd taken of the park and its surroundings when I first moved here. "Oh, right. Back when you were stalking me."

Without any real effort, he pounced, twisting and turning my body at his whim. I was on my back before I could even think. "Yeah. When I was stalking you, Brat," he said, sitting on me. "You took a picture of that fountain and that really pretty hotel. Or at least your pictures made it look pretty."

I smiled, trying to push him off me, but my moves were useless against him. "That's the Plaza Hotel. It doesn't need me to make it look pretty. It's amazing, and I'm quite sure I'm in love with it."

"I still haven't seen any of that stuff, you know?" He pinned my arms above my head before inching his face closer to mine. "You're a bad host." His lips brushed against my lips, softly at first before he deepened the kiss. Emotions and heat swirled inside me.

Thank God I was already lying down because my knees would have buckled completely the instant he started that kiss. I struggled to remember what we were talking about before he erased all my thoughts. "Host? I'm not a guy, and you're not my visitor. You live here now."

A gorgeous dimple flashed on each cheek. "True. But I still think you should show me around. I have Thursday off."

"Well, I don't. I have to work."

"So call in sick," he suggested, and my temper started simmering. "It's my only day off this month."

"I'm not calling in sick!" I shoved at him, and he relented. Sliding his body from mine, I pushed up from the bed into a sitting position. "Wait. Is Thursday really your only day off this whole month? Seriously?"

His head cocked to the side, sympathy glimmering in his eyes. "We only get two days off a month, Kitten. And they're usually travel days."

"That's insane," I said, my shock taking over. "I mean, I knew you were gone half the month for games, but I guess I never realized that you didn't have any real days off." Jack's baseball schedule wasn't his fault. It's not like he controlled it. It was one more thing to adjust to in our new life together.

He shrugged. "I know it's a lot. But listen." He reached for my hands. "I have Thursday off. I would love to go look at new places if we have time, and I want you to show me some of your favorite spots in the city. OK? Maybe you can take a half day?" His thumb caressed my hand. As if sensing my hesitation, he added, "We'll make this work."

"I know. It's fine." I attempted to mask my concern.

"No, it's not. What's wrong? What are you worried about? Is it the other girls?"

I shook my head. "No, it's not that. At least, not right this second." I faked a smile. "I don't know. Maybe it's just that we'll barely see each other for the next few months?"

"You could always quit your job and come with me. Then we'd never be apart." He smirked as my stomach dropped and my pulse quickened.

"Don't say that. You know I hate when you say shit like that," I warned as heat rushed to my cheeks.

"Ah, Kitten. I'm just messing around."

"Well, don't," I snapped, my tone harsh and laced with bitterness. This wasn't the first time Jack had mentioned me not working. I flashed back to meeting Gran and Gramps for the first time when he'd said the same thing. "Not with my job, OK? It's important to me. I *want* to work. And if that means we don't get to be together that often during your season, then," I shrugged again, "I guess we won't be together that often."

"I just want you to be happy," he admitted sweetly but it was too late. Jack picked the one topic that forced me to react in such a vicious way that I wanted to reach across the bed and rip his heart out. My defenses crawled into every crevice of my body, spreading its barbed wire protective coating all around.

"Then don't ask me to quit again. Not even in a joking way. It tears me up inside." My work was the one thing I had that was all for me. It wasn't about Jack. It wasn't about us. It wasn't about anyone or anything else. "Photography is my passion, Jack. It owns pieces of my soul, my guts, everything inside of me. My entire being comes alive whenever I stand behind that lens shooting, and I worked really hard to get to this point."

"I know you have. And I'm sorry," he backpedaled. "I just meant that I'll miss you. I want you with me all the time. I hate traveling, and I'll just wish you were there. But we'll never have that as long as you're working."

I whipped my head in his direction, my gaze glaring. "I can't not work, Jack. Don't you get that? How can you, of all people, not get that?"

I learned a long time ago that no one was going to do things for me. If I had a dream I wanted to reach, I had to claw my way toward it and grab it on my own. I wouldn't give up what I'd worked so hard to achieve. I wouldn't let anyone take it from me. Jack, of all people, had to be able to relate. He worked just as hard as I did to get the things he wanted. Both of us had been let down by the few people in the world you're supposed to trust implicitly. All the unfulfilled promises from my dad ran through my mind, but the constant disappointment I'd felt growing up paled in comparison to both of Jack's parents choosing to leave him.

"I do get that. What the hell are you talking about?" He tugged at his hair.

"If I stopped taking pictures and stopped working, I'd be lost. I wouldn't know who I was without it," I admitted, the very thought causing my insides to feel pitted and empty.

"How do you think I'm going to feel when my baseball career is over?" He sat up straight and faced me.

"But you said once that you'd give it up. For me! How could you say that?" I couldn't imagine giving up that part of myself for anyone. Not even Jack.

"Because, goddammit, it's the truth! I'm going to be a fucking mess without this sport. I don't know who I am without baseball, and it's going to take me some time to figure it all out when that day comes. But I'll be able to do it as long as I have you."

I shook my head, disbelief running amuck through me. "Listen to me," he demanded. "One day baseball will end. It's a fact. And that day is going to be one of the worst days of my life. But if I have to go through the end of my career without *you*?" He huffed. "Then you might as well just put me out to pasture like one of those old fucking cows. Because there is no me without you. Jack Carter does not exist as a full person without Cassie Andrews."

My chest heaved as I fought back the hot tears that threatened to pour from my eyes as he continued. "Without you, I'd be a shell of a man. A hollowed-out, empty, lifeless carcass. And I know that because I've been there. I lived through it. I lived through losing you due to my own stupidity, and I can never explain to you what that felt like."

I allowed my tears to fall, but I couldn't say anything yet.

"Cass, I don't want you to stop working. I don't want you to give up anything for me. But I need you to know that I've learned from losing you. I know how bad it feels to not have you in my life, and I never want to experience that again."

I sucked in a breath. "I can't imagine my life without you, Jack," I wholeheartedly admitted. "Even when we were apart, I always hoped that we'd find our way back to each other. But I don't like feeling pressured to choose between you or my job. It's not fair, and it's a decision I don't want to have to make."

"Because I won't win?" he asked, his voice soft but firm.

"I don't know," I answered honestly. "But I can't believe we're fighting already."

"We're not fighting. We're just figuring things out."

"No. I'm pretty sure we're fighting."

I Won't Let Anything
Happen to Her

Jack

I knew what Kitten meant last night, even if she didn't. She felt like choosing between her job or her heart was like being asked to literally choose me over herself. I wanted to blame her, but I couldn't. She didn't know what it was like. Not really. To live without the one person you knew you were meant for. I'd experienced the pain of being forced to live without her while I had achieved my biggest dream.

It wasn't enough.

Having baseball but no Cassie didn't make me happy. I was pretty sure it was the same for her with photography and no me; she simply hadn't realized it yet. She hadn't really been forced to. At least not from the perspective I had been. I fucked up. I lost her. It's different when you're the one who made the mistakes.

I tried not to wake Cassie as I dialed the office where Matteo worked. I purposely woke up before her alarm was set to go off to handle this.

"Good morning, Mr. Lombardi. It's Jack Carter."

"Good morning, Mr. Carter. Is everything working out with Matteo?" His accent echoed through the phone.

"That's what I'm calling about actually." I attempted to explain before he interjected.

"If Matteo's not working out, we have plenty of other drivers."

I released an irritated breath. "No, Mr. Lombardi, Matteo's fine. I wanted to see about booking him longer on the days I have home games."

"Ah, how much longer?"

"I need him to stay at the field from the time he drops Cassie off until we leave." I didn't want to tell this guy my reasons for needing Matteo to stay. I wanted to keep that business as private as possible. "So, that's probably an extra four or five hours. Is that possible?"

"How many days a week do you have home games?"

"We have about thirteen home games a month, with usually six or seven of them in a row."

I heard scribbling and the sound of papers being shuffled on the other end of the line. "That shouldn't be a problem."

"Are you sure? Because if it is, I'll need to look into other options." I needed a straight answer with no bullshit. If this guy wouldn't give me Matteo's time, I'd take Matteo from him and hire him exclusively. Or find someone else to do the job.

"It's fine. Just make sure you give Matteo a copy of your schedule so we can write him off in the books."

"Great. Can you have Matteo call me when he checks in?"

"Not a problem, sir."

"Thanks." I clicked the phone off before breathing out a sigh of relief. I'd half expected more of a battle for Matteo's time. I appreciated it didn't come to that. Now I needed to talk to Matteo. I needed someone who wanted to watch out for her, and he needed to be able to put Cassie's safety above his own. Maybe he wouldn't like the idea of his pretty little model face being put at risk. I guess I'd find out.

"Hey, you're up early." I turned around to see Cassie standing in the doorway, watching me. She looked so beautiful standing there that I couldn't resist her. I eagerly walked toward her, wrapping her up in my arms, and squeezed. I kissed her neck, breathing in the smell of her skin.

"I'm so sorry about last night." She tilted her head up to look at me. "I think I just get really defensive when it comes to my job."

I looked into her green eyes, pushing the hair back from her face and tucking it behind her ear. "I know. It's OK. I get it."

"I hate fighting with you." Her lips jutted out in a pout, and I smiled.

"I told you we weren't fighting. We're just figuring things out, OK?" I leaned down, planting a kiss on her cheek. "So listen, I talked to Matteo's boss this morning, and he's fine with him staying for the games. I'm going to meet with Matteo later today to make sure he can handle it."

She released a breath. "Handle it how?"

"I just want to make sure he's up for it. I'm not going to ask him to do this for us if he isn't comfortable doing it. He does have a choice in the matter."

"Well, how nice for him," she said, her voice laced with bitterness.

I dropped my hands. "Am I doing something wrong, Cass? I'm just trying to make sure you're safe and protected when I'm not around. Is that not OK with you?"

This girl is driving me fucking crazy.

"No." She paused before looking at the floor. "God, I'm sorry, Jack. I don't know what's wrong with me." Her eyes closed as she dropped her face into her hands. "I'm not used to anyone looking out for me the way you do. It's a bit of an adjustment for me is all. I'm sorry."

"Don't be sorry. Please don't fight me on this. I won't be able to concentrate on the field if I think people are harassing you or being mean or hurting you."

"I know." She nodded her head in agreement before swallowing. "I'll try to be less crazy. I love you."

"You're not crazy." I smiled. "And I love you too." I kissed her lips before she pulled away.

"I need to get ready for work." Her face softened.

"Go then. Stop wasting time fake fighting with me." I smacked her ass, and she yelped.

"Jack!"

Half tempted to chase her ass right into the bathroom, the sound of my phone ringing distracted me. "Hey, Matteo," I said into the phone, after seeing his name and number appear on my screen.

"Good morning, Jack. Mr. Lombardi said you wanted to talk to me?"

"Yeah. Is there any way we could meet a little bit later to go over some stuff? I'll pay you for your time, of course."

"Hold on one sec." The phone sounded like it got tossed onto a desk. "I have a couple clients this morning, but I'm free around eleven. Is that too late?"

"No, that's perfect. Meet me at Sal's?" I suggested.

"Yeah. Sal's it is," he replied, his voice excited.

"OK, Matteo. See you then."

I pressed End, dropping my phone on the small counter before walking into the bathroom. I peered around the shower curtain at Cassie and became instantly aroused.

Down, boy.

"I'm having lunch with Matteo at Sal's. I'll text you afterward to let you know how it goes, OK?"

She turned her body to face me, embarrassment spreading pink across her cheeks. "Great. Now get out of here before you make me late for work. I know what you're thinking, Carter."

I loved it when she called me by my last name. Her voice always sounded extra sassy, and it turned me on even more.

"Can you blame me? Fuck, woman, look at you. Sexy as hell," I teased, knowing I was making her uncomfortable. But she looked beautiful all naked and wet, and now all I could think about were the things I wanted to do to her.

She pressed her lips tightly against each other. "'Kay. Get out now. Bye. Thanks."

◇

I walked into Sal's, the smell of pizza making my stomach growl.

"Hey! Jack! Good to see you!" Sal stood in the kitchen area, waving at me through a pass-through window. "And hey, nice game the other night." His boisterous voice reverberated throughout the small building.

"Thanks, Sal."

"So what can I get ya?"

"I'm going to wait until Matteo shows up, and then we'll order something," I said, before sitting down at one of the tables.

"Matteo's coming? Ha! I haven't seen that little shit in weeks!" He flung some pizza dough into the air before catching it on his fist and spinning it wildly.

"He's not really that little."

"No, he's not." He chuckled. "So, how's he working out for you and Cassie? Everything good?" He eyed me while pressing down on the dough, creating the perfect thin crust.

"It's all good so far. Thanks again for the recommendation."

"No problem, no problem." He waved a hand at me as the bells on the door chimed. Matteo walked into the pizzeria, a huge smile spread across his face.

"Matteo! Why don't you come visit me? You don't like my food?" Sal teased before coming out from the kitchen to greet his cousin.

I watched the two men embrace and realized in that moment how much I missed my little brother, Dean. I wished he was done with school so I could move him out here, but he probably wouldn't leave Gran and Gramps. Dean was always the better grandkid.

"Ah, you know I love your food. I've just been busy." Matteo nodded in my direction.

"I've heard. Busy's good." Sal slapped Matteo on the back. "You two let me know what you want to order, OK?"

"I'll just take a slice, Sal." I hesitated, patting my rumbling stomach. "Better make it two."

"Same here," Matteo said, following my lead.

"I'll just make you guys a whole pie. It's not like the two of you won't finish it." Sal laughed before walking back into the kitchen.

I smiled, waving Matteo over to sit with me. Once he was close enough, I reached out my hand. A quick, firm handshake later and Matteo was seated across from me. "So, I need to talk to you about something," I started, leaning my elbows on the tabletop.

"Yeah, Mr. Lombardi mentioned that you want me to keep the car there during the games, is that right?"

"Yeah, but there's a bit more to it than that."

"What's up?"

I pushed back into my chair, thinking about how to word it right. "Some fans were heckling Cassie last night at the game. And I guess the other wives are really mean and don't do anything to help. The press is taking pictures of her and posting them online. I would really appreciate it if you would take her to the games and sit with her so she's not alone."

"So, you want me to drive her to the field and then stay for the game with her?"

"Yeah. But I also need you to watch out for her. And if anyone fucks with her, I need you to be OK with handling it."

"Like a bodyguard?"

"If it comes to that, yeah." Matteo shifted in his seat, and I added, "That's why I wanted to talk to you. If you're not comfortable doing this, I'll find someone else."

"I never said I was uncomfortable," he responded in a sharp tone that caused my defenses to flare.

"Well, I figured I'd ask you because you're obviously strong, and I assume people find you intimidating."

I don't.

He laughed. "I actually don't have a problem with it at all. I just need to know my boundaries."

"What do you mean?" I jerked my head toward him as my muscles tensed.

He better not be talking about his boundaries with Cass. I'll beat his ass right here in his cousin's restaurant.

"I just mean, what exactly do you want from me? If someone heckles her, do you want to me to knock his teeth out, get him to shut up, or do nothing?"

This was my idea and I hated it already. The thought of someone else defending my girlfriend was agonizing. I should have been the one protecting her, but I was willingly handing that job over to another guy. A guy who looked like a fucking magazine model.

"I don't think you should cause a scene unless it's absolutely necessary. Don't overreact, 'cause that will only lead to more bad press." He nodded as I continued. "I basically don't want Cassie to be alone at the games anymore. I figured she'd make friends with the other women on the team, but since that doesn't look like it's going to happen . . . I need to make other arrangements for her safety."

"I understand."

"And all this is fine with you? I need you to be sure," I asked, waiting to sense any hesitation on his end.

"I'm sure. It's not a problem."

"Great." I smiled, happy we'd come to an understanding. "Listen, that girl is my world, and I can't stand the thought of anyone hurting her. I'd handle this myself if I could play the game and be by her side at the same time, but I can't."

"You need me to start tonight?"

"Yeah, if you can."

"I cleared my schedule already."

"Perfect. I appreciate you watching out for her."

"I won't let anything happen to her. I promise." His expression turned serious, his mouth narrowing into a thin, tight line, and I believed him.

He Can Drive Me Anytime

Cassie

Matteo arrived at my office promptly at six, just like Jack texted he would. He waited for me downstairs with the car while I finished up some last-minute photo editing. Tonight's game would be the first game he'd attend with me, and I was nervous. Not to be alone with Matteo, but because now I'd be photographed with some guy who wasn't Jack.

It wasn't like Matteo wasn't a good-looking guy. He was downright gorgeous. I started wondering if this was a good idea after all. Were we unintentionally giving everyone more ammunition against me?

I sighed before heading down in the elevator, the stress of the situation starting to gnaw at me. I hated the things I had to think about now before I even walked out the door. All the added drama affected my ability to be happy. I was too concerned with everything around me to simply sit back and enjoy Jack's time on the field.

I hated this.

I spotted Matteo the moment I exited the elevator. He smiled, and I couldn't help but smile back in response.

"I get to be your date tonight," he said with a wink.

Date?

"Yeah, I guess so," I said, silently berating myself for agreeing with that word choice.

I walked toward the car, and when Matteo pulled open the back door, I declined, opening up the passenger door instead. "I hate sitting back there while you drive me around. It's dumb."

"You sure?" he asked with surprise.

"Yeah." I nodded before sliding in and closing the door behind me.

I fastened my seat belt as Matteo scooted into the driver's seat, starting the sleek Town Car with a flick of his wrist. "This should be fun, huh?"

"I hope so. Honestly I think it might create more drama at first, but hopefully that will die down in time."

"More drama how? Because I'm going with you?"

I wondered how exactly to phrase what I meant. Matteo was stupid hot, but I wasn't about to tell him that. "Matteo, it's not like you're ugly. So I'm sure it's going to cause some sort of chaos."

He laughed, and I noticed a hint of color creeping into his cheeks. "You think I'm pretty?"

"No," I choked back. "I said I think you're not ugly."

"Well, thanks." He grinned. "I think you're not ugly either."

Unsure of how to respond, I flashed a quick, tight-lipped smile instead. The last thing I wanted was to make things uncomfortable between us, so I dropped the subject altogether and reached for my phone. I typed out a quick text message to Melissa before gazing out of the car window at the city whizzing by in a blur.

"So, tell me what I'm in for tonight," he asked.

"Um, well, we have the chatty fans and the mean wives."

"Oooh. Tell me about the wives." He glanced at me before returning his focus to the highway.

"They're just really nasty. They won't talk to me."

"At all?"

"At all."

"What'd you do to them?" he asked with a chuckle.

"Shut up!" I pursed my lips together before swatting his shoulder with my hand. "I didn't do anything to them except join their stupid team with my boyfriend."

"How dare you!" he exclaimed, his voice animated and I laughed. "So do they just completely ignore you?"

I nodded. "Pretty much. It's like I'm not even there."

His lips formed a slight snarl. "You women are rather mean to one another. Why is that?"

"You're asking the wrong girl. I'm not one of those women. Unless you're mean to me first; then I'm a bitch. But really, you asked for it, so you can't blame me," I smiled innocently.

"Well, this oughta be fun."

◇

We pulled into the parking lot at the stadium, and I nervously looked around. People swarmed all around our car, but no one paid attention to who was in it. I glanced at Matteo before opening my door and sliding out.

He exited and stood next to the door, not moving.

"What are you doing?" I asked.

He glanced down at his work attire and then back at me. "I need to change my clothes."

"Oh. I didn't even think about that, but good idea."

I turned my back to the car as he scooted into the backseat to change. I thanked him in my head for being smart enough to bring a change of clothes. He would have looked ridiculous wearing slacks and a tie at the ball field.

"Ready?" he asked from behind me, and I jumped. "Sorry."

"It's fine." I turned to look at him and wanted to scream. Nothing this guy wore covered up his good looks. "You look so different," I said, noting his jeans and long-sleeved white shirt that hugged the muscles in his shoulders and arms perfectly. The ink from his tattoo showed a little more now, although I still had no idea what it was.

"Thanks." He arched an eyebrow. "I think?"

"I've never seen you in jeans. You look cute."

Shit.

"I just mean, you look nice in jeans. It's a different look from your dress slacks." I fumbled, trying to make my statement mean nothing, but clearly making it worse.

I picked up our tickets at the window, and we headed in. My nerves should have calmed with Matteo by my side, but they were heightened. Heads turned in our direction when we passed by. His good looks called attention to us, and that was the last thing I wanted.

"You ready for this?" I asked before we headed out of the tunnel and down the aisle.

"Don't worry, Cassie. I've got your back."

I swallowed my apprehension and stepped into the light of the outdoors and the rush of the crowd. I walked down the steps, inching toward our row of seats as Matteo followed right behind. My heart raced as I braced for hateful words or taunting that never came. I released a breath before pointing to our seats.

I noticed all the mean wives staring at Matteo, their jaws agape at the sight of him. I sat down and faced them, suddenly filled with confidence. I pasted an obviously fake smile on my face and said, "Close your mouths, ladies. You look ridiculous," before turning my back to them.

They gasped and whispered to each other, and I decided not to give a shit. At least not for tonight.

"That was awesome." Matteo leaned toward me, whispering.

"I'm sure I just signed my death warrant with the baseball wives, but I don't care."

I looked around the stadium and down toward the dugout for any signs of Jack. I hated when he didn't pitch. It wasn't as much fun watching the game when he wasn't playing. And the bullpen for the pitchers couldn't have been any further away from where our seats were. The way the bullpen was situated, I rarely even caught sight of him.

Someone cleared her throat, forcing me to look up. "Trina. Where were you last night?"

"Sorry, girl, I had to work. Who is this?" She extended a tanned hand toward Matteo as she eyed me curiously.

"I'm Matteo. I'm Jack and Cassie's friend. It's nice to meet you." He paused, clearly enamored with the beautiful woman. "Trina, is it?"

"Yes. It's nice to meet you as well." Everything she said sounded prettier with her accent. "May I sit next to you, Cassie?" she asked before tossing her purse in the seat to my left.

"Like you have to ask. Please sit your bony ass down next to me."

"I thought you said all the wives were mean?" Matteo's voice flirted as Trina leaned over me.

"They are. They're horribly mean. Everyone except for me," Trina said, her cleavage on full display beneath her sand-colored V-neck blouse.

My phone beeped and I reached for it, noting a text message from Melissa.

Who is that hot piece of ass sitting with you?

She'd attached a picture of Matteo leaning toward me. I typed back:

That's Matteo. He's our driver.

Holy hell. He can drive me anytime he wants!!!

Her response made me laugh out loud. Matteo peered over my shoulder at the text message. "Who said that?"

Embarrassed, I hid my screen and shoved my phone into my purse. "My best friend, Melissa. She's crazy."

"So," Trina asked softly. "What I miss last night?"

"Oh, just some fans giving me shit. And the wives sitting here doing nothing while it all happened. I hated that you weren't here."

"I saw the paper." She frowned, an expression that looked unnatural on her face.

"Has that ever happened to you?" I hated the way hope coursed through me, but I desperately needed someone to relate to how my mind raced and my pride hurt.

"Of course." She placed her hand over her heart. "But I'm already in the public eye a lot for work, so it's different."

"Different how?"

"I'm used to it. I've dealt with this kind of shoddy stuff for years. I feel bad for you because I know how uncomfortable it feels."

"That's it! That's the perfect word for it." I looked between Matteo and Trina. "It's so freaking uncomfortable."

She placed her hand on top of mine. "I know. And I'm sorry you're going through it, but you'll be OK. Don't let them get to you."

"I'm trying. It's a lot easier when you're here," I said meaningfully.

"Hey! What am I, chopped liver?" Matteo interjected.

I answered "yes" as Trina answered "no" at the same time.

Cheers filled the stadium as the sound of a bat cracking echoed into the night air. I snapped my head toward the field in time to see the small white ball fly over the wall in center field and into the stands. The crowd screamed and hooted wildly, and the three of us clapped and high-fived each other like we'd just hit the ball.

"I miss a lot of the games for work. I'm sorry," Trina shouted above the noise.

"Speaking of . . . apparently you know my boss, Nora? She loves you and said to tell you hello."

Trina's face lit up at the mention of Nora's name. "No way! I love Nora. She's your boss? You are one lucky girl. She's brilliant."

"I know. She's really great."

"So that's the magazine you work for! That's smashing, Cassie. Truly."

"Thanks," I said, reaching out to pat her shoulder.

Trina's cell phone vibrated against the seat before she picked it up and looked at the screen. "Oh, excuse me. I need to take this."

I watched as she climbed over the row and into the aisle behind us before walking out of view.

"She's beautiful," Matteo said.

"I know. And she's so nice. Her accent kills me. I want her to call me every night and read me a bedtime story," I said with a laugh.

"I want in on that deal. Except I don't want it to be on the phone."

I rolled my eyes.

"What?" he asked defensively.

"It's just typical, Matteo. That's all."

I hated typical, which is why I attempted to steer clear of Jack in the first place back in college. I'd labeled him as the most predictable kind there was. I had been wrong.

"Ah, come on, she's a beautiful girl. I'd have to be blind to not be attracted to her."

"Well, I'll let you know if it doesn't work out with her and her boyfriend." I winked.

"Would you?" He nudged my shoulder teasingly, and I looked back toward the field.

Trina never came back, and Matteo and I spent the rest of the game making idle chitchat and wondering where Trina disappeared to. I realized that having him there made me less concerned with my surroundings, and who violated my space.

When the game ended, I stretched and almost lost my balance. Matteo's strong arm grabbed my back, holding me steadily in place. "Thanks," I said, before moving away from his grip.

"Can't let you get hurt or Jack will kill me."

I shrugged, unable to disagree when, amid the chaos of people shuffling around, I heard someone shout, "Replace Jack already, Cassie?"

I shook my head in disgust. I wanted to yell back, "If I'd replaced him, then why the hell would I be at his game?" But I didn't. I hated not defending myself. I convinced myself that I discouraged the heckling by staying silent.

Matteo tensed behind me, his body closing the space between us defensively. "Are you OK?" he whispered into my ear, and I jumped.

I swatted near my ear. "I'm fine. Don't do that."

"Sorry. Just making sure you're OK."

"If they're gonna insult me, they could at least be creative about it." I tried to smile, but disgust twisted my lips instead.

He followed close behind me until we reached the private entrance to the clubhouse. "I'm going to wait for Jack down here. We'll meet you at the car."

"OK. I'll see you at the car." He nodded before walking away.

◇

I rounded the last corner when I spotted Trina sitting on a bench. "Hey," I shouted toward her, hearing my voice echo off the walls.

She stood up and walked toward me. "Sorry about that. I got stuck on a bunch of phone calls, and now I have to leave for Brazil in the morning for some big photo shoot."

"I'd say that's insane, but I get it." I shrugged, understanding all too well the last-minute trips and how unplanned work can come up suddenly. I hadn't experienced it yet firsthand, but watched my coworkers handle it without complaint.

"Kyle won't be happy." She frowned, and I half smiled sympathetically. "He hates it when I'm gone. I think he secretly wishes I'd stop modeling and pop out some kids."

"Would you do that?" I asked, remembering the argument Jack and I had last night.

"One day, yeah. But not right now." She let out a deep sigh. "It's hard though, trying to balance working and being there for Kyle. He's on the road so often and he needs so many little things taken care of. I feel awful that I'm not around to handle it, but not awful enough to give up my career for him."

I nodded my head, letting her know that I understood everything she said, but I didn't want to get into it any deeper at that moment. There was a time and place for that discussion, and it wasn't right then. At least not for me.

"Do you think I'm a horribly selfish person?" She closed her eyes tightly, as if she didn't want to see just how selfish she might be.

"No. Of course not." I touched her shoulder and her eyes reopened. "Why do we have to give up our careers for theirs? I mean, why is it one or the other?"

"Because it's really hard to work and have a relationship at the same time. Neither one of us is in a typical sort of job, really." She cast a glance toward the mean girls. "None of them work anymore. I heard that Kymber gave up some huge career to be a wife and mom," she lowered her voice, "I think that's probably part of the reason why she's so ugly to us. She's full of resentment."

I nodded. "I don't ever want to be like that."

Trina laughed. "You won't, Cassie. No matter what happens in your life, you'd never treat people the way she does."

The door opened with a loud bang and Jack walked out, a cautious smile on his face. "Hey, Trina. Kitten." He planted a kiss on my cheek and pulled me away.

"Hi, Jack," Trina smiled. "I'll see you later, Cassie."

"Oh, wait." I stopped abruptly. "Can we exchange numbers? I want to be able to text you. Especially if you disappear like you did tonight. I was a little worried."

"I know. I'm sorry. Here."

I typed her number into my cell phone before giving her a quick hug and catching up with Jack. He tossed his muscular arm around my waist and pulled me tight, our hips pressing against each other with each step.

"How was everything tonight?" he asked.

"Better actually," I admitted, knowing that I'd been far less stressed with Matteo around.

"Anyone give you any shit?"

"Not really."

He squeezed me and kissed the top of my head. "So it was a good idea then, right?" he asked as we headed toward the dark car where Matteo waited, once again wearing his work attire.

"What was?" I smiled playfully, thankful for the times my mind allowed the past to fade into the distance.

"Having Matteo go with you to the games. Admit it was a good idea."

I leaned my head on his shoulder. "It was a good idea. Thank you."

Two Bedroom on the Twenty-Third Floor

Jack

Cassie couldn't take the day off, but she promised to meet me for lunch. Unsure of what to do with my rare few hours of freedom, I went online and searched for available rentals near the Plaza Hotel. I printed out a list of places on both the Upper West Side and the Upper East Side. I didn't know the difference between the two, but Cassie would.

After calling a few of the numbers, I set up an appointment to view a place on the East Side after she got off work. I looked over my baseball schedule for the next three weeks, paying close attention to all the days I wouldn't be here. The team traveled for an eleven-day road trip soon, and I wondered if Cass would be able to make it to any of the away games.

I knew it was a shitty thing for me to think, but it sort of sucked that Cassie worked full time. It meant that we'd never be together when I played on the road. And I was going to be gone an average of seventeen days each month. That's a long time to go without seeing your girl.

I'd never admit that to her though, and I knew that wanting her around me all the time was selfish. Especially after everything

I'd put her through. She'd moved to New York to follow her own dreams, and I wanted to be supportive.

Aside from my own pride-filled bullshit, I honestly hated the idea of her being here alone. The press and the fans stressed me out, and I needed to know she was protected when I wasn't around. We needed to move somewhere with a round-the-clock doorman sooner rather than later—and before I lost my damn mind.

Maybe I'll buy her a dog? I've always wanted a dog. Jesus, Carter, is anything not about you?

Pulling on my ball cap, I walked out of the apartment building and toward the subway station. The cool breeze whipped across my face, and the sunshine was so bright I almost turned back for my sunglasses. Cassie texted me directions to the restaurant where we were meeting for lunch since I had no fucking idea where I was headed or what I was doing. I was half tempted to call Matteo and have him drive me, but I knew Cass would ream my ass for not getting the "New York City experience," as she liked to call it. Plus, I needed to learn my way around.

I followed the stairs underground, stopping at the first vacant vending machine I could find. I pushed a ten dollar bill into the slot, and a blue-and-yellow Metro Card popped out. Glancing around, I watched as people slid their cards into the electronic readers before walking through the turnstiles. Memories of visiting Disneyland as a kid flashed through my mind as I slid my card through. The light turned green and the turnstile unlocked with a click.

I pushed through it, feeling like a fucking lost tourist and hoping no one would recognize me. Walking down another set of stairs, I reached the subway platform.

What a trip.

The lighting was dimmer and the air damper down here. A guy at the far end of the platform banged on some drums and the sound traveled up and down the station. The idea of having my back un-guarded didn't sit well with me, so I pressed against the wall and waited for my train to arrive.

The brakes squealed as the subway pulled in, the driver's voice fading in and out. When the doors opened, I waited for everyone to exit before I jumped inside. Virtually empty, I had my choice of seats. I grabbed the seat closest to the doors. Two stops later, I hopped out and headed up the set of stairs; the sunlight practically blinded me so I averted my eyes to the ground.

"Aren't you that super-hot baseball player?" Her voice stopped me in my tracks, and I looked up to see those familiar green eyes staring right through me.

"Aren't you the smoking hot girlfriend of said baseball player?" I licked my lips and her mouth fell open. I loved fucking with her.

Cassie dropped her sunglasses over her eyes and pulled me away from the subway exit. "Come on." She giggled, and I wanted to make out with her like some lovestruck teenager in the back of a movie theatre.

"I thought we were meeting at the café?" I reached down for her hand, interlocking her fingers with mine.

"Nora gave me the afternoon off. She wouldn't take no for an answer, so I'm all yours, Carter."

"She probably knew I'd get lost."

"Probably." She smiled. Her lips were so tempting I wanted to suck them into my mouth and never let them go. "So how was your first subway ride?"

Shaking the visual from my mind and willing my dick to calm down, I refocused my thoughts. "Interesting."

"But amazing, right? I mean all the different people from so many walks of life gathered in one place together. I freaking love the train stations."

I shook my head with a huff. "You would."

"What does that mean?" She swatted my shoulder.

"It just means that you see the beauty in everything. Even the ugly, dark, disgusting subway stations."

"I just think they're cool. A little scary sometimes, but still cool."

Cassie pointed to the red-and-white checked awning up ahead. "That's where we're eating."

"I gotta be honest, Kitten. I feel like we're betraying Sal."

"No!" she whined. "We're not, I promise. This place isn't even Italian. It's French."

I stepped ahead of her to open the restaurant door when a woman's voice said, "Oh my God, are you Jack Carter?"

I turned to face the woman as Cassie stopped midstep.

"Oh my God, you ARE Jack Carter! I'm a big fan. You're an amazing pitcher. Can I get a picture with you, please?"

I glanced at Cassie and saw her lips form a tight-lipped smile. So I pulled her close to me and put a polite but firm smile on my face as I told the woman, "I'm sorry, but I'm about to go eat with my girl. Some other time."

"Please! Just one picture? Or an autograph? Can you sign something for me then?" I watched as she buried her hands into her oversized purse, searching for God knows what.

"Please understand, I'm just trying to have some personal time right now. I'm sorry." I turned my back to the overzealous fan and held the door open for Cassie.

"Sorry, babe," I said, stroking her hair.

"It's OK. Why didn't you just give her what she wanted?"

The hostess smiled but didn't interrupt us. Instead she grabbed two menus and waved us toward the back of the small café as we followed her lead. "I didn't want to."

I pulled Cassie's chair out for her before sitting down across the table and removing my cap.

"Your waitress will be with you shortly," the petite brunette said before she bounced away.

"What do you mean, you didn't want to?" Cassie leaned forward, her hair flopping in front of her eyes as I swept it away with my fingers.

I sucked in a breath. I hadn't told her any of this yet, this part of my master plan, but I guessed now was as good a time as ever. "I'm trying to limit my contact with them."

Her eyes narrowed. "You're trying to limit your contact with whom? Your fans?"

I leaned across the table. "Just the female ones."

There. I admit it.

I wanted to limit my contact with my female fans whether I was on or off the field. I never wanted to give them or the press anything to talk about, write about, or post about.

"Jack." She closed her eyes for a moment before meeting my stare. "You can't ignore your fans. It's mean and they'll end up hating you."

I leaned back against the hard chair and shrugged. "If I'm mean to them, they'll leave me alone. And if they leave me alone, they won't have anything to say. And if they don't have anything to say, then you'll never have anything to worry about."

She shook her head. "I don't want people to hate you."

"So what are you saying? You're OK with me talking to them?"

"Of course I'm OK with you talking to them. I just don't want you to sleep with them." A slight laugh escaped her lips. "Or make out with them or do anything with them."

I reached over, taking her hand in mine. "I won't ever make that mistake again. I'll prove it to you every day for the rest of our lives.

I wanted to ignore them for you, so you could see I'm trustworthy and not be worried."

"I don't want you to go to those extremes for me. It's not right. And the trust part will just come in time. OK?"

"OK." I agreed, bringing her hand to my lips.

When we were done eating, I settled our bill with the waitress and waited for her to bring me back the change. She approached our table, a weird look on her face.

"Is everything alright?" I asked.

"Here's your change," she said, handing me the soft leather bill holder. "And I'm really sorry, but there's a crowd outside waiting for you to leave."

I glanced at Cassie as the surprise flashed in her eyes.

"We wouldn't let them come in, obviously. But they know you're here. We're really sorry." The waitress stared at her feet.

"It's fine. It's not your fault," I tried to reassure her before looking back at Cass. "You OK?"

Cassie nodded and looked at our waitress. "How'd they know we were here?"

"Someone posted it on that Spotted website."

I frowned. "I don't know what that is."

"It's this website where people can put where they spotted a celebrity or an athlete. Someone posted that you two were eating lunch here."

I leaned my head back slowly. "Gotcha. Thanks." I pushed my chair back before stretching. Running my fingers through my hair, I grabbed my cap and placed it firmly on my head.

"You ready?" I asked Cass, reaching my hand out for her to grab. She stood slowly, peering outside.

She exhaled. "OK, there's not that many people outside. There's like ten."

"They're going to want me to sign stuff. Do you mind or do you want me to blow them off?" I'd do whatever the hell she wanted me to.

"Of course you should sign stuff." She smiled.

I gripped her hand, leading her toward the door. I pushed it open, holding it for her to walk through before following behind. The sound of my name filled the air around us as people crowded to get close, shoving their camera phones toward us. Instinctively, I wanted to protect Cassie from the rushing bodies, but I ended up only tightening my grip on her.

"Ow, Jack." She winced, pulling her hand from mine and shaking it.

"Shit. Sorry, Kitten."

"It's OK." She smiled.

"Jack, how about a picture?" A woman shouted above everyone else. I'd have to have been blind to not notice her good looks.

"Sure," I said, remembering Cassie's words.

Reluctantly I posed, keeping my hands to myself, but this chick draped herself all over me like a cheap fucking suit. Disgusted, I removed her hands from my body. "No more pictures, but I'll sign whatever you want," I announced to the group, frowning at the one who'd just ruined pictures for the rest of them. Forcing a big smile on my face, I signed papers, taxi receipts, and a couple of baseballs.

"Cassie, Cassie honey. Look this way." My attention turned to the long-haired, greasy-looking guy with a professional camera taking pictures of Kitten while she waited for me to finish. I watched as she reacted to the sound of her name, which clearly caught her off guard, and she searched the crowd for the one calling out to her.

"Leave her alone," I shouted in his direction, and he glared at me. He fucking glared at me, aimed the camera back toward Cass, and clicked the button. I imagined jumping over everyone and breaking that camera across the side of his fucking skull.

"You're so pretty when you smile, Cassie. Won't you smile for the camera? Who was with you at the game last night? Cassie? Did you and Jack make up? Why were you mad at him?" The dirtbag was relentless.

"I said leave her alone," I threatened, my patience fading.

Cassie suddenly appeared at my side, whispering in my ear, "That guy's creeping me out."

"We'll go," I whispered back. "I have to go. Sorry." I made my way through the crowd, which had grown in number since I started. I pushed lightly through the people, signing a few scraps of paper on the way, never letting go of Cassie's hand.

We walked down the sidewalk and I glanced back, noticing the guy still taking shots of us, following our every move. "That guy's following us. He must be paparazzi."

"When he called out my name," she paused, "that freaked me out. And all those questions. It's weird when people know about your life like that."

"I know. Come on, let's get a cab." I stopped walking and the guy did too.

That's right, asshole. Keep your distance.

"I got this." She winked at me before stepping out onto the edge of the busy street.

She looked sexy as hell hailing down a cab, her hip jutted out as she waved her arm. The cab pulled up like a speeding train before slamming on the brakes and we hopped in.

"Is he following us?" Cassie asked softly.

I glanced back. "Nope. I think he knows I'll deck him," I said with a laugh, and she kissed my cheek.

When the cabbie stopped in front of a gold-trimmed apartment building with a uniformed guy standing outside the revolving door, I smiled, my comfort level growing already.

This is what I'm talking about.

I helped Cass out of the cab, and we walked toward the door.

"Can I help you?" the doorman asked.

Good. He asks what you're doing here before you go in. I like that.

"We have an appointment with Ruth."

"Have a good day," he nodded, allowing us to enter.

A middle-aged woman greeted us the moment we walked in. Her voice was so raspy it sounded as if she smoked twenty packs a day. "I'm Ruth. You must be Jack and Cassie. It's nice to meet you. We happen to have a vacant two-bedroom apartment on the twenty-third floor that I want to show you. Are you ready?"

I turned to Cassie. "Twenty-third floor? It's my number, babe. That's a sign."

Baseball players are nothing if not superstitious.

Cassie smiled, following Ruth into the elevator that flew us to the twenty-third floor in no time. Ruth led us down the hall, unlocked the door, and waved us in. "I'll just be over here, so you kids take your time looking around."

Holy shit.

This place was gorgeous. I knew Kitten was already sold by the look on her face. "Can we afford this?" she whispered.

"We can. Easily. It's not as much as you think."

"I find that hard to believe."

I could see why. Cassie started on about granite countertops and stainless-steel appliances, and squealed when she walked into the master bathroom. I didn't know half the shit she was talking about, but the smile on her face was priceless. I'd take out a fucking loan to live here if I had to.

"I think we can fit ten apartments the size of yours in here," I teased, before walking onto the balcony. The city rushed by down below, and the buildings provided the perfect landscape. I bet Kitten would love to photograph things from up here.

"A balcony? Heaven. I'm in heaven." Her face crinkled with delight.

"I wanna do bad things to you on this balcony, Kitten."

"Shocking," she said as she rolled her eyes.

"So you like it?" I asked, grabbing her by the waist and pulling her to me. Before she could answer, I pressed my lips against hers, feeling her body go limp in my arms. I pulled away from her slowly, letting the kiss linger before finishing it with a peck against her cheek.

"It's seriously gorgeous, Jack. I think I could live here forever."

"Even if it's a little further from Central Park than you wanted?" I asked just to be sure, already knowing what her answer would be.

"It's perfect. And the park isn't that far away."

"I'm sold then."

"You didn't even see the master bedroom. Or the guest room. Did you even look around?" She ran her fingers through my hair.

"I don't need to. If you like it, that's all that matters." I stepped inside and shouted toward the open front door. "Ruth." She peered around the door frame and smiled. "We'll take it. What do we have to do?"

Getting Caught

Cassie

Jack talked Ruth into letting us move in as soon as possible, saying he wanted to know I'd be safe while he was on the road for eleven days. The move kept my brain occupied, so instead of focusing on the fact that Jack would be gone for so long, I thought about packing instead. It stopped me from my small freakouts about Jack and cheating. I didn't want to worry about him doing that, but sometimes you can't help the way you feel.

We spent the following week packing up our small apartment, and I stayed away from the field when Jack wasn't pitching to have more time to get everything in order. I realized that I didn't like staying home when Jack's team played a home game. I thought I'd feel differently because Jack wasn't pitching, but I didn't. I wanted to be where he was, whether he was playing or not.

But being away from the field also meant that there were no pictures of me online and that small reprieve brought a sense of normalcy back into my life I'd almost forgotten. It's amazing how quickly we adapt to things in our lives when we believe we don't have a choice in the matter.

I closed the top of a box, taping it shut as Jack walked through the front door. I smiled, jumping to my feet to greet him. I wrapped my arms around his neck and nuzzled against his warm skin. "Hi, babe. How was the game?"

"I don't like it when you're not there," he admitted, and a part of me melted with his words.

"Me either." I closed my eyes, breathing in the smell of him.

"And we lost." His tone turned grumpy and annoyed.

"I'm sorry."

He leaned down, giving me a quick peck on the mouth before walking into the kitchen. "I'm hungry, Kitten, and everything's packed." He opened and closed our cupboards.

"There's pasta in the fridge that I made for dinner. Just needs to be heated up."

He turned toward the refrigerator and opened the door. "Oh, here," he said, reaching into his back pocket. He pulled out a folded-up piece of paper and tossed it at me.

"What is it?"

"It's the detailed travel itinerary for the next few games."

"Oh." I unfolded it. "Is this my copy or do I need to write this all down somewhere?"

"That's all yours. I have mine in my locker."

"Thanks." I scanned the paper looking for his flight time. I breathed out with relief when it read six p.m. "I'm so happy that your flight isn't until six."

"I know. It's only about two and half hours to Miami from here so we lucked out." He flashed a quick dimpled grin before the microwave beeped, signaling his food was ready.

I nodded and scanned the bare living room. "I didn't think it could look any smaller in here, but it actually does. Which really makes no sense."

"Our new place is going to feel like a palace to you."

"I may never leave our bathroom," I teased and he raised an eyebrow. "You don't even know what I'm talking about because you didn't even look at it. Just wait until you see it!"

I started getting really excited. Our new apartment looked amazing, and I couldn't wait to begin living there. "Matteo knows we're moving, right? You told him?"

He nodded before swallowing a mouthful of food. "I told him. He knows exactly where it is."

I started going through the checklist in my head. Utilities changed over and turned on, old apartment cleaned, movers booked, house packed, and address updated online and with the post office. "Kitten?" Jack's voice broke through my overly organized brain.

"Hmm?"

"Did you hear a word I said?"

I shook my head. "Sorry. What'd you say?"

"I asked if you thought about coming to any of the away games."

"I was going to ask you if I could come to the Chicago series." I plopped down on the couch.

"Ask me? Kitten, you can come to every fucking game if you want. You don't have to ask me."

"Well, I've never been to Chicago." I smiled, picturing Cloud Gate, the famous stainless-steel bean-shaped sculpture that people always talked about. I wanted to photograph that bean.

The couch dipped as Jack sat next to me. "Alright, but listen. Chicago is a really big city that sometimes isn't safe. Since you'll be alone, I don't think you should take the El around town. Just take cabs."

"The L?" I asked.

"It's Chicago's train system, which I'm sure is fine but I'll lose my shit thinking about you riding around on it alone."

"I take the trains in New York alone all the time. It can't be that different."

"It's probably not. But I'd feel better if you just took cabs."

"OK. I'll take cabs." I agreed before feeling small nerves tingle up and down my spine. I needed to get used to traveling to strange places alone. Not only was it a part of dating Jack, but it was a part of my future career as well. My job assignments were almost always guaranteed to be in unfamiliar territory.

"I'm not kidding, Kitten. And as much as I want you there, now I'm freaking out at the idea of you being there alone." His eyebrows pulled together.

"I won't be alone. I'll be with you."

He shook his head. "Not really. I'll be at the field most of the time. I don't think there's a day I'm even around for lunch. We're gone before then."

"That sucks." I understood now why the wives didn't go to the away games.

Jack's shoulders squared as he faced me. "I know it's a lot of alone time. You don't have to come."

"I want to. I should at least see what it's like, right? Maybe I'll like having time to explore," I offered, unsure of whom I was trying to convince, me or him.

The tension on his face remained. "Maybe we should fly Matteo out so you aren't alone?"

I jerked my head back in surprise. "No! We're not bringing Matteo! Are you insane?"

"It was just a thought."

"Well, stop thinking like that. I don't want Matteo to go everywhere I go." I imagined the field day the local press would have with that.

Jack reached over, grabbing my hand in his. "I worry about you is all."

"I know, but at some point you need to let me be a big girl and take care of myself. I was perfectly fine here before you came, you know." His expression fell, and I knew I'd hurt him. "That's not how I meant it. I just meant that I didn't need a babysitter before."

"You weren't being hounded by the press or fans before either."

"That's true," I admitted, my stomach fluttering with the thought.

"I know you think I'm crazy, Kitten, but I can't function if I'm worried about you." He lowered his head, and a horrible feeling crept over me. I hated being the source of his pain.

"I don't think you're crazy, but I hate that I cause you so much stress."

His dark eyes turned to my face. "You don't cause me stress. I cause me stress because I can't relax when it comes to you. Because I love you so damn much." ·

I didn't know how to respond. Jack made me fully aware that I was his number one priority in life, and I'd never experienced that feeling before. I stared at him, allowing my own feelings for him to circulate throughout every ounce of my body. Feeling heavy with my own emotions, I longed to lighten the mood.

"Does it matter what time I land on Friday?"

He brought my hand to his lips and kissed across my knuckles. "Even if you book a flight that gets in when I do, I'm not allowed to ride with you to the hotel. So don't worry about trying to coordinate your flight with mine or anything."

"Alright. I'll just fly out after work then."

"So you might miss the game?"

"I shouldn't. We have summer Fridays in the office now so we get to leave early."

"What the hell are summer Fridays?" he scoffed.

I smiled. "This whole freaking city goes to the Hamptons on the summer weekends. So everyone gets off early on Friday so they can drive up there."

"Shut the hell up."

I laughed. "I'm not kidding."

"Could you imagine if we did that shit in LA? What would we have, Malibu Fridays?"

"Beach house Fridays!" I yelled.

Jack smiled and tilted his head. "You're so adorable. I love you so much."

His words pierced like an arrow into my lungs, causing me to catch my breath. "I love you too."

"What time do the movers get here tomorrow?"

"Eight." I looked around one last time. "I got everything, right?"

Jack turned his head in all directions, scanning our tiny living space. "Looks like it to me. You did good, Kitten."

"Thanks." My cheeks warmed with his compliment as his hand cupped my face.

"We should leave this place with a bang."

"What do you have in mind?" I sucked at my lower lip.

"I think you know." He pushed off from the couch before slipping his hands under me and lifting me up. "I think I have two quarters in my pocket." His tongue swept across my lips as he carried me into our tiny bedroom one last time.

◇

We moved into our new apartment the following morning, and Jack was on a flight that evening. But not before building our new bed frame, two sets of bookshelves, and a new dresser. He promised he'd put together everything so I wouldn't have to.

I adored the man he was becoming for me.

For us.

Chicago Friday finally rolled around, and I landed at Midway airport around four. Jack's game at Wrigley didn't start until seven thirty, but he was already at the field. I hopped a cab to the hotel like Jack insisted and watched the city come into view. Even through the backseat window, I sensed the difference between this city and New York. I assumed they'd be similar, but they weren't.

Both cities had numerous tall buildings, but that was pretty much where their similarities ended. While New York appeared dirty and lived in, Chicago was spotless and trash free, newer maybe. And where New York buzzed with constant energy, Chicago exuded more of a gentle hum.

I checked in at the hotel on the bank of the Chicago River and ordered room service while I killed time before the game. I looked out the window at the water down below and the city that surrounded me. Chicago had a style all its own, and I smiled as I thought about capturing it with my camera. I'd have plenty of time for that tomorrow.

When I arrived at the stadium, I almost spent the entire evening staring at the WRIGLEY FIELD, HOME OF THE CHICAGO CUBS sign. It was such a classic piece of baseball memorabilia that I found myself awed by it. I took a few shots of the aged red-and-white sign, loving everything about it, before picking up my lone ticket waiting for me at guest relations. I passed through the dark entrance, lost in the excitement of a new-to-me stadium.

Once inside, I wandered alone, going the wrong direction at first before turning around. I wondered if any of the mean girls would be here. Aside from Trina, there wasn't anyone I wanted to see. Three text messages later, and I found out Trina was still out of the country on her job. I scanned the row of green seats searching for mine. I dropped into my chair before looking around. I found myself surrounded by a few pretty, college-aged girls, but no one that looked familiar. My shoulders relaxed at the absence of any mean girls. I didn't realize how stressed out they made me feel until they weren't around.

Without the distraction of the usual fans or the mean wives, I concentrated completely on watching Jack play. The way he focused always impressed me. He seemed like another person entirely when he stood on that mound of dirt. He blocked out every sound, every shout, every yell, and zoned in one hundred percent on the batter standing sixty feet away.

And when he gave up a hit, he gathered his composure and refocused his energy, unlike some of the other pitchers who became completely rattled when someone got a hit off them. In a game in which your state of mind could make or break you, Jack had the ability to keep it together. His temper off the field never translated on it. Jack always moved forward, putting the last play behind him and focused on the next one.

His passion and sheer respect for the game he loved only made me love him more. I admired the way Jack played ball. It showed a lot of internal character to pitch the way he did. He was focused, determined, and played with a full heart. How can you not love that?

When the game ended, I asked three different security guards for directions to the visiting team's locker room. With my ID card in hand, I wandered underground and waited for Jack to emerge. It was odd being the only person waiting. Players started to walk out of the locker room, each one flashing me a quick smile before walking away. I wondered if they even knew who I was. I hadn't really met any of the players since Jack, and I didn't spend time with them socially.

Trina's boyfriend Kyle walked out, and I smiled. "Hey, Cass. Jack's on his way out," he said, before giving me a quick hug.

"Thanks. Tell Trina I miss her."

He laughed. "I sure will. See you later." He waved as he walked down the corridor out of view.

Jack walked out moments later, his hair still wet from the shower. I wrapped my arms around him and squeezed. "Great game, babe."

"Thanks," he whispered before kissing my lips.

He led me outside where the team bus rumbled. "I'm sorry you have to take a cab back to the hotel."

"It's fine."

"It's not fine. I should be able to ride with you instead of sending you off alone at eleven o'clock on a Friday night."

"I'll be fine. Don't worry." I tried to reassure him, but I sensed that he was uncomfortable.

"I'll wait with you until you get a cab." He grabbed my hand and walked me toward the busy street.

"You don't have to do that, Jack. I don't want you to get in trouble."

"Half the team isn't even out of the locker room yet. It's fine."

Hailing a cab took longer than I anticipated. It was a Friday night and the majority of the taxis driving past me were already filled with passengers. I started to worry that Jack would have to leave me alone when an empty cab came our way and Jack hailed it.

"Thanks, baby." I craned my neck up to give him a kiss before hopping inside.

"I'll see you at the hotel," he said before shutting my door for me.

I arrived before the team bus, so I stepped inside the grand lobby and waited. I almost headed into the bar when Jack's warning coursed through my mind.

Don't look in there, Cass. Jack told you not to look.

But the team's not even here yet. What could I possibly see?

I argued with myself mentally before caving and turning my head to peer inside the bar area. I spotted the three college girls who were sitting near me during the game. One of the girls waved her hand in my direction as if recognizing me from earlier, and I quickly averted my eyes.

Holy shit. Those girls were sitting in the player ticket section?

The team barreled into the hotel lobby, making a loud scene as they entered. I scanned the burly men, searching for Jack. Kymber's husband passed by me without a glance, and I watched as he turned into the bar.

No fucking way.

I observed the scene unfolding like a car crash before my eyes. I couldn't look away if I tried. He sauntered into the bar as one of the blonde girls hopped up from her stool and into his arms. She giggled as he gripped her ass, giving it a couple of smacks, much to her delight. She wrapped her legs around his waist, planting kisses all over his lying, cheating, rat-bastard face. Two more players, both married, entered the bar and a similar scene unfolded. I wanted to puke.

My jaw dropped wide open as all the feelings of Jack cheating on me poured into my bloodstream. My stomach churned, threatening to empty its contents all over the shiny tile floor. Jack suddenly appeared in front of me, his expression grim. "I told you not to look in the bar, Kitten. I told you."

"Holy shit." I shook my head, still shocked at the blatant display of infidelity and my own hellish flashbacks.

Jack grabbed my arm and led me toward the elevator. "That's why I said no bar. And that's why we're on a different floor than they are. So you don't have to see that shit. Come on."

I stumbled as I tried to keep pace with Jack, who was clearly desperate to remove me from the area. "I can't believe they act that way in public. Aren't they worried about getting caught?"

Jack eyed me. "Not here."

"Huh?"

Jack's lips tightened. "We're not talking about this here. Wait until we're in our room."

"Oh." I sighed.

Stepping out of the elevator, we walked down the long corridor toward our room. I ran my fingers across the wallpaper as Jack pressed the card key into the slot. With two clicks, he pushed on the door, holding it for me to enter before he followed. He lay down on top of the bed.

"They aren't worried about getting caught because everyone already knows."

"You're trying to tell me that Kymber the bitch knows her husband is a cheating piece of shit?" I asked, my tone clearly reflecting my disbelief.

He huffed. "Not in so many words, but yeah."

"So she knows he's cheating on her, and what? She just doesn't care?"

I couldn't fathom how anyone in their right mind wouldn't care about being betrayed in that way. What kind of relationship was that anyway?

"I don't know if she really knows, but I know she suspects it."

"And she doesn't care enough to find out for sure?"

"She probably doesn't really want to know the answer. The reality is that a lot of these guys cheat on their wives, Kitten. It's a really shitty fact, but it's the truth. And yeah, the wives usually know, but they just pretend it's not happening."

"Like they're in denial?" I shook my head, still trying to comprehend it all. I thought about Kymber and her crew of mean girls, and felt sorry for them.

"Either that or they just pretend it's not happening because they like their lives."

I shook my head, refusing to believe such craziness. "No way. All the material things they get are more important to them than being respected, or treated well, or truly loved?"

"I think it's really easy to get accustomed to a certain lifestyle. And they'd rather not give it up." He tousled his dark hair before pressing his head against the wall.

That entire concept seemed foreign to me. I wondered what caused a person to convince themselves that the trade-off was worth it. Who needed self-esteem and self-worth when you had big diamonds and expensive clothes? "Well, don't you get any ideas, Mr. Carter, because that kind of crap will never fly with me."

My eyes started to mist, my heart aching with the realization that he already did do that to me. The whole cheating, my knowing about it, basically accepting it, and welcoming him back with open arms. It all happened.

"Kitten, I would never do to you what they're doing to their wives. I think they're assholes. Especially the guys with kids." He patted the bed. "Come here."

I moved to lie down next to him, and he wrapped his arm around my shoulder. "I know you aren't like those other women.

And I wouldn't like you if you were." His lips pressed against the side of my head. "I made a mistake before, but it won't happen again. I know you'd leave me forever if I did and I can't . . ." he paused, "I *won't* lose you again."

Shouldn't She Be Hotter?

Cassie

Jack and I fell into a comfortable routine over the next six weeks. Matteo accompanied me to every home game, and the heckling basically stopped. Until Jack garnered his first lost for the team, that is. That night I was forced to hear a few choice things about how much "Jack sucked" and how I needed to "get his head on straight." The hard-core fans were rabid. When you won, they loved you so fiercely you could do no wrong. But the moment you lost, they stepped all over you on their way out the door.

We talked on the phone constantly when he traveled. He wanted me to come to as many away games as I could, but it wasn't as fun as I thought it would be. I spent most of my time wandering alone in a strange city or eating by myself in restaurants. From the outside, it seems so glamorous to be the girlfriend of a major leaguer, but it's mostly sort of lonely. Not to mention the fact that seeing the other players constantly cheat on their wives made me sick to my stomach.

I had small bouts of insecurity every now and then, but I did my best to keep my fears in check. Jack tried his best as well, staying on the phone with me until all hours of the night, opting for room service instead of going out with the guys, no matter how many times I told him not to.

Baseball kept Jack gone for literally half of each month. The most consecutive number of days he'd been home at one time was seven.

Seven.

Trust was a tricky thing. At times, it seemed like a living, breathing entity that I shaped, built, and conformed to fit my needs in that moment. And other times, it moved like an uncontrollable emotion that ebbed and flowed like the tides in the ocean. One day I'd be perfectly fine and the next I'd be a wreck, convinced that Jack was no better than his teammates.

I wished our relationship were easier, but we were a work in progress. The hardest part was being OK with that. I had a choice when Jack first came back. I didn't have to let him through my front door, but I wanted to. I needed to move forward and believe that he wouldn't hurt me again. My heart longed to accept his actions and take a leap of faith, but my head refused to give in.

Stupid head.

Jack being on the road didn't mean that the online posts about us stopped. They didn't. And no matter how hard I tried to convince myself not to read them, I usually couldn't resist. My own curiosity killed me. I'd read the things written about me or Jack and I'd swear I'd never read them again because they caused me so much anguish. It became a vicious self-deprecating cycle, and I needed to work on my willpower.

And Melissa, bless her heart, didn't always help matters. She kept tabs on every site that posted about me or Jack, and even though she claimed to not share them all with me, it seemed like she alerted me to a new post every day. I was exhausted simply hearing about it all.

Determined to stay focused on work and not the press, I scanned the Internet at my desk, searching through old photographs and news clippings for another photographer's research. An e-mail alert from Matteo popped up on my screen.

Want to grab lunch today? I have no clients and Jack's still out of town.

I almost typed back "Yes," but stopped myself. I enjoyed Matteo's company, and we'd become really good friends, but I knew what would happen. Someone would see us together and take our picture. That picture would be plastered all over the Internet within minutes and most likely printed in the paper the next day with some false headline and trumped-up story from an "anonymous source."

I hated feeling like I couldn't go anywhere with anyone when Jack was out of town, but all it took was one headline that screamed "While Jack's Away, Cassie Will Play" to stop me. The headline was printed above a picture of me and Matteo laughing over dinner and resulted in a number of Internet accusations, not to mention my needing to reassure Jack that absolutely nothing fishy was going on between Matteo and me.

That was a nightmare I had no intention of repeating. I quickly typed a response back to Matteo's e-mail:

Working on a project. Sorry. See you when Jack gets home.

Hopefully my last line made it clear that I wouldn't make plans with him until Jack was back in town.

I worked straight through lunch and by the time I left the office, I was famished. After sweating through the humidity on the non-air-conditioned train ride home, I decided to stop at a café.

"Good evening, Cassie. You want to order something to go?" the short round man asked. I'd only been here a handful of times, but Roman always remembered me and greeted me by name.

"Actually, Roman, I think I'll eat here tonight." I smiled as he pressed his hands together with delight.

"You go ahead and sit anywhere you'd like."

"Thanks." I looked around at the empty tables before choosing one in the far corner near the window. Roman appeared at my table, an iced tea in hand.

"You need to see the menu?" he asked.

"I think I'll just get your famous East Side sandwich and fries."

"You got it, pretty lady!" He grinned and it stretched across his whole face, forcing me to smile back in return.

I rested my back against the wooden chair and watched the people dash by. New York was such a busy city all the time. Day or night, snow or sun, people always rushed around.

My phone vibrated against my hip pocket. Pulling it out, I read the text message from Melissa.

Cute top.

What the hell?

I looked around anxiously with the sudden wish that she were here for a visit and simply hiding from me. I typed out a response:

What are you talking about?

You're on that Spotted website again. Spotted: Jack Carter's girl-friend dining alone near her apartment in Sutton Place.

Immediately, I was lightheaded.

You're joking.

Before I typed anything else, my phone beeped again. Melissa sent a screenshot of the website to my phone, complete with a picture of me staring out of the window I was actually looking out of.

Damn it.

I grabbed my purse, dropping more than enough cash on the table to cover the bill, and looked around for Roman. "Roman, can I get it to go? I need to get home. Something came up. Sorry."

"Sure, Cassie. No problem. Tell Jack I said hello." He transferred my food from the plate he carried into a box before handing it to me.

"I will. I left the money on the table. Thank you." I smiled before rushing out the door.

I looked over my shoulder the entire walk back to my apartment. I couldn't get there fast enough. Every step reminded me how exposed my life had become. From behind my sunglasses, I glanced at the passersby, wondering if the cell phones they held were actually being used to help splash my life across computer screens all over the country. Every tourist with a camera now seemed a potential accomplice in my media hazing.

Once inside the safety and security of our apartment building, I allowed myself to crumple.

"Are you OK, Miss Andrews?" the doorman asked, his big bushy moustache bouncing as he spoke.

"Sorry, Antonio. I'm just a little freaked out by all the online posts and stuff. They can't come in here, right?"

"No, ma'am. They can't come in here." He straightened his back. "I won't let them."

"Thank you," I muttered, averting my gaze outside, thankful that no one stood gawking or staring.

Insisting that my every step was tracked, I'd become paranoid. The press, the fans, the pictures; it never seemed to stop. There was little reprieve. Little sanctuary. I tried to pretend it didn't matter, but the constant pressure was getting to me. Pieces of me were being chipped away at daily. Why was I up for public consumption? I wasn't even the celebrity in the relationship.

I called Melissa from the elevator as soon as the doors closed. "Are you OK?" she answered instead of saying hello.

"No. I'm freaking out. How the hell does this whole town know who I am? And more importantly, why do they care?"

"Because you're Jack's girlfriend. And he's the number one pitcher for the team right now. You know how people get with stuff like this. They're obsessed with celebrities' personal lives."

I exhaled, unlocking my apartment door and walking inside. "But I can't even get dinner without someone posting it online. Even you know I'm not that interesting." I tried to laugh.

"But they don't know that. All they see is the girl who has the hot and awesome Jack Carter's heart. They don't know what you guys have been through."

"But they act like they do." I sprawled across the couch. "They post all sorts of shit claiming to know everything about us."

Melissa laughed. "Yeah, and we both know how accurate those postings are. They're almost as good as the ones on that hot wives website."

My heart beat in double time. "What hot wives website?"

"Shit." She paused. "I'm sorry, Cass. It's just a stupid website."

"What's on it?" I asked, before sitting up to grab my laptop from the coffee table.

She hesitated and I knew she was keeping something from me. "Pictures."

"What else? Tell me," I demanded.

"No really. It's just pictures mostly, but they rate you."

"Rate me how."

"Based on hotness."

I typed a description into the search engine as hundreds of disgustingly named websites turned up. I added "athlete" into my search and bingo. I clicked on the first link listed and my name appeared, along with four recent pictures of me. There was a description that stated Jack and I met back in college but broke up for a brief time before getting back together after he was traded. A paragraph described what I did for work, but didn't mention where.

Thank God.

A rating scale of one to ten stars waited at the end of the post to be voted on. Underneath the star rating, mine currently sat at six, by the way, was a comment section.

"I found the website," I breathed into the phone.

"Oh God. No. Cass. Don't," she pleaded through the phone.

I clicked on the Comment link as my stomach turned.

"I heard she cheats on Jack every time he's out of town with that Matteo guy. Maybe someone needs to help Jack get back at her. I volunteer."

"I saw her making out with that guy who's always with her at the games. I would have taken a picture, but I didn't have my phone with me. Next time."

"My friend went to school with her in California and said she was a bitch to everyone there and no one liked her."

"I thought baseball players were supposed to have hot girlfriends. Where'd he find this one—she's disgusting. And she should probably go on a diet."

"Hello? Cassie?"

"I'm here." I sniffed.

"Do we have to go through these one by one? Obviously you don't cheat on Jack when he's away. You were not making out with your super-hot driver, but if you'd let me I totally would. You were not a bitch to anyone who didn't deserve it in college, and you're not fat or ugly. These are all jealous girls who all think they want what you have."

My eyes filled with tears as I asked my best friend, "What do I do?"

"You've got to stop reading it. Right now," she insisted, and I clicked the small red X at the top of the screen, closing the page. "And I'll stop telling you anything anyone is saying. None of it matters anyway, and it's tearing you apart."

I nodded, knowing she couldn't see me. "You have to help."

Melissa was right. These posts and judgments wrecked me. I tried to not care and be stronger, but it was hard when it was constantly shoved in your face. And it was even harder when the things posted were blatant lies.

"I will. No more texts or picture messages, OK? I promise. You'll feel a million times better once you stop reading the things they're posting."

"I can do that," I said, obviously trying to convince us both.

"I know it's hard to stay away, but trust me, you'll be better off."

"Thanks, Meli." My phone beeped and I pulled it from my face, staring at the screen. "Hey, I have to go. Jack's calling on the other line."

"Alright. Talk to you later. Love you!" she shouted before I clicked over.

"Hi, babe," I answered.

"Kitten." His voice purred into my ear. "I miss you."

I released a breath. "I miss you too. How was the game today?"

"Eh, we lost. They outhit us."

"Sorry, babe."

"It's alright. I'll be home soon, and I have a surprise for you," he teased through the phone.

I smiled, tucking my feet underneath one of the pillows on the couch. "What kind of surprise?"

He laughed. "I got in touch with my buddy Jake. I saw that he had a concert coming up at Madison Square Garden. So I reached out to him for some tickets."

"Jake who?" I asked, never hearing about this friend in a band before.

"Jake Wethers," he answered.

"From The Mighty Storm?" I choked out before bolting upright.

Jack laughed again. "Yeah, you've heard of the band?"

"Shut up, Jack. Everyone's heard of the band. How the hell do you know Jake Wethers?"

"We have some mutual friends back in LA, and we met a few times over the years. We just hit it off and stayed in touch. You'll love him."

"Holy shit, I already love him," I said. "I can't believe we're going to a Mighty Storm concert! And I can't believe you freaking know Jake!"

"So I did good?" he asked, his voice a mixture of sweet and cocky.

"Better than good. I can't wait to see you."

"You just remember that you love me and not Jake Wethers, got it? I love Jake but I'll kick his ass if I have to."

"It's hard enough dating you. The last thing I need is to date a freaking rock star," I moaned.

"Yeah, and Jake's no picnic like I am," he said, and the irony wasn't lost on me.

"Oh, I'm sure. Because dating you has been a real walk in the park," I joked, my insides still giddy with the knowledge that Jack and Jake were friends.

"I'm gonna go grab some food, Kitten. I love you. See you tomorrow."

"Love you too," I said, before hanging up my phone and collapsing back onto the couch.

◇

Jack walked through the front door with a wide grin on his face, and I practically knocked him over in my excitement. "God I missed you," he breathed into my hair, tangling his fingers in it.

I kissed each of his dimples before pressing my mouth to his. "I missed you too," I said, before sweeping my tongue across his bottom lip. He tasted like warm cinnamon, and I sucked his bottom lip into my mouth, nibbling gently.

Jack dropped his bag onto the floor with a loud thud and lifted me from the ground with one arm. He walked us into our bedroom and tossed me onto our new bed. "Get naked," he demanded with an arched brow.

"You first," I toyed, staring at him.

With a cocky grin, he shrugged and then pulled off his black T-shirt. I wanted to lick every inch of his tanned chest and abs. He unfastened his shorts and removed the rest of his clothes in one swift motion. I took in every delicious ounce of him, my eyes roaming from head to toe.

"Your turn," he said, not moving from where he stood at the end of the bed.

I lifted off my white tank top before scooting out of my shorts and underwear. Then I unfastened my bra and dropped it to the side of the bed. Jack was on me, licking, nibbling, and kissing my body like a man starved for it.

"I need you," he breathed against my skin before licking my neck.

I didn't want the foreplay; he'd been gone for so long that I craved his touch. I pulled at his body, aching for him to enter. I didn't want to wait a second longer without having him inside me.

"Jack," I breathed out, as he kissed my breasts and moaned against them. "Jack, get in. I want you. Now."

His mouth moved up to mine, his tongue moving in and out of my mouth passionately. He was feverish, and I was desperate. "Say it again. Tell me you want me."

He kissed my mouth harder as his body moved around mine. I tried to force him inside, but he resisted. My fingertips dug into his lower back as I attempted to guide him. "Say it."

"I want you, Jack. I need you."

"Where?" His hands grabbed at me all over. "Where do you want me?"

"Inside me. I want you inside me now," I breathed and moaned in unison.

With one deep thrust, he pushed himself inside of me. I moaned, the pleasure mixing with pain. "Oh God. You're so deep."

He moved in and out, pushing deeper with each thrust until he could go no further. I wrapped my legs around his waist, taking him as deep as he could go. "I'm not going to last, Kitten."

I tightened my grip, pushing my hips against him harder and faster as he grew inside of me. I maneuvered my body and Jack flipped us over so I was now on top. Taking him even deeper from this position, I cried out with pleasure. I looked down at Jack, his eyes locked on mine. "You feel so fucking good," he groaned.

I leaned forward, thrusting my tongue into his mouth while working my hips up and down in a rushed pace. The feeling of him inside of me was unlike anything else, and I moaned as he pressed against the right spot. Bursts of feeling shot through my body as I screamed out with the pleasure he gave me. I worked my hips against his as he moaned, his hands gripping mine forcefully. He throbbed against my insides as he groaned in raspy breaths. Our movements slowed and he pulled me against his heaving chest.

"It's nice to have you home," I whispered against his chest.

He huffed. "It's nice to be home."

"I love you, Jack." I loved Jack more than I'd ever loved anyone in my life, but dating him was hard. I wanted to tell him about all the Internet sites and the things they posted, but he had enough to concentrate on during the season. So I stuffed my unhappiness deep inside, hoping to God it would stay there.

He ran his fingers through my hair as he leaned up to plant a kiss on the top of my head. "I love you, Kitten."

Not Cut Out For This

Cassie

I could rarely attend Jack's afternoon home games because of work, so I was following a game online when my cell phone sang its Melissa ringtone. I reached for it, silencing it immediately. I answered it quietly, "What's up, girl?"

"I know we said no more, but I have to tell you something."

My chest tightened as I held my breath. "What?"

"Chrystle sold her story to a tabloid."

My stomach dropped. "What story exactly?" I managed to ask through my shock.

"Oh, the one where you're a home-wrecking whore who stole her husband after she lost their baby to a miscarriage."

My head started to pound as the walls of the office spun around me. I clutched the phone tight against my cheek, willing the bile rising in my throat to subside.

"Cass, are you there?"

"I'm here."

"There's more."

"More?" I choked out, wondering what more there could possibly be.

"There are pictures online of their wedding. And pictures of you. And the article is filled with lies. People are eating it up, Cass.

Believing every word of that lying bitch's story. The message boards online are blowing up calling you a home wrecker and the devil. It's crazy!"

My body started to tremble with fury. I hated Chrystle so much for everything she'd done to come between me and Jack. And here I'd thought she was out of lives for good. "Why won't she just go away?"

"'Cause she's a money-hungry publicity whore. I'm going to fucking kill her. Straight up murder the bitch."

I managed a chuckle through my rage-filled tears. "Me first."

"Cassie, can I see you please?" Nora shouted across the bustling office floor.

"Meli, I have to go. My boss is calling me." I tossed my phone into a drawer before my nervous legs walked me into Nora's office. Her walls were covered with various magazine covers from over the years and pictures of Nora with celebrities and local politicians.

"Close the door and come sit," she said, not looking up as I entered. I did as she requested, shaking as I collapsed into the over-stuffed white leather chair. "Talk to me about this article that just came out."

"What do you want to know?" I asked, my eyes instantly welling.

She leaned forward onto her elbows and looked directly at me. "How much of it is true?"

"I just found out about it, so I'm not quite sure what it says."

"Was Jack married to this person?"

I nodded. "Yes."

"And she got pregnant." I could tell she assumed those parts of the story were accurate.

"No. She lied to him. She told him she was pregnant, but she never was. The minute Jack found out, he left her."

"So he didn't leave her for you?"

"He was with me first." I suddenly wanted to defend what Jack and I had in the past, before Chrystle came along and fucked it all up. "We were together when he met her."

"So he cheated on you?" she asked matter-of-factly.

"Yeah."

"Did she know about you?" Nora eyed me, and I sensed that an idea was coursing through that brain of hers.

"She knew about me. She didn't care. She said that she always wanted a baseball-playing husband, so that's what she got." Anger and embarrassment collided within me as I struggled to keep my emotions balanced.

"Do you want to address this article publicly? We could make a statement on your behalf, disputing all of this woman's claims and accusations." Nora folded her hands together and rested her chin on top. "Or we could run a counter article on you and Jack."

I hadn't even thought about defending myself. In the past months, I'd learned to keep quiet when it came to all the things people wrote about me. I was told standing up for myself would end up making me look worse, which I never understood, but I had to agree with because I didn't know what else to do.

"If you fight back they'll attack even harder," Melissa's mom had advised me at one point. "Don't give them any more ammunition. People like that love getting a reaction out of you. So when they don't get what they want, they eventually move on." But they hadn't moved on.

"Is that what you think I should do?" I asked Nora. "Make a statement? Won't it make it worse?"

Her brow furrowed. "Possibly. Let me think on it for a couple days."

"OK."

"I worry about you. I don't know how you put up with all of this crap. Being with this guy sure has its downfalls, doesn't it? I hope he's worth it."

My lungs constricted as if all the air had been sucked out of the room. I wanted to choke, but couldn't. I struggled to keep my composure as the tears spilled out. And just like that, I broke down. I couldn't take it anymore. The bad press, the constant harassment, the online sites judging me every day. It had become too much weight to carry.

"Oh dear." Nora pushed back from her desk and walked over to me. "I'm sorry. I just meant that it's a lot to take."

"I know. It's not what you said; it's how I feel," I tried to explain through my sobs.

"Why don't you take a few days off? Go clear your head. Hell, take a vacation or something. Get out of the city for a while."

I wiped at my eyes and sniffled. "Maybe I'll fly home. Are you sure that's OK?"

"Absolutely. We'll come up with a game plan when you get back." She squeezed my shoulder before returning to her chair.

"Thank you, Nora." I forced a smile before walking out of her office. I gathered my things, typed a quick out-of-office notification for my e-mail, and turned my computer off. I stopped at the lobby store, grabbing a copy of the tabloid as my legs wobbled. The wedding picture of Jack with Chrystle caused me sharp stabs of pain as I stared at it.

Mortified, I tucked the tabloid under my arm and walked outside. I couldn't take the subway home, I'd never last surrounded by all those people, so I called the only person I could think of while I walked back into the lobby.

"Matteo, can you come get you from work and bring me home?" My voice was shaking as I practically begged.

"Of course. Are you OK, Cassie?"

"Yeah. I just need a ride home please." He knew I was lying, but he didn't press the issue.

"I'll be there in ten minutes."

Matteo arrived right on time, and I headed out of the lobby doors toward the car. He rushed out of the driver's seat, concern written all over his face. He took me by the hand, opening the door for me and closing it softly. Once inside, I buckled myself in and waited for the inquisition that never came. If he had a million questions, he wasn't asking any.

Matteo pulled the car up in front of my building as hordes of cameramen surrounded it. "Oh my God," I said, the shock clearly written all over my face.

"Cassie, what's going on?" Matteo asked.

The press realized it was me in the car, and it took less than two seconds for them to swarm the side I sat on, cameras flashing nonstop, practically blinding me, even in the daylight. "I got this," Matteo said before exiting the car. I heard him demand they move as he opened my door and helped me out. I lowered my head upon exiting, refusing to make eye contact with anyone.

Reporters shouted questions while Matteo wrapped a protective arm around me and pushed through the crowd.

"Did you know she was pregnant?"

"Did Jack leave her for you?"

"Were you having an affair with Jack while he was still married?"

"Do you think stress made her lose the baby?"

"Leave her alone!" he shouted, trying to get me into my building.

Once inside the building, the doorman blocked the reporters while Matteo shielded me from view and pressed the button on the elevator. He stayed by my side until it opened. "Thank you," I said through watery eyes.

"Are you going to be OK? Are you sure you want to be alone right now?" He held the elevator door open with his hand.

"You have to go get Jack soon, right? I'll be fine until he gets home. But I might need you to drive me somewhere later. I'll call you if I do," I said, knowing I was being cryptic.

"Whatever you need, I'll be there for you," he reassured me.

"Thanks again." I swallowed before allowing the doors to close and block everything but my own reflection from view.

In the security of our apartment, I collapsed onto our bed, tucking my knees into my chest. I allowed my tears to spill out onto my pillow. I couldn't believe this was happening again. I'd never experienced someone so vindictive and cruel, and I hadn't even read the damn article yet.

I flashed back to being at Fullton, when reports started coming in about Jack getting married and how I was portrayed as the woman left behind. I thought I'd never experience pain and humiliation like that again, but this was far worse. Now that Jack played in the major leagues, everything was amplified. Our lives weren't simply a local story anymore; they were national news. And this Chrystle story garnered everyone's attention.

My stomach twisted and turned as I tried to block it all out, but failed. My cell phone rang, causing me to jump as I looked at the number flashing on the screen. I didn't recognize it, but answered it anyway. "Hello?"

"Is this Cassie Andrews?" a male voice asked on the other end of the line.

I hesitated. "It is."

"I wanted to ask you a few questions about the article today for our website, OK?"

"No, it's not OK. How'd you get this number? Don't call again."

Horrified, I ended the call as quickly as I could. I guess I should have been surprised it took them this long to track me down, but I was completely losing it. I didn't want the press to have my phone number. I hated it enough that they knew where we lived.

I closed my eyes after putting my phone on silent, falling into the comfort of sleep. The sound of the door slamming woke me.

"Cass? Cassie? Where are you?" Jack's voice was frantic as the sound of his footsteps beat against the wood flooring. I stayed silent, knowing that he'd eventually find me in here.

"Kitten. Are you OK?" He curled next to me in the bed, holding my shaking body in his arms. All I wanted to do was run. *Literally.* "Talk to me, Cass."

"Are they still downstairs? The press?" I avoided looking at him.

"Yeah. They're fucking vultures."

I pushed off the bed and walked into the kitchen. I opened the cupboard and pulled out a glass. Filling it with water, I gulped the entire thing down. "How did you hear about the article?"

"The team's publicist saw it and alerted me. He's putting out an official statement on my behalf."

"What is your statement?" I asked, placing the glass down on the cold granite countertop.

"I don't know." He shrugged.

"What do you mean, you don't know?" I started getting pissed, the heat rising in my belly.

"The team makes a statement, and I'm required to go along with it," he told me, trying to make me feel better but failing miserably.

"What if you don't agree with it? What if it's a horrible, stupid statement? You're just supposed to smile and nod your head?"

"That's what happens, Kitten. They put out a statement that's best for the team, and I'm supposed to agree with it. I have no say."

I turned my back to him, storming into our bedroom. "That's fucking ridiculous! This is your life we're talking about! And my life. These are horrible lies about you and about me. We can't just sit here and agree with some statement you didn't even make."

He followed right behind me. "What do you want to do? Make our own statement?"

I grabbed my running shoes from the closet. "I have to get the fuck out of here." The heat spread quickly throughout my entire body as my temper flared beyond control.

"What are you doing? Where are you going?"

"You're not the only one with a temper, Jack. Just because I don't go around putting my fist in people's faces doesn't mean I don't lose my shit!"

"Running away isn't really showing you have a temper. It just shows you have . . ." he paused, "legs."

I laced up my gym shoes. "Just leave me alone."

"See? Legs for running away instead of staying here and talking it out!" he yelled, his voice frustrated.

"I can't think clearly when I'm around you. I need to be away from you." His eyes. His face. They all distracted me from my internal thoughts.

I slammed the door and walked down the stairs to our gym, thankful it was empty. I turned on a treadmill before plugging into my iPod. The music of Imagine Dragons blasted in my ears as I started running faster and faster, all the frustration from the last few months pouring out in beads of sweat across my forehead. Wishing I could stomp out all the blog posts, newspaper articles, gossip columns, message board threads, and Chrystle from my memory with each step, I slammed my feet against the moving surface.

After an hour of running on pure adrenaline, nothing changed. I didn't feel better, relieved, or calmed. The same pressures and hurt remained. I realized this was something I could no longer ignore.

I wasn't happy.

The past four months had helped dissolve my strength into a puddle of self-doubt and misery. Being with Jack meant accepting all the other things that came with it, and I hated it. My head pounded as I walked back into our apartment. Ignoring Jack, I moved past him and into the shower. He tried to follow me, but I closed and locked the door. I took my time, hoping the hot water would wash away my doubts, but nothing helped. Afterward, I towel dried my hair before emerging with another towel wrapped around my body.

Jack sat on our bed, watching my every move as I quickly changed into a pair of jeans and a tank top.

"I didn't sign up for this, Jack." I snapped my eyes shut, willing the online pictures and tabloid article to disappear from my mind.

"You didn't sign up for what exactly?" he asked cautiously, his head tilting to one side.

I sighed. "I didn't sign up for this life. This constant invasion of privacy . . . this scrutiny. This judgment. People get to say and write whatever they want about me, and I just have to sit here and take it. I can't deal with it anymore."

The tears started to fall, and I didn't bother to stop them. "Did you know that my pictures are plastered all over websites where people get to vote on whether or not they think I'm hot enough for you?" I screamed through my frustration.

Logically I knew it wasn't Jack's fault, but my embarrassment overruled all logic at the moment. "Do you know how horrible that feels? To be judged on my looks by a bunch of fucking strangers? Heaven forbid I'm actually a good person who loves her boyfriend and works hard and treats people well. But that doesn't count. None of that matters!"

I threw my hands out, shaking my head. "It's all about what I wear and how my hair looks and how much weight I need to lose. Why do people think it's OK to tear apart the way I look? Did you know there's an entire thread on the baseball website dedicated to hating me? Not liking me, but *hating* me. What the hell did I even do to anyone?"

"What? Why didn't you ever tell me?" he asked. "I'll have administration get that shit taken down right now! I will not have any threads about you on a baseball website. Unless it's good stuff." He forced a small smile, his dimples barely showing.

"I've been called every name in the book. Whore, slut, gold digger, ugly, fat, bitch, cunt, tramp, cleat chaser . . . and I can't fucking take it, Jack. I don't know how anyone does."

"What are you saying, Kitten?" He took two steps toward me, and I instinctively stepped back.

"I don't know what I'm saying." My heart battered against my chest as I denied the truth. I knew exactly what I was saying . . . I just apparently couldn't form the actual words.

He started nervously pacing. In all honesty, my nerves even overwhelmed me in that moment. "Don't do anything stupid, Cass. You know we're no good without each other."

I nodded my head as more tears escaped. "I'm not sure we're any good with each other either."

"You don't mean that. You're just upset." Jack's voice shook as he shoved his hands into his front pockets. When I didn't respond, he begged, "Don't do this. Don't you dare give up on us."

"I feel like I'm losing myself." I turned away, unable to bear the look in his eyes. "Being in this relationship with you is completely fucking with me," I admitted, the tears falling down my cheeks without mercy. Guilt rushed through me as my words spilled out. I never intended to admit all of this to him during the baseball season. I wanted to be strong enough to get through it on my own, to talk to him when the season ended, but I couldn't take any more. My insides had wound up so tight I thought they might shatter. Chrystle's accusatory article was the last straw.

Jack stepped closer, his arms resting on my shoulders as he turned me toward him. "You don't get to quit," he said, reaching for my chin with shaky hands. "You don't get to walk away from this."

I wanted to throw up. My feelings contorted inside of me, the conflict raging once again. Part of me wanted to bolt as quickly as I could from everything Jack Carter, while the rest of me wanted to tangle myself up in his arms and never let go.

"I need to figure out how to be with you and still keep my sanity. I feel like a crazed lunatic. Like I have absolutely no control over my life. I can't keep living like this." I sobbed until my vision blurred.

He led me toward our couch, pulling me down with him as I cried into his chest. How had I become so twisted up and confused? I knew I loved Jack, but I wasn't sure I could be with him like this any longer. I pulled away from his grip, wiping my eyes with the back of my hand as he returned to the view, as gorgeous as ever.

He cupped my cheek, moisture filling his dark eyes. "I don't want to be here without you. We can fix this. But we can't fix it if you walk away. I can't make us work by myself."

"I just need to find some sort of balance. Between your work and my work and all the pressure that comes along with it—" I stopped as I tried to gather my thoughts. "It's just too much. I need to get myself together. I'm falling apart here."

He leaned his head into his hands, his fingers tugging at his dark hair. I watched his chest rise and fall, his head shaking before he turned to look at me. "Fine," he started with a ragged breath. "Get yourself together, then. But don't you fucking quit on me. After everything we've been through, please don't let this break us."

Tears ran down my cheeks with his words. I loved Jack, but this was about me. Loving Jack put my own self-worth at risk. A girl could only take so much bashing and criticism from so many fronts until her self-esteem started to take a nosedive. And that wasn't healthy for either of us.

"I'm going to take a few days off from work and go stay with Melissa." The words flew from my lips effortlessly. I hadn't even talked to Melissa, but I knew she would welcome me.

He lowered his head, the look of defeat replacing any hope he once had. "OK, Kitten. You go."

I nodded, reaching for my cell phone and dialing Matteo's number. "Hi, Matteo, it's Cassie. Can you get me to JFK as soon as possible, or are you busy?"

Matteo asked me to hold for a moment while he rearranged his schedule with another driver. I waited, avoiding all eye contact with Jack. Matteo came back on the line, informing me that he'd pick me up in twenty minutes and he'd call me when he was downstairs. I thanked him before I ended the call and turned the ringer back on.

Whether I wanted to or not, it was time to pack.

I sensed Jack watching me from the doorway of the bedroom we shared as I tossed pieces of clothing into my open suitcase. Deliberately, I forced myself not to look at him. He could take the broken parts of me and shatter them even further. If I looked at him, I'd question everything. He could make me stay, and I desperately needed to go. After adding two more pairs of shoes, I zipped up the suitcase and lifted it from the bed.

"Let me help you," he offered from behind me, his breath gliding across my back.

"It's fine. I have it," I said tightly, refusing to face him.

"How long will you be gone?" he asked, his tone desolate.

I shrugged, unsure of my actual plans. "I don't know. A few days. A week, maybe. I'll text you," I offered with a glance in his direction.

Jack's face turned sullen as the color drained instantly from his cheeks. He reached for me, his fingers tightening around my wrist, stopping all forward movement. "You are coming back. Right, Kitten?" A look of powerlessness covered his face.

My stomach dropped to my feet with his question. I took a few short breaths before responding, "Yes, Jack. I'm coming back."

It wasn't a lie, but the truth was almost as painful. Of course I would come back, but I wasn't sure what I'd be coming back to. "I have a job here."

His eyebrows pinched together, tears filling his eyes as he let go of my arm. My phone rang, breaking the sorrow-filled heaviness in the room. "Hi, Matteo. OK, I'll be right down."

"I need to go." I leaned toward Jack and planted a soft kiss on his cheek before turning to walk away.

He gripped my wrist from behind and yanked me around to face him. "Get over here," he said roughly as he pulled my body effortlessly into his. Before I could situate my arms, his were wrapped around me, pulling me tight against his heaving chest.

Oh my God, he's crying.

"I love you more than anything. You need to know that before you walk out that door." The warmth of his breath fluttered against my skin. My eyes met his, and the tears that rolled down his cheeks caused my heart to shatter.

"I love you too." My current dysfunction had nothing to do with my feelings for Jack. I loved him more than I ever thought possible. But sometimes love wasn't enough, and in order to be with him forever, I needed to make sure I could handle whatever came my way.

"I'll do anything to make you happy. Anything, Kitten. You just tell me what I need to do and I'll do it. Tell me what you want and I'll give it to you. You want to file a lawsuit against Chrystle, I'll start the paperwork tomorrow. You want me to quit baseball? I'll stop playing."

It pained me to hear his voice sounding this desperate, this needy. "That's not what I want," I choked out, my jagged heart beating out painfully piercing beats. "Right now I just need some space."

He peeled his arms from my body, and I instantly craved their attention again, but refused to give in. "OK. Space," he breathed out in response, his cheeks tearstained. "But not forever. I won't let you quit on us. I know this is all my fault. One fucking mistake that never goes away. I'm so sorry about all of it."

"I know you are," I whispered. "I am too."

I pulled my suitcase out the front door, leaving Jack behind.

◇

I walked out of the elevator, noticing the gaggle of press still gathered outside our building. Seeing me, the cameras started flashing against the glass of the window as they fought over one another for the best shot. Matteo lunged through them on his way to reach me. Blocking me from view once again, he grabbed my suitcase while keeping a tight hold on my body.

Stepping outside, I was bombarded by the press shouting their questions.

"Where are you going, Cassie?"

"Did you and Jack split up?"

"Is he going back to Chrystle?"

"Why are you leaving?"

"Why are you crying?"

I wanted to scream at the top of my lungs for them to shut the hell up and mind their own business. They didn't know anything about our relationship and their stupid assumptions drove me nuts. Matteo opened up the passenger door, and I shook my head, opting for the rear seat, which had privacy glass on the windows. I watched as some of the paparazzi scattered, and I assumed they were heading for their cars so they could follow me.

He opened the door for me and ushered me inside. "Are you OK?"

I wiped the tears from my cheeks. "I will be."

"Are you and Jack alright?" he asked as he pulled the car onto Second Avenue.

Unsure of how much I wanted to confide in Matteo at the moment, I opted for the easy way out. "I'm not sure."

Matteo checked the rearview mirror a few times before I asked, "Are they following us?"

"I don't think so. I can usually tell if they're around us because they drive like assholes, but I don't see anyone."

"Good."

"Cassie?" His voice questioned and I simply looked in his direction. "You know I'm here if you need me."

I forced a polite smile. "I know. Thank you."

We drove the rest of the way in silence. My brain turned inside my skull, causing more confusion, questions, and pain. I closed my eyes as the sound of my cell phone beeping filtered into my ears.

I read the text message from Jack.

I love you. I wish there were different words that I could say, but no one's been clever enough to invent any yet. So it's all I've got. But it's everything. I love you. I want to spend the rest of my life with you. Please come home soon.

Half tempted to ask Matteo to turn the car around, I turned my phone off instead. Another text message like that, and I would go back. I'd never leave.

And I'd probably become a shell of a person who secretly resented everything her life had become. Because the problems and issues would still remain. I needed to fix this. I needed to fix me. Before I knew it, the car screeched to a stop in front of the airline terminal. I pushed out of the backseat with the help of Matteo's outstretched, muscular hand.

"Come here," he said, pulling me against his chiseled body.

God, he smells good.

"You'll be OK." He patted the length of my hair, his hands sliding down my back slowly. Matteo had never touched me like that before. I sensed deliberation in his movements, but did nothing to stop him.

Why aren't I stopping him?

"I hate seeing you cry," he whispered in my ear, before wiping my cheek with his thumb.

Pull away, Cass.

I didn't move. Nerves surged through my body like waves in the ocean. Forceful and without remorse, they ebbed and flowed from my head to my toes. My knees started to shake as my heart rate quickened.

Pull aw—

Before I could process another thought, Matteo's soft lips pressed against mine. I tensed quickly at first, shock and disbelief sprinting through my head. I squeezed my eyes shut, allowing the difference in his kiss and his touch to overwhelm my senses. His mouth opened and his tongue pushed up against my lips, begging for entry.

Instantly, my eyes shot open as I pushed away from his Adonis body. I wiped his taste from my lips with the back of my hand before covering my mouth from view. My mind raced to piece together what the hell had just happened and why I'd allowed it.

Fuck, what if someone saw that?

I quickly scanned the area, noting the absence of prying eyes and cameras. I couldn't be certain there wasn't someone hiding, but it looked all clear.

Thank the stars.

"Oh God, Cassie. I'm so sorry." His eyes widened as a look of horror crossed his face. "It broke my fucking heart to see you crying. You're too beautiful to cry like that. I just wanted to take your tears away and make you happy."

I processed his words.

I think.

What is he saying exactly?

I refused to move for what seemed like an eternity, but I'm sure it was only a few seconds. "Um," I stuttered, "I . . . I have to go."

I reached into the open trunk of the car, pulling at my suitcase. "Cassie. Look at me," Matteo said forcefully. I released my grip on my suitcase, turning to face him. "Please don't tell Jack. I'm so sorry. I never should have done that."

"Then why did you?" I yelled as embarrassment and anger all competed for the gold medal in my emotional Olympics.

His long, tanned fingers gripped the edge of his jacket. "Oh, come on. Don't make me say it out loud."

"Say what out loud? What the hell are you taking about?" I didn't have time for this. Not tonight. I was already coming apart at the seams; I couldn't take any more shit from anyone.

Here, Matteo, pull this frayed piece of fabric and watch me fall into particles of skin, clothing, and hair in a big heap on the ground.

"I like you. I didn't mean to and I know we can never be together, but fuck!" He started pacing.

"What do you mean, you like me?" I shouted at his back. "You don't fucking like me. We're friends. That's all we've ever been. That's all we'll ever be," I insisted.

His jaw worked under his fingertips as he continued to pace. "I know. Like I said, I fucked up. I didn't mean to go and fall in love with you—"

I interrupted, refusing to hear another word. "You are not in love with me! Do you hear me?" I inched closer to his body, my anger rising. "Say it!"

He stopped pacing and shook his head. "Say what?"

"Say you're not in love with me! You just think you are because we spend so much time together, and you're supposed to protect me. But you're not in love with me. Not really. So I want you to fucking say it." I jabbed my finger into his rock-hard chest repeatedly.

He shrugged his shoulders, no words leaving his lips. I jabbed at him again. "Say it!" And then I lost it. I started crying out of pure frustration. "Say it, damn it!" I insisted, stomping my foot on the concrete.

He took a step toward me, and I firmly placed my hand against his stomach, stopping him cold. "Do you feel something for me? Anything at all?" his voice pleaded.

I wanted to kick him in the nuts right then and there and tell him that pure hatred raced through my veins for him. And well, that was *something*. But it would have been a lie. "Matteo, I do not feel anything for you other than friendship. I love Jack. I've always loved Jack."

"So you're not attracted to me? This is purely a one-way street?" His lips formed a snarl, and I fought down the urge to sock him in the jaw. He'd pushed all the wrong buttons tonight.

"I'd have to be dead to not be attracted to you!"

"I knew it!" he shouted, pleased at my apparent revelation.

"But it's not the kind of attraction that means anything!" I yelled back, my frustration boiling over so hot and thick I thought my skin might blister.

He shoved a hand through his hair in frustration before leaning toward me. "What the fuck does that even mean?"

"It just means that yes, I think you're hot. But so does anyone with eyes! You're a good-looking guy. Of course I'm attracted to you," I explained, intentionally lowering my voice before continuing. "But I don't want to be with you. I don't want to leave Jack for you. It's not the kind of attraction that makes me question anything in my life, if that's what you're asking."

His gaze dropped to the ground, looking like all the wind had just been sucked from his sails. "Oh."

Guilt seeped into my bones, making itself at home. Scenes of our time spent together ran through my mind like a sports highlights reel. Had I given him the wrong impression? Did I lead him on? Did I make Matteo think there was something between us?

"Look, I'm sorry if I've ever given you some impression that I wanted more from you. I don't. And I don't say that to hurt you, but I'm in love with Jack. I want that to be very clear."

"You didn't." He paused, exhaling a breath so large his chest caved inward. "You didn't lead me on. It's just that I don't really spend any time with anyone other than you."

"That's what I'm trying to tell you. You don't love me, Matteo. I promise you that you don't. You just think you do because we're always together. Maybe we should look into hiring another driver when I get back into town?"

The idea of a new driver filled me with a sliver of relief. The lines of our relationship had blurred so often that I suddenly appeared blinded by it. Matteo worked for us, but the friendship we formed often took precedence. Lines needed to be clear again—business first, friendship second. But how would I ever explain that to Jack without him suspecting something?

His face twisted as he pushed off the curb, standing above me. "Please don't fire me. I love working for you guys. This is literally the best job I've ever had. Give me another chance. Please, Cassie. I'm so sorry. It will never happen again. I promise."

I couldn't give him any answers, so I didn't. Right now, I needed to get the hell out of New York and away from everyone. "I have to go."

"Are you going to tell Jack?" His handsome face looked nervous; it seemed strange to see him looking so undone.

"I don't know," I admitted. I considered keeping the kiss from Jack, and that fact alone nearly wrecked me. Omitting the truth was still being dishonest. I'd be doing the number one thing I'd insisted Jack never to do me: lie.

"He'll kill me." Matteo rubbed his temples.

"Yeah." I couldn't disagree. "He will."

I Don't Care How Much It Costs

Jack

Watching Cassie run out our door last night practically tore me in two. I knew I had to let her go, but it fucking killed me to stand there and watch it happen. I hoped Melissa would be able to talk some sense into her. Despite all of the torment and pain I'd caused in the past, I knew Melissa still believed that Cassie and I were meant to be together. I thought I could count on that much.

I convinced myself that Cassie just needed some time away. She'd see everything clearly in a few days, and she'd come back home to me. I knew that being in the public eye could be unbearable at times, but hopefully it was worth putting up with in order to be together.

Right?

I knew what I wanted. And what I wanted was to spend the rest of my life with Cassie. I've always known it, but having her leave like this only solidified the fact that I refused to live my life without her in it. I wanted her to know how serious I was about us. Nothing and no one would ever come between us again. I didn't know shit about jewelry, but every guy knew about Tiffany's. The ring Chrystle sported on her tiny finger had been her late grandmother's, so all of this ring-shopping business was new to me. And I wouldn't have it any other way.

I hustled down the busy New York streets toward the shop six or so blocks away. I pulled my hat down low and donned sunglasses, hoping no one would recognize me and try to stop me for pictures. Two steps from the Tiffany's store a voice shouted, "Jack Carter?" and my feet stopped moving. "Oh my God, are you Jack Carter?"

I looked up to see a teenage girl practically dancing off the sidewalk. "Hi." I smiled, not wanting her to draw attention to me, or the store I was about to walk into.

"Can I get a picture with you? Please?" Her voice shook.

"Sure." I leaned toward her as she tried to take a self-portrait of us. I grabbed the phone from her shaking hands. "Here, I'll take it." I reached out my arm as far as it would go before clicking the button on her phone.

"Thank you so much. Oh my God. I can't wait to show my dad. And all my friends. They think you're so hot," she gushed.

"Just your friends think I'm hot?" I teased, hoping to ease the teen's nerves.

She laughed, her face turning a bright shade of red before squeaking out, "Thanks again. Bye."

I turned around, scanning the area for photographers and passed the Tiffany's entrance just to be safe. When no one else approached me, I turned back around and hastily walked through the revolving door. Once inside, I wanted to puke. Talk about overwhelming. Glass cases lined the entire length of the store. Where the hell was I supposed to start?

"Hello, sir. May I help you find something?" A brunette stepped in front of me with a fake smile.

"Um." I froze. "Engagement rings."

Her fake smile deepened. "Right this way."

She led me past a crowd of people hovering over something and directed me toward a display of cases. "All of our engagement rings are here. Let me find a specialist to help you."

"Thanks," was all I muttered in response.

I glanced down. No wonder girls loved this shit. Diamonds of all sizes and colors sparkled like the lights at the baseball stadium. Everything seemed so fancy and showy—neither of which was Kitten's style. I continued to scan the flashy rings when a voice broke my concentration.

"Good afternoon. My name is Elizabeth. Sasha told me you were looking for engagement rings. Do you have a specific style in mind?"

Yeah. The kind that fits on her hand and makes her say yes when I propose.

"Um, no. I have no idea what I'm doing."

"How about we start with a price range. Do you have a certain amount you are looking to spend?" She smiled, her overly white teeth blinding me.

"It doesn't matter."

Her face lit up. Like seriously . . . Lit. The. Fuck. Up. Like I'd just told her she'd hit the jackpot.

"OK. So then, is there a certain shape she likes?"

"Honestly." I paused. "Elizabeth, was it?" She nodded. "I have no idea what kind of shape she likes. I'd just like to get her a ring that fits her personality."

"Alright then. Is there a shape you like? There's round, cushion cut, princess."

"I don't know what any of that means other than round. Why don't I just look at these, and I'll tell you which ones I like."

"Of course. You go right ahead."

Holy hell, salespeople are annoying.

I wandered around the cases searching for the one ring that looked right. I passed by all the so-called "fancy" diamonds, assuming that Cassie would probably hate a big pink or yellow diamond on her finger.

I stopped at a case filled with more subtle pieces. They looked more classic, timeless even, and I liked the look. And then I noticed it. A round diamond surrounded on all sides by smaller diamonds. The band held diamonds as well.

"Elizabeth, can I see this ring please?" I looked up, searching for her.

She smiled again, rushing over. "Which one?"

"The round one right there with all the diamonds around it," I said, pointing.

"Beautiful choice. Now this band comes with either a two-and-a-half-, three-, or four-carat diamond in the center."

"You lost me," I admitted.

"The size of the diamond. The center one for this band can accommodate any of the sizes I mentioned."

I contemplated her words, but still had no idea what they meant. "Can I see the difference in sizes? I have no idea how big or small that is."

"Of course, let's go in the back."

She led me toward a private office in the back, the ring I picked out coming with us in a small white paper bag. "Please sit." she motioned to the black leather chair, and I sat down.

Elizabeth unfolded a black velvet ring holder and gently placed the diamond ring inside before unfolding another small envelope and pouring out three diamonds. She arranged them flawlessly on the velvet with her tweezers.

I sat back and admired them. "OK, I think she'd hate the four-carat one. That thing is enormous and would take up her entire hand."

I released a long breath, wanting to choose the right ring at the right size. I pulled at my shirt to relieve the pressure that raced through me. "What size do you like best with that band?"

"Honestly I think the three carats is divine. And the band itself is gorgeous. They complement each other beautifully."

I nodded in agreement. "I think you're right. Let's go with the three carats."

"Great!" She smiled. "One more question. Do you want this particular diamond, or would you like me to look for a better one?"

"What do you think?"

"Honestly?" She placed a black contraption against her eye as she examined the diamond. "I think it's a beautiful diamond. I don't see any inclusions, scratches, or marks in it."

"So it's not a piece of crap, right?"

She laughed uncomfortably, clearly stunned by my language. "No, sir. Definitely not. We don't carry any crap in our store."

"Great. Then I'll take it."

Strength

Cassie

I told Melissa I didn't want to talk on the drive back from LAX. I leaned my head against her car's passenger window and closed my eyes part of the time, and watched the palm trees fly by the rest. When I walked through the door of our old apartment, relief filtered through every weight-induced crack in my bones. The pressure I endured living in New York had become such a constant companion that I'd stopped being aware of the heaviness that bore down on me.

I looked over my shoulder at Melissa and took a long, deep breath, filling my lungs before virtually crumpling on the couch.

"Can we talk now?" she asked, tossing me a bottle of water from the fridge.

I stared at her, wanting to confess everything, but not really knowing where to start. "It's just a relief to be away from everything and everyone. I had no idea how stressed out I was until I wasn't there. You know?" I buried my head in my hands.

"I have something for you," Melissa smiled before disappearing into her room.

My eyes crinkled as I wondered what she could possibly have for me. She didn't even know I was flying out before last night. She reappeared with a small, red mesh bag in her hand and sat down next to me.

"I was going to mail it to you, but now I don't have to. Open it," her bright blue eyes danced as she watched me.

I pulled at the satin strings and poured the contents of the tiny bag into my hand. A brass ball chain holding an old silver key appeared. Confused, but still liking the concept, I eyed my best friend, "It's cool. Did you get one for you too?"

She rolled her eyes before grabbing the key out of my opened hand and turning it over. "Read it."

I inspected the tiny letters stamped onto the top, holding it close to my eyes. It read, STRENGTH. I smiled, pulling my head through the open space of the necklace without unlatching it. I watched the key fall between my breasts and loved that I would be able to hide it under my clothing if I wanted to. "This is really awesome. Thank you."

"There's a story that goes along with it," she started and I turned my attention toward her. "So I bought you this particular word because I think with everything going on in your life right now, you could use the extra STRENGTH. But there will come a day when you'll see someone who will need your key and your word more than you do. And when that day comes, you have to pay it forward and give your necklace to them."

My breath hitched. "So I have to give it away?" I asked, rubbing my thumb along the gift I wasn't ready to part with just yet.

"Yep. That's the whole concept behind these necklaces. That we give them away at some point. When someone needs your word more than you," she reached for the key, touching it briefly before letting it go. "But not right now. You need it right now."

I inhaled sharply before exhaling. "This is really cool. I mean, all of it. The necklace. The word. Giving it away. The whole concept and idea. I love it. Thank you so much." I leaned into her and squeezed as much as I could without getting up.

"I knew you would. And you're welcome. So, are you going to tell me what's going on? You didn't fly out here at the last minute for no reason."

My smile dropped as my bottom lip jutted out in a pout. "Stop trying to psychoanalyze me."

"No way!" She shook her head. "That's what I'm good at. Plus, I like pointing out all your broken parts," she added with a smile.

"So you can be thankful it's not you?"

"Bitch! No. So I can help fix you." She nudged against me. "What did Jack say about the article?"

"Not much, really. I think he's just worried."

"We're all worried." She placed her head on my shoulder, and I leaned against it.

There were two quick knocks on the door before it opened and Dean burst through. "You told him I was here?" I whispered to Melissa.

"No," she whispered in response.

"Sis. What's going on?" Dean practically sprinted to me. I loved it when he called me that, even though it wasn't official.

"How'd you know I was here," I asked, before he snatched me up from the couch into a bear hug. I missed Dean and seeing him forced me to realize just how much.

"Jack called me, out of his mind. Told me to go check on you and make sure you were OK. He said he thinks you broke up with him. Is that true?" Dean's voice was filled with disbelief.

"What? You did what?" Melissa asked through her surprise.

"I don't know what I did. I just left and told him I didn't know if I could do this anymore."

"Jesus, Cassie! Are you trying to fucking kill the guy?" Melissa shook her head. "After everything the two of you have been through?"

"Why is it always about Jack and how my decisions affect him? Why isn't it ever about me and what all of this bullshit does to me?" I broke down, the tears spilling out as I leaned back onto the couch.

Dean dropped onto the other side of me, wrapping his arms around me, "I don't want you guys to break up."

"I'm a fucking wreck on the inside. Can't you see that?" I looked at him before looking away. I hated disappointing Dean. "Chrystle's stupid article pushed me over the edge. I can't take another picture of me with 'home wrecker' or 'man-stealing slut' written across it." I buried my head in my hands, pressing my palms against my eyes.

"What does any of that have to do with Jack, though? I mean, really?" Melissa's forehead creased.

"It has everything to do with Jack!" I shouted, throwing my hands up in the air. "I'm only dealing with all of this because I'm dating him. This keeps happening to me because I'm his girlfriend."

"So if you two weren't together, then no one would post stuff about you?" she asked.

I breathed out a loud, annoyed breath. "Obviously! They wouldn't care about me if I wasn't with him."

Melissa's hand rested on my thigh. "Well, then. You should definitely let these strangers dictate your love life."

"Don't be a jerk." I narrowed my eyes.

"I'm not. I honestly can't believe I'm sitting here listening to this. You would walk away from Jack just to stop some stupid gossip?"

I shook my head. "You don't know how it feels. I know it probably seems like I shouldn't care, or I should let it roll off my back, but people read those things and they believe them without question. They shout mean things to me all the time at Jack's games. New York might be a big city, but it feels really small sometimes. Everything that gets posted, I have to deal with. Not anyone else. Me." I pointed at my chest. "And it sucks."

Dean reached for my shoulder. "Cassie, leaving Jack isn't the answer."

I shrugged. "All the harassment would stop."

"Do you honestly think you'd be OK *not* being with him?" Dean pleaded, his voice becoming more agitated.

"I don't know, but I'm not OK right now and I'm with him."

Melissa cleared her throat. "You know you're not a real person to them."

"A real person to whom?"

"The people that post on those websites, they don't know you. They don't know anything about you. It's really easy for people to talk shit about someone they don't know. Especially when it's someone they think they'll never see in real life."

I'd never been one of those types to write nasty things online about people I didn't know. Did I read gossip sites and watch shows about celebrities? Of course I did. But I always remembered there were two sides to every story, and I never trusted what was reported. Melissa's mom instilled that in both of us from a young age. Occupational hazard, she called it.

I sniffed, wiping away a tear as Meli continued. "You know this. You've just never been at the receiving end of it like this before. Last year was bad, but it was nothing like this. It's horrible and hurtful, but people do it because they can. They hide behind a computer screen where no one else can see them. They aren't held accountable for their words. They can type them, press enter, and walk away."

"But I read those words and they stay with me. When someone takes a picture of me at lunch eating a burger with a caption that says, 'Maybe she should lay off the burgers' . . ." I looked down at my thighs before staring ahead at the wall.

"I know. We grew up out here, surrounded by celebrity rumors and paparazzi and all the craziness. You know that people enjoy tearing other people down. They get off on seeing you fall apart," Melissa added with a snarl.

"I've never understood that. Why do people love seeing other people in pain?"

"I don't know. Because people are petty, shallow, and jealous? Because they think they want what you have and when it's not so glamorous, they're happy it's not all it's cracked up to be?"

Dean sighed and I directed my glossy gaze at him. "It's mostly girls, you know."

"Mostly girls what?" Melissa shot back, her tone defensive.

"It's mostly girls who read those magazines, watch those shows, and post on those websites. You girls love taking each other down a notch."

I nodded in agreement. "It's so true. You're absolutely right."

"Well, that's never gonna change." Melissa rolled her eyes and exhaled loudly. "Girls are competitive bitches."

"But why? Why are we like that? I mean, if all those people who talked shit actually got to know me, I'm pretty sure they'd like me." I looked between Melissa and Dean, longing for reassurance.

Melissa grabbed me by both of my shoulders. "That's what I'm trying to tell you! They don't know you. And they never will. You're someone they see on TV, or in a magazine, online, or at a game even. You're not someone who has dinner at their house on Sunday night!"

"So you're saying I should start planning dinners with strangers?" I choked back a laugh.

"Bitch. I'm saying that these people suck. They suck. Not you. And you're punishing Jack for what these people are doing to you."

"She's right, Sis," Dean added with a smile. "People always posted things about Jack on Facebook and online and stuff. They were mostly lies, but Jack never read any of it. So it never affected him."

"I tried to stop reading it all. Then this stupid Chrystle thing came out." I turned to Melissa. "How can she say all these things, anyway? They're outright lies."

"It's not like it's a reputable magazine. It's a trashy tabloid. They're sort of known for printing half truths." Melissa tilted her head.

"Can I sue her for defamation of character or slander? Something . . ." I pondered out loud, before propping my feet up on the coffee table.

"It wouldn't be worth your time and effort. In those kinds of cases, you have to prove that you were affected by her story. You would have to prove that your character was defamed, by say, a loss of job or income due to the things she said." She stopped to take a drink of water. "Same thing with slander. You have to prove that her statements were made maliciously to cause you harm. And you have to prove the harm it actually caused."

I dropped my head back against the couch pillows. "I swear she knows all this before she does it. It's the same shit she did to Jack with the annulment, knowing he would have to prove her claims were false."

Dean made a quick sound of disgust. "I'm convinced that little bitch knows exactly what she's doing before she does it."

I yawned, covering my mouth with my hand before wiping at my tired eyes. "I'm so tired. Dean, can I come over and see Gran and Gramps tomorrow?"

"You'd better. They know you're here."

We all stood up at the same time, and I hugged Dean tight, thankful he stopped by, before walking into my old room. I looked around at the empty walls; the memories still existed within the confines of this space, even if the mementos didn't. The front door closed and Melissa knocked softly before opening my door.

"Do you miss living here?"

I smiled. "I miss you."

"Duh." Her face crinkled with pleasure.

I moved to sit on the bed and patted the empty spot next to me. "So, tell me what the freaking deal is with you two." I nodded my head in the direction of the door Dean just exited. Melissa shrugged her shoulders and I leaned into her. "I know you like him. Why are you torturing him?"

"Who said I like him?"

"I can tell you like him. What I can't figure out is why you won't tell him that."

"I don't know," she admitted before changing the subject. "But I do know that you're taking your frustrations out on the one person who would literally do anything for you. Breaking up with Jack won't fix you or make you better. It will only break you more. And you know it. So stop pretending like you don't."

"Nice subject change."

She hopped off the bed, leaving me with her words before blowing a kiss into the air and closing the door behind her. *Brat.* I hated how well she knew me.

◇

I woke up the next morning feeling refreshed. I couldn't remember ever sleeping so soundly. I rolled over and reached for my cell phone when I realized it wasn't near me. I'd turned it off before I left New York and hadn't turned it back on. *No wonder I slept so well.*

Normally I'd search frantically for my phone, but I decided it was nice to be disconnected and left it turned off in my purse. After brushing my teeth, I walked into the living room. Melissa was sitting on the couch, watching TV. "Morning."

She clicked it off before turning to face me. "Morning. Hungry?"

"Starved," I admitted. I couldn't remember the last time I ate anything, and I hadn't been hungry at all last night. But now my empty stomach growled and twisted.

She chuckled before standing up and making her way into the kitchen. "Well, I only have cereal and toast. That's gonna have to do." She popped her head out from behind the cabinets. "Unless you want to go out to eat?"

"No, thanks. Cereal and toast is perfect."

"Go sit down. I'll get it." Melissa shooed me away with her hand, and I made my way to the table.

"You know what I think the worst part about all of this is?" I watched as my tiny best friend balanced bowls, milk, and cereal boxes in her arms.

"That you're an emotional mess who thinks her life would be better off without Jack Fucking Carter in it?" She cocked an eyebrow in my direction, and I frowned.

"No. Smartass." I took a deep breath before finishing my thought. "It's that I'm supposed to stay quiet. While people post all these things and say whatever they want about me and Jack, I'm not supposed to defend myself. And I hate the way that feels because I feel like I'm being bullied in a way, you know?"

"You are kind of being bullied," she agreed, setting everything on the table before plopping two pieces of bread into the toaster.

"So I feel like by keeping my mouth shut, I'm telling all these people that it's OK to do the things they're doing. Like my silence condones their behavior. It doesn't feel right to keep quiet. It should be OK for me to stand up for myself." I poured cereal into my bowl until it overflowed onto the table. I picked up the scattered pieces and popped them into my mouth.

"That's why people in your situation normally have a PR person, or a publicist, or a lawyer on their side. Those people speak out on your behalf. Which brings me to something I want to talk to you about anyway."

"What?"

"As your personal publicist, it's my job to—"

I laughed, mocking her tone. "As my personal publicist?"

Her lips narrowed, her eyes squinting. "Give me a break, Cass. If you ever hired someone else to handle your PR, I'd disown you. And so would my mom. I can handle this for you."

Melissa worked at her mom's publicity firm in the summers and would join the staff full time as soon as she had her degree in hand. I asked Melissa when we were still in high school why she bothered applying to colleges when she could learn everything she needed to by working with her mom directly. But Meli's mom insisted she have the college experience and wouldn't let her start working at seventeen. I remembered her saying, "You have the rest of your life to work, Melissa. Don't be in such a hurry to get it started. Go live. Have fun. Enjoy college and everything that comes with it."

I leaned my elbows on the table. "Go on."

"Well, I was thinking," she started.

"Always dangerous," I interrupted.

"Stop interrupting me! This is serious, Cass! I'm trying to help you!" she shouted, her annoyance clearly growing.

I puckered my lips, stifling a chuckle, "I'm sorry. Go on. I won't say anything." I marked an *X* across my chest with my finger.

She breathed out. "OK. So I was thought about this all night and I think it's brilliant! You and Jack should do some sort of interview together. Like a human-interest story on what it's like being a professional athlete and for you, what it's like dating one. And you can address all the Chrystle accusations and lies, as well."

"Meli, people who lose their house in a flood, or an entire community wiped out by some freak super storm . . . that's a human-interest story. Not the girl whining about how hard it is to date an athlete and how mean people are. They'll only hate me more."

"Not if it's done right." Her bright blue eyes looked into mine, her eyebrows raised.

I shook my head wildly. "We're not a human-interest story."

"But you are. Those tabloids wouldn't sell if people weren't interested. And trust me, they're interested."

My chest tightened. "You think people would care about our side of the story?"

"Hell yes, they'd care! But the story will have two purposes. The first will be to put that little lying bitch in her place. And the second will be your public image."

"My public image?" I tried to follow, but I was confused.

"If people see you as a real person, with problems just like they have, then maybe they'll stop being so mean. If they hear about all the things you and Jack have gone through as a couple, they'll sympathize with you instead of hate you. You won't be someone who's unattainable and only seen from a distance. You'll be relatable. It's hard to hate the girl you'd be friends with if you knew her." She smiled, quoting my feelings from last night.

"I don't know if we're even allowed to do something like that. I'd have to get permission from the team's publicity department first. And who the hell would even want to run a story like that?"

Melissa rolled her eyes, my question apparently stupid. "Right now? I bet I could get almost anyone to run that story. But you work for a freaking magazine, Cassie! A human-interest magazine," she reminded me pointedly.

"But those aren't the types of stories we print."

"You mean to tell me your magazine doesn't ever profile anyone local? Don't you ever do puff type pieces on New York's elite?"

I pursed my lips together before responding. "Actually they do. But it's online only and never in the actual printed version."

A wide grin appeared on Melissa's face as her hands clapped together. "That's fine. Online can be just as effective. Think your boss will go for it?"

I shrugged. "Yeah, I do, actually. She mentioned something about it before I left. But I need to talk to Jack first."

"He's an easy sell. He'll do anything if it means keeping you happy."

Love Makes A Life Worth Living

Cassie

fter almost an hour of arguing, I convinced Melissa to drive me over to Gran and Gramps's house. I still didn't know why, but she still wanted to keep her distance from Dean, and meeting Gran and Gramps was not part of her master plan.

"Can we stop by the store real quick so I can pick up some wine?"

"Yep. I'll get some too. I'll need it," she suggested, pulling into the supermarket parking lot.

I looked around at how spread out and spacious everything seemed. New York was so compact. I'd forgotten how different Southern California was. And I really missed the palm trees. My heart squeezed as I took in the sight of them.

"You coming?" I asked Meli before shutting the car door.

"I'm coming, I'm coming." She typed out a text before throwing her phone into her glove compartment.

After grabbing two bottles of wine and a small flower arrangement, we headed toward the checkout stand. Pictures of Chrystle and Jack's wedding suddenly appeared in my vision as the tabloid sat in the wire rack, mocking me. My heart pounded, and I couldn't step forward; my legs trembled forcefully.

And then another sight caught my eye. More pictures of Jack and Chrystle, feeding cake to each other and posing with their bridal party. "Melissa," I tried to squeak out, but all sounds failed me.

"Oh shit. Cass. Cassie?"

I turned to face her, my body numb and eyes already tearing up. She scooted our items up on the conveyer belt. "We'll take these, thanks."

"Can I see some ID?" the clerk asked, and Melissa thankfully pulled her license from her wallet.

I stared at the newer, more mainstream magazine in horror. Chrystle had sold her story to not only one magazine, but two. What else had she done? "Do you want to grab that?" Melissa asked through my shock.

I managed to shake my head when the clerk said, "Do you know him? Jack Carter? He used to live here, but he plays for the Mets now. Can you believe all the stuff him and his new girlfriend did to that poor girl? It's crazy. I guess fame makes you do horrible stuff."

I turned to face her, multiple emotions running through me like a fucking tornado. She gasped as she noticed my face, her mouth twisting into a slight snarl. "Oh my gosh. You're her! Jack's girlfriend, Cassie. Right?" Her eyes narrowed with accusation.

I opened my mouth to say God knows what when Melissa rescued me. "What? Cassie lives in New York with Jack. Why the hell would she be here?" She grabbed the receipt, stuffing it in the bag before tugging me by the wrist toward the door.

"Jesus, Cassie."

I snapped out of my wedding-photo daze. "Sorry." I apologized, although I wasn't quite sure what for.

"No." Meli shook her head. "That was brutal."

"Welcome to my life." I extended my hands with a shrug.

My mind raced with thoughts about Chrystle and thoughts about Jack, and how even all the way across the country I couldn't get away from the media nightmare I now lived in. I wanted to focus on being happy right now, excited to see Gran and Gramps. I let those thoughts take over.

"You'll love Gran and Gramps, Meli. They're awesome." I looked at her, a large fake smile plastered on my face.

"I don't want to love them," she responded without even a glance.

"What the hell is wrong with you? After we fix me, we really need to do some work on your dysfunctional ass."

That garnered a glance. A nasty, wicked one. She pulled her car up to the curb and I hopped out, excited to see the family waiting inside for me. Dean popped his head out from behind the screen door, his eyes meeting mine. I widened mine, and he figured out what I was trying to convey and bolted through the door and to the side of our car.

"I'm glad you came, Melissa." He smiled at her, grabbing the bag from the store.

"You've only been trying to get me here for months." She turned a pointed glare at me.

What the hell?

"Cassie?" Gran's voice spilled out from an open window.

"Is the kitten here already?" Gramps voice quickly followed.

I arched my eyebrows at Dean. "*The* kitten?" I asked with a laugh.

"Don't ask. He started calling you that after you moved. We think it's funny, so we never correct him."

Dean opened the door for us, and as I stepped inside my heart immediately filled with love. Nothing had changed since my last visit, except for the three new black-and-white photographs on the wall.

Melissa pointed at them. "Cass, you took these, right?"

"Yeah," I answered with a small smile before tossing a quick glance at Dean. I turned my head, noticing one additional new portrait. It was taken the day Jack signed to play for the Diamondbacks. Five people were in the photo, and I was one of them.

"You're practically family already," Melissa said as she glanced at the picture.

If a heart could grow in size, mine enlarged on the spot. I'd been more at home here with this family than with the one I was supposed to call my own.

Grabbing the bag from Dean, I started walking toward the kitchen.

"I'll show you around the house." Dean grabbed Melissa by the hand, leaving me alone.

Gran and Gramps sat at the table, drinking out of coffee mugs. Gran scooted out of her chair and shuffled toward me, her arms outstretched. "Oh, Cassie. It's so good to see you. We miss you." She kissed the side of my cheek and hugged me as tightly as her frail arms could.

"I miss you too. Here, I brought these." I pulled out the flowers and the wine.

"The kitten is here!" Gramps practically shouted before wrapping his burly arms around me, the smell of tobacco lingering on his clothes.

I breathed him in, the scent reminding me of being here with Jack. "Gramps! I miss you the most. Don't tell Gran," I whisper-shouted near his ear.

"I heard that!" Gran yelled out from the sink where she worked on arranging the flowers in a vase.

"Come sit," Gramps said as he plopped back into his chair.

"Should we open the wine?" Gran asked, still arranging the flowers.

"I'm OK. We brought those bottles for you guys to enjoy with dinner. Save them." I winked at Gramps, and he grinned.

Gran placed her hand on my shoulder as she passed me to sit down. She sipped from her mug before eyeing me. "So, dear, how is everything?"

My smile faded quicker than I intended. "It's good. Everything's good," I lied, as the realization that being around Jack's family without Jack was harder than I anticipated. I missed him. And I knew I couldn't get anything past Gran.

Gran reached out a hand, touching my fingers gently. "We saw that dreadful magazine. Why won't she just go away?"

"I don't know, but I've wondered the same thing."

"Jack said you're having a hard time dealing with it all. Tell us what's going on." Gran had a way of making you talk about the things you wanted to avoid.

I looked into Gramps's tired eyes, the worry lines around them increasing. "He's right. I'm just having a hard time dealing with all the press and the Internet sites."

"Why? What do they say?" Gramps asked through his confusion.

"Just a bunch of mean stuff about how I'm not hot enough for Jack. I'm too fat. They take my picture and basically say whatever they want about it. They just make things up. And now with the whole Chrystle thing, I feel like I can't take it anymore."

"Cassie, you know how much we love you, right?" Gran asked, and I nodded. "It broke our hearts what Jack did to you. We were so disappointed and sad. But to know that you've taken him back after everything, we can't tell you how happy that makes us." She reached out to squeeze Gramps's hand.

"The press sounds dreadful. Truly awful. And I can't begin to imagine what it must be like to deal with that on a daily basis. But, dear, one day, all of that will fade away. The press, the Internet, the websites, Chrystle," she paused, "they will all be things of the past."

She leaned forward, cupping my face in her hand. "I know you can live your life without all of those things, but can you really live your life without Jack?"

They already knew the answer as I blinked back the tears. "I think I'd be miserable without him."

"Because you love him," Gramps called out, joy animating his voice.

"Of course I love him."

"Then don't give up. One day you'll look around and realize that all the things you thought mattered so much, really didn't matter much at all." Gran eyed Gramps, the love between them apparent. "What matters the most is who you love. Because when everything else is a distant memory, the people you love are all that's left. And love is the single most important thing we can do in our lives. Give it. Receive it. Teach others how to do it."

My eyes filled with tears again. "Love is the most important thing? Above everything else?"

"Absolutely," Gramps said with a crooked smile. "It's funny the things you think will last forever when you're young. I figured I'd work until I died. But even work stops at some point. And you find yourself looking around, taking stock of your life, and you realize that you don't give a shit about where you worked, or what you did to bring in money, but you care about the lives you touched. The love you shared. The family you created. You care about who is standing beside you when the shit hits the fan."

Gran swatted at Gramps twice, presumably for each time he cursed, but missed. "It's true," she said. "The older you get, the more you realize that it isn't about the material things, or pride or ego. It's about our hearts and who they beat for. I know your heart beats for Jack in the same way that his heart beats for you. I don't think one can survive without the other. Do you?"

I wiped at the tears rolling down my cheeks, their words striking a chord inside my soul. How could I ever think I'd be OK without Jack in my life? I might be able to distract myself for a little while, but eventually I would realize that my heart lay vacant and cold. "No. I'd be miserable without him."

"Then you have to figure out a way to let all the other stuff go. You have to let Jack carry some of the load for you. If you keep things from him, he can't help."

Gramps raised his hand before quickly adding, "I know you ladies like to think that we can read your minds, but we can't. We don't know anything that's going on in those heads of yours unless you tell us."

I nodded. "I know you're right. It's just easier said than done right now."

Gran didn't miss a beat. "If you quit on Jack, you're giving everyone what they want. Chrystle wins. And I would hate to see her win at anything." Her eyes narrowed. "But you and Jack would be the real losers because you'd lose each other. People spend their whole lives searching for the kind of love that the two of you share. That's what life is all about."

Gramps chimed in, "Love is life. If you miss out on love, you miss out on life."

Melissa and Dean shuffled into the kitchen, goofy smiles on both their faces. "Gran, Gramps, this is Cassie's best friend, Melissa." Dean beamed with pride as he introduced her to his family.

Gramps grinned. "Hi, Melissa. You're just as pretty as the kitten," he said with a wink, and Melissa couldn't help but smile even wider.

"It's nice to meet you." Gran extended her hand before glancing in my direction and whispering, "This one's going to need a little work on the Dean front, isn't she?" I nodded, wondering how the hell Gran seemed to instinctively know everything.

After a couple hours of polite conversation and Gran force-feeding us sandwiches, Melissa and I said good-bye. Dean stood on the porch with a pout on his face as he watched us leave. She begged him for some time alone with me, but he claimed he wanted to spend time with me too. They compromised on girl time tonight and Dean time tomorrow. I laughed at their conversation.

"You like them, don't you?" I asked Melissa as she lowered the car radio.

"They are pretty great. How was your alone time with them? Dean insisted we let you guys talk by yourselves." She sounded slightly annoyed by Dean's suggestion.

"I appreciated it," I admitted, hoping to relieve her irritation. "They're so awesome. They always seem to know just what to say and how to say it."

"What did they say this time?" she asked, her eyes focused directly in front of her.

"They talked about the importance of love. And how in the end, it's all that really matters, and it's all you have left when everything else is gone."

"They sound almost as smart as I am," she said, and I smacked her shoulder with the back of my hand. "Hey!"

I watched as we passed the restaurant where Jack and I had our first date, the quick jolts of pain to my heart reminding me how much I missed him.

"So, did they fix you?"

"I still need to figure out how to find some balance, but all of you are right. Breaking up with Jack won't solve anything in the long run. I'd regret it eventually, and I'd probably never get over it."

"You know, Cass, Jack isn't the only one who changed. I mean, you changed him. But he changed you too. Whether you realize it or not, it's the truth."

Hearing Melissa say those words solidified what I'd known for some time. She'd told me the same thing back in college, but it seemed to carry more weight now. I felt like I'd grown up twenty years in the span of the last two.

"You're right. I honestly can't imagine my life without him. And I don't want to."

"Then you need to stop running away from him when things get rough. You do that a lot, and eventually he's going to get pissed."

"I don't run away," I sniped defensively.

"Really? You left the state! You're either running away or shutting him out completely. And both of those things suck."

I watched the palm trees blur into green streaks across the sky blue backdrop. Melissa was right. "I'll work on it." I'd bottled so many of my emotions inside because I didn't want to burden Jack with them. And I needed to learn how to clear my head with Jack in the picture instead of pushing him out of it.

Melissa's phone started to ring. "Can you see who it is?"

I grabbed for the phone and noticed Jack's name flashing across the screen. "It's Jack."

"Speak of the devil. Answer it."

My stomach dropped to the floor. "Hi," I answered nervously.

"Where's your phone?" Jack's voice was tight and agitated.

"I left it in the apartment. Why? What's wrong?"

"Check it as soon as you get back and then you fucking tell me," he said tersely.

"Jack? Hello?" I pulled the phone from my ear to look at the screen. "Holy shit, he hung up on me."

"What's going on?" Melissa sounded worried.

"I have no idea. He told me to check my phone." My head started to spin as I wondered what the hell could have happened.

Don't

Jack

My cell phone beeped, signaling I had a new text message. Instead of a return phone number, the sender was an anonymous e-mail. I considered not opening the message, knowing that nothing good could come from an anonymous source. After a short battle with myself, I clicked the message and a picture popped up.

What the fuck?

Matteo kissing Cassie displayed on my screen and violent urges instantly ripped through my guts. My temper flared as a fire blazed through my every pore. I wanted to tear Matteo's fucking head off. How dare he put his lips on my girl? How dare he fucking even think about touching her?

But she let him. She wasn't pushing him away in the picture, she was kissing him back. Fuck, even her goddamn eyes were closed!

I dialed Cassie's number, but it went straight to voice mail. Again. Where the hell was she? I forwarded the picture message to her cell.

She'd bailed on me in the middle of all the Chrystle drama and now this. How would she explain this? I looked at it, clear as day with my own two eyes. Matteo's filthy fucking lips stuck to my beautiful Kitten's. Have I been fooled this whole time?

I walked into our bedroom and pulled out the velvet ring box I'd buried in my sock drawer. It creaked as I opened it to peer at the shiny diamond inside. How could she do this to me? To us? Shaking my head, I squeezed my eyes closed before opening them again. The image of Matteo kissing Cassie plagued my every thought.

I snapped the box shut and pitched it forcefully through the opened closet door. It crashed against something with a loud thud, and I walked out of our room not caring what happened to the contents.

Maybe it was all an elaborate ploy, her inability to handle the press? How long had she and Matteo been sneaking around behind my back? Had I forced them together by asking him to keep her safe during my games? Was this all my fault? I wondered how long I had until the media got ahold of that picture. With my luck, it was already posted everywhere.

I dialed Melissa's cell phone, determined to reach Cassie. I listened as it rang three times. Cassie answered, and she sounded nervous when she said hi. I asked where her phone was, unable to hide my anger. Her voice rose, and she actually sounded confused and worried when she told me she left it at Melissa's apartment and asked what was wrong.

"Check it as soon as you get back and then you fucking tell me," I said and ended the call. I didn't want to hear another word out of her mouth until she looked at the same picture I had. I waited. And grew more agitated with each passing minute. The press was already having a field day with all of Chrystle's accusations, now they'd have even more to talk shit about.

On top of it all, now I needed to find a new driver. Matteo's work here was finished. No matter what the story, I didn't want to see his face anywhere near mine again.

I paced our apartment, my anger growing as my patience wore thin. Half tempted to call Melissa again, my phone suddenly rang. I answered the call, but said nothing.

"Jack? Are you there? It's not what it looks like, I swear." She pleaded through the phone, and I found myself surprised at my lack of sympathy.

"So, he didn't kiss you? 'Cause it looks like he's kissing you."

She hesitated. "Yes, he kissed me, but . . ."

I cut her off. "How long?"

"How long, what?" she asked, her breathing shaky.

"How long has this been going on?"

She inhaled sharply. "What? Nothing is going on, Jack, I swear. There's nothing between me and Matteo. He kissed me, and I pushed him away."

"It doesn't look like you're pushing him away in this picture. Did you like it? His lips on yours. Looks like you might like it."

"I pushed him off of me, Jack! I told him no! I told him I loved you." She started to cry.

It tugged at my chest, the sound of her crying, but I pretended not to care. "Why didn't you tell me about the kiss?"

"Because we haven't even talked. Because it meant nothing. He apologized. He was scared to death of losing his job with us."

"He should be. 'Cause I'm either going to fire him or fucking kill him." *Or both.* "You know what, Cass, I don't blame another guy for falling for you. I don't. But you . . . I never expected this from you, of all people. I feel like I don't even know you."

"Don't say that, Jack. Of course you know me. I love you. I'll come home tomorrow. We'll fix this. I'll tell you everything."

"Don't." I stopped her rant.

"Don't what? Don't come home?" She sounded like she couldn't believe what I said.

"I don't want to see you," I admitted, my guts feeling like they had just been shredded.

"What? Don't do this. Jack, please," she begged.

I leaned against the granite countertop, thoughts racing, emotions clashing. I was pissed off. I'd worked so hard to break down this girl's walls, but no matter what I did, it was never good enough. She always ended up blocking me out, and I didn't deserve it.

"This is bullshit, Cassie! I haven't done anything since I came back into your life except try to be a better man for you. I try every single day to do right by you. It's all I want, to be good enough. To make up for the mistake I made. I'd do anything for you."

My frustrations mounted as I vented. "But you walk around here constantly keeping shit from me. And when things finally get to be too much for you, what do you do? You run away. I know you're used to being let down and disappointed, but we're supposed to be a team. We hold each other up when the other one's about to fall. We don't run away and leave our other half to fend for him or herself."

She stayed quiet, clearly having no defense for her actions, so I continued. "You left me here to deal with Chrystle and her shit all alone. I know you're hurt and angry, but I am too. Did you even once stop to think about how I felt? How her article affected me and made me look? No. Because you left me here and took off."

"I'm sorry. I'm so sorry," she said with a sob.

"Yeah? For which part?" I asked, and could hear her sobbing in the background.

"I'm sorry for all of it, Jack. You're right. I don't deal with things well and I promise I'll work on it."

I exhaled through my nose as I stared out the balcony window. "It's more than that. You keep things inside and . . ."

"Because I don't want to bother you with stuff I think is stupid. I don't want you to worry about things when you're on the field. You have enough to worry about."

"You don't get to decide what's stupid and what isn't. If it's bothering you, then you need to tell me. You need to communicate with me. I fucking tell you everything. I share everything with you because I don't ever want there to be another secret between us again. I don't like keeping things from you, and I don't appreciate you keeping things from me."

"I don't know what to say other than I'm sorry. I know I'm not good at being an open book, but I'll try to be better."

"And I know I let you down before and you don't trust me completely. But this goes beyond that, and I think we both know it." She sniffed, and her breath hitched repeatedly as I continued. "After tonight's game, we'll be on the road for few days. I think we should take this time to figure out what we both want."

"I know what I want," she insisted.

"I don't," I lied. Of course I wanted Cassie, but I was hurt. I lost her trust in one terrible decision-making moment, but she lost pieces of mine every time she shut me out, kept me at distance, or didn't care enough about our relationship to stay put and fight. I wanted to know we were solid, but her actions only confused me.

"OK," she said with hurt in her voice. "I'll do anything to fix this, Jack. Tell me what you need me to do."

I took a long, deep breath. It was finally my turn.

"Prove it," I said before ending the call. Now she would know how it felt to be on the other end of that fucking request.

I immediately dialed the car service where Matteo worked and asked for the owner. "Hi, Mr. Lombardi, Jack Carter here. I need to cancel all services with Matteo and request a new driver starting today."

"Of course, Mr. Carter. Did Matteo do something wrong?"

The media would inform him soon enough, if he didn't know already. "I just want a new driver. Do not send Matteo here today or I'll lose my shit. Do you understand?"

He cleared his throat. "I, uh . . . understand."

"Thank you."

"Do you still require the driver to stay for the duration of the games?"

"No, I do not."

I pressed End on my cell and typed out a text message to Matteo for good measure.

You're fired. Don't show your face here again and stay the fuck away from Cassie.

I tossed my phone down, not expecting a response when it beeped right back.

Jack, I'm really sorry. Can I come there and talk to you?

I cracked my neck from side to side, the idea of seeing Matteo igniting the flames of my temper.

Not a good idea, man. Not right now.

It will take 2 seconds. Please. I know you want to kill me. Let me explain.

Explain? Explain how his lips touched my girlfriend's? What the hell was there to explain? Maybe he wanted me to kick his ass? I glanced at the clock on the wall. I had time.

Fine. But don't say I didn't warn you.

My body tensed all over as the image of him kissing Cassie burned into my mind. Within minutes, he knocked on my door. I hesitated, knowing that if I started hitting him, I wasn't sure I'd be able to stop.

I opened the door, the dejected look on his face almost made me feel sorry for him. *Almost.* I clenched my hands, balling them into fists as my mind raced. I stepped back from the door, not wanting to be near him. I didn't invite him in.

"Jack, I'm really sorry. There's no excuse for my behavior. It's just that she looked so sad and so distraught that it killed me to see her like that. I just wanted her to be happy. My emotions took over, and I got all jumbled up inside."

He had feelings for her.

I glared at him, willing myself to stay calm as he continued. "I feel horrible and I know you can never forgive me, but you need to know that Cassie stopped me. She shoved me away and put me in my place."

Good girl.

"I never meant to disrespect you or your relationship. Somewhere along the way of looking out for her at the games, my feelings got involved. But she doesn't have any feelings for me. She made that completely clear. I know you'll never forgive me, but I hope you'll forgive her."

I don't know why, but that kindhearted comment set me off. "Don't tell me what to do with her. She's none of your business."

His expression tightened. "You're right. I just wanted to apologize to you and tell you what happened. I really am sorry Jack."

I swallowed my pride. And then I almost choked on it. I couldn't blame him for caring about her when that's exactly what I'd asked him to do. No wonder the lines got blurred. He protected her so often that he didn't know how to turn that part off. "I understand how your feelings for her grew." The tension between his brows lessened slightly. "I don't forgive you right now for kissing her. But maybe in time I will."

He nodded. "Thank you. That means a lot." He turned to leave.

"Matteo," I called out. "Thanks for coming by."

A real man owned up to his mistakes and confronted them. Even when I warned him not to come here, he still insisted. It was hard not to respect that kind of integrity. Not to mention the fact that I liked Matteo. Maybe I could grow to like him again. Maybe.

Game Changer

Cassie

I sat on the floor staring at my cell phone as Melissa practically danced around me. "What the hell is going on?" I pulled up the photograph of Matteo kissing me on my phone and held it up to her face. "Oh shit. When the hell did he kiss you?"

"The night he drove me to the airport." I shook my head, wondering how I was going to fix this.

"Why didn't you tell me?"

"I forgot," I admitted.

"You forgot?" she asked incredulously.

"I was so caught up in everything else that I completely blocked it out. It wasn't important. I shoved him off me and told him I loved Jack. End of story."

"End of story?" She shook her head, her fingers tapping along the base of her hip. "Shit, Cassie. This is bad."

I glanced up at her. "I know."

"How pissed is Jack?

"Pretty pissed. But he's mad about other stuff too. He basically said that we're supposed to be a team, but I'm not being a team player."

"You have to fix this," Melissa demanded, as if telling me something I didn't already know.

"I'm aware. Get this." I paused to look her straight in the eyes. "He told me to *prove it.*"

A sharp laugh ripped out of Melissa's mouth before she tossed her hand in front of it. "Sorry," she mumbled from behind her hand. "But that's some ironic shit, right there."

"Tell me about it." I rolled my eyes.

Melissa sat down next to me on the floor, our legs pressing together. "First things first, you have to fire Matteo. I mean, you should do it so Jack knows you're serious."

"I'm pretty sure Jack fired him the minute he hung up on me. But if he didn't, I will." I leaned my head against the wall. "Do you think I should call Matteo and make him go over there? He needs to tell Jack that I didn't do anything. He created this mess!"

Melissa shook her head, "I don't know. Jack might turn it all around on you and get pissed that you reached out to the guy. Plus, I wouldn't really send Matteo over to talk to Jack right now. Unless you want to go his funeral later."

I sighed, my fingers shaking as I reached for my phone to type out a text message.

You have to tell Jack I didn't do anything. You have to fix this.

"Who are you texting? Matteo?" She cocked her head to the side, her lips pursed together in a disapproving gesture. "Do you not listen to a word I say?"

I shrugged as my phone beeped.

Already got it covered. I'm so sorry.

"Well," she tapped her finger against her hand impatiently, "what'd he say?"

I moved the screen of my cell in her direction and waited for her to read his brief response. There was nothing more I wanted to say to Matteo, so I placed my phone on the floor.

"I hope you enjoyed knowing the guy."

"This sucks. And all of it could have been avoided if I'd just stayed put and actually talked to Jack instead of running away."

"Don't beat yourself up, Cass. You needed to get out of that scene. It took you all of two seconds of being away from Jack to realize you couldn't live without him."

"Do you think this picture's in the tabloids already?"

"Absolutely."

"Fuck."

"So we have Chrystle's crazy allegations," she held up one finger, "and a picture of you and Matteo kissing," a second finger joined the first, "and photos of you leaving the apartment with a suitcase when Jack has games at home."

"Looks bad, right?"

She twisted her mouth. "It doesn't look good. But you need to worry about Jack first and everyone else after. I'll reach out to your boss and talk to her about my ideas for the human-interest story on you and Jack. I'll fill her in on all the details she needs to know about Chrystle, and I'll work Matteo in there too. You said she's cool, right?"

"She's phenomenal. And she wants to help, so I think she'll welcome any ideas you have. You might want to word it that you heard she wanted to run this story so she thinks the whole thing was her idea," I suggested with a smirk.

"Couldn't hurt."

"But what if Jack says no to the interview? I mean, what if he doesn't forgive me?"

She slammed her palms against the tile floor. "If he doesn't forgive you, I'll fly out there and personally kick him in the nuts! After everything you've forgiven him for, he can absolutely get the fuck over this."

"What if he doesn't?" Nervous butterflies flapped their wings in my stomach. I hated being on this side of things. It was so much easier being the one who was mad. It sucked being the one someone was mad at.

"He may be a stubborn asshole, Cass. But he loves you. He will forgive you and get past this. He might murder Matteo, but I think we all expect that."

"Even Matteo expects that." I laughed.

"So, when are you leaving?"

I stared straight ahead at the photographs covering the walls, wondering how the hell she knew me so well. "Tomorrow."

"Will Jack be there?"

"No. He'll be on the road."

"Well, that gives you a little time to get yourself together and prove it." She nudged my shoulder with hers. "Although I do think taking back the little cheating liar proved plenty, but what the hell do I know?"

"You know a lot, and I love you. What would I do without you?"

She faced me, her bright blue eyes shining. "You'd be lost forever, searching for me." She laughed. "It's been nice being here and not being online, right?"

I breathed deeply, not realizing the truth before she asked. "Between that and having my phone off, it's been way less stressful." I cocked my head to the side. "I mean, it was before the whole Matteo kissing thing."

"Just remember when you get back, no gossip sites. We're still not reading them."

"Not reading them, check," I wholeheartedly agreed.

She held her pinky out in the space between us and I wrapped my pinky around it.

◇

I stepped into the terminal at JFK and turned on my phone. I scrolled to Matteo's number, and, since I could never use him for a ride again, especially now, I deleted it. Hopefully this would help prove to Jack that the dreaded kiss truly meant nothing to me. I wouldn't talk to Matteo again for the rest of my life, and that was fine with me.

After getting my suitcase, I waited in line for a cab, and once inside, I started to feel sick. Being back in New York after spending time in LA was like being in a different universe. My life appeared so different depending on which state I was in. I couldn't hide in New York. And even though there were a hundred times more photographers in Southern California, it seemed easier to get lost there. Or maybe I simply knew the hiding places better?

We pulled up to my apartment building where three paparazzi waited outside. They had to know Jack and I were both out of town, so why were they here? I tried to be nonchalant, but they recognized me right away as I pulled my suitcase from the trunk.

"Where's your boyfriend, Cassie?"

"How long have you been cheating on Jack?"

"Why isn't Matteo driving you?"

"Where have you been?"

"Did you really make Jack leave Chrystle?"

"Did you go away with Matteo?"

Back in the middle of hell, I lowered my head and walked through the revolving door, resisting the urge to scream in their faces. I kept my back to the cameras while I waited for the elevator doors to open and swallow me whole.

Walking through our front door, I noticed the mess Jack left. Dirty dishes sat in the sink. Maybe he didn't think I'd come home so soon? Or did he think I wouldn't come home at all? I cringed inwardly at my thoughts and cleaned up the mess. I wanted to text Jack that I made it back, but remembered that he'd asked me to leave him alone. I hated being in our home without him.

I couldn't win. I hated being in LA without him. I hated being here without him. It was time for me to stop holding Jack accountable for things he didn't do. And if I truly didn't want to live my life without him in it, I needed to act accordingly. Be strong and trust that he was tough enough to deal with my emotional baggage. My choosing to keep things from him only placed a heavier burden on my shoulders. And Jack never asked me to do that. That was a choice I made to make things easier on Jack, but in the end, it only made me resentful.

I spent the next couple of days on the phone with both Melissa and Nora, working out the potential details for the magazine article. Nora was thrilled to help but made it clear there was a need for the story, especially now. She pressed me to firm up a date as soon as possible, insisting that the longer we waited to speak out, the more potential things had to escalate. I promised her that I'd ask Jack as soon as he came home, and then hoped he'd still speak to me. Melissa and Nora were also up to something, I sensed it, but neither would admit a thing.

◇

I was restless the entire day Jack was due to come home. Pacing while I waited, I practically held my breath for him to walk through the door. A bottle of wine called out to me while I paced, so I stopped and poured myself a glass. I desperately needed to ease the tension running through me.

I stepped outside on the balcony and leaned on the railing, the summer heat beating down on my bare shoulders. Lights switched on and buildings lit up from the inside out as I sipped my wine, watching the city come alive. This city held its own kind of magic. You just had to know where to look.

The front door slammed shut, and I whipped around to see Jack standing in the entryway staring at me. I wanted to leap into his muscular arms, but resisted and just walked slowly back inside. He looked so damn good in his travel attire of black slacks and a white collared shirt with a black tie. I was tempted to rip his clothes from his body and throw them in a pile on the floor.

"Hey." He nodded curtly in my direction, his voice devoid of any emotion.

"Hi," I answered softly, terrified that this could be the end.

"When'd you get back?" He glanced around at the kitchen and the living room.

"A couple days ago."

He dropped his bag at his feet and opened the fridge. Pulling out a beer, he twisted the top off before taking a long swig.

"Jack, listen," I started, unable to wait any longer before working things out between us.

His eyes widened as he moved to our kitchen table. Pulling out a seat, he plopped down. "I'm all ears."

"I am so sorry for everything. I should have told you about the kiss the second it happened, but I just wanted to forget it. And I'm sorry for running out on you without even giving you a chance to talk. I've realized that I really suck at talking things out, and I promise you that I'm going to work on it. If you'll let me, I mean."

My chest tightened as I looked at him, trying to gauge his reaction before I continued. "Leaving you here all alone to deal with the fallout of Chrystle's article was wrong of me. You were right when you said I didn't take your feelings into consideration." I averted my eyes briefly before looking back at him. "I didn't even think about how you felt. I only thought about myself. And I'm so embarrassed to even admit that to you, but it's the truth."

I took two short, steadying breaths. "Jack, I know I'm not perfect, but I'm really hoping you're not ready to give up on me yet. I don't have gifts or love letters or anything like you had. But what I can give you is my word, my promise, my vow to you. Which I will back up with actions, by the way." I forced a slight smile and thought I saw his expression soften.

"I promise to stand by you and not run away when things get tough," I told him solemnly. "I promise to always talk to you about the things that are bothering me, no matter how stupid and insignificant I think they are. I promise to be a better team player. Because there isn't a game on earth I want to play if you're not by my side."

My eyes filled with tears as my emotions overwhelmed me. "I love you. I don't want to be anywhere without you. You told me once that I was your game changer, but the thing is, you're mine too. It took me a little time to realize that, but I finally did. You're my game changer. Because nothing else matters if you're not with me."

Jack pushed back from his chair and walked over to me. "I love you, Kitten."

I stood up and pulled me to him, crushing my chest against his. We squeezed each other like we'd never touched before, all space disappearing between us. "I'm so sorry, Jack. I know I'm a pain in the ass."

He nodded. "Yeah, but you're my pain in the ass."

"Do you forgive me?" I pressed my wet face against his shirt.

"Of course, I forgive you." He tilted my head up and pressed his lips against mine.

"There's more," I pulled back from the kiss.

"More what?" he asked.

I hesitated, nervous that he might hate the idea. Jack had always been a private person, and I wasn't convinced he'd be willing to invite the public into our personal space. "I want to fix everything. I want people to stop hating us and believing the things they read and think they see. The magazine said they would be willing to interview us. They'd call it a local human-interest story, but it really would be our way of setting the record straight. Nora and Melissa both think this will help our public image. Especially in light of Chrystle's accusations and the Matteo picture, but they want to do it as soon as possible."

"Do we get to throw Chrystle under the bus?"

"Every step of the way. We can address whatever we want. Nora said we would have a lot of creative control, but she'd make sure we came out on top. What do you think?"

"Let's do it."

"Really?" I thought he would argue more, or be more concerned.

"Really. I think this is the best way for people to hear the truth. And since it's the magazine you work for, I trust it will be done right."

"Me too."

"So you set it up, and I'll be there."

"Your next day off is Monday. Can we do it then?"

"I'm all yours."

"I'm excited for people to learn about the real us. Maybe they'll stop being so judgmental," I said hopefully.

"Who cares? Is it time for make-up sex yet?" He bit his bottom lip suggestively, and I instantly craved every inch of his skin on mine.

"Absolutely." I leaped into his waiting arms, desperately pressing my lips against his.

"Don't forget your quarters," he teased.

I Can't Believe I Did That

Cassie

I hopped out of bed Monday morning filled with anticipation. The interview was supposed to take place here in our apartment, but Nora asked to see us in the office first. The request was a bit unusual, but since she was doing us this huge favor, I agreed. Not to mention the fact that I still was getting paid time off.

Tossing my long hair into a ponytail, I stared at the bags under my eyes before dabbing some concealer on them. I hurried through the rest of my makeup routine as Jack hopped into the shower.

"Do we have a new driver, or should I just call us a cab?" I cringed at bringing up the whole Matteo and driver situation.

"I never hired a new person. I've just been using random drivers."

"So, do you want to call the car company or grab a taxi?" I pressed my lips together to spread my lipstick.

"Whatever you want. I don't really care."

I frowned to my reflection at Jack's apparent indifference. "We'll just take a cab." I finished getting ready as Jack got dressed and disappeared into the living area. I hated how it took him absolutely no time to look gorgeous.

By the time I got ready, I caught Jack reading online, a sour look spread across his face. I crept up behind him and tossed my arms around his shoulders before looking on the computer screen. A nasty article titled a "Home-Wrecking Floozy" was on the screen. Obviously, it was about me.

He shook his head, his hand reaching up to grab mine. "I'm so sorry, Kitten. I had no idea these were the kinds of things people were saying about you."

I leaned down and kissed his cheek. "It's not your fault, babe."

"Yes, it is. This whole thing is my fault. No wonder you flipped out. This shit is horrible."

I shrugged. "None of that matters. It's all lies anyway, and we both know it."

"You really don't care?"

"I care about how you feel about me. Not a bunch of people I don't know. At least I'm trying not to care what they think," I admitted honestly.

◇

I pulled Jack by the hand into the magazine offices. He had never been up there before. "Where's your desk?" he whispered as my co-workers turned to eye us before saying hi and excitedly introducing themselves to Jack. I spotted Joey in the kitchen, hanging back and looking clearly uncomfortable, and I offered him a slight smile. He smiled back but stayed put.

I pointed toward the far wall. "Over there. I'll show you after."

I rapped on Nora's oversized door. "Come in," she called out.

We closed the door behind us. Nora stood up and came around her desk to introduce herself to Jack. "It's nice to finally meet you."

"You too. I've heard a lot of great things," Jack said respectfully, and I was impressed.

"So, I know we were supposed to shoot the puff piece today," she began, and my heart raced.

Supposed?

"But this just came up, and I wanted you to be the first to read it." She handed us each a copy of our magazine with a cover photograph of a girl I didn't recognize.

"That's Vanessa," Jack said as he opened the magazine and flipped to the article.

"Chrystle's best friend, Vanessa?" I asked and he nodded.

"Read the interview. I think you'll find it quite illuminating," Nora insisted.

I skimmed through it before my jaw dropped and I was forced to stop. "Holy shit, Jack. Do you see the part where Vanessa says that Chrystle planned this whole thing from day one?"

I read directly from the magazine copy:

"Chrystle knew every player who got drafted and had the potential to eventually play on our team. She researched Jack and learned everything about him before he even played here. She was obsessed. She knew he was raised by his grandparents, that he had a younger brother, a girlfriend, what kind of car he drove. She found out his parents weren't in his life, and she said no one could live through that unscathed. Chrystle believed that everyone had a weakness and she was convinced she'd just stumbled upon Jack's. When I mentioned that he had a girlfriend, she didn't care. Unless Jack moved to Alabama *with* his girlfriend, Chrystle considered him fair game."

My stomach turned. "Jesus, Jack." I looked at him, his eyes still scanning the magazine in his hands.

"And the minute Jack arrived, sans girlfriend, she put her plan in motion. She practically stalked him, waiting for the opportunity to seduce him. She knew where he lived and who he lived with. Some nights she would wait outside their apartment in case they all went out somewhere. She wanted to follow them and make it look like a coincidence when they all showed up at the same place. She was relentless. I feel like Jack didn't stand a chance against her. He had no idea what he was up against because most normal people aren't that manipulative and determined. She wasn't going to stop until she had what she wanted. And what she wanted was Jack."

The interviewer of the magazine asked, "Why? Why Jack?" And Vanessa responded:

"Because he was going to make it all the way to the major leagues and she knew it. Anyone who watched him play and knew anything about baseball knew it. Most of the guys on the team would never get that far, and she once said that she refused to be saddled with any of them. That they were all just loser head cases waiting to happen. She wanted the money, the celebrity, and the lifestyle that went along with being the wife of a major league ballplayer. It really is as simple as that."

Reading all of Vanessa's words horrified me. Anger, sadness, and pain all raced through my body. I wanted to go back in time and protect Jack from this nightmare ever unfolding. No one deserved to be treated this way.

I reached out my hand, placing it on Jack's thigh as he turned to me, shaking his head. "Unbelievable."

Nora clapped her hands together and leaned her chin against them. "The rest of the interview basically talks about how she faked the pregnancy, the miscarriage, and then how she dragged out the annulment."

"Oh, I want to read the part about the faked pregnancy," I said a little too enthusiastically. I scanned the questions and answers, searching for it.

"She got a local doctor to go along with her plans by basically framing him. She told him that she knew he had an affair in the past and she threatened to tell his wife if he didn't help her. She claimed to have proof and numerous witnesses. The poor guy was terrified of losing his family so he did whatever she asked. He falsified paperwork and prescriptions for her. She came home from that first doctor's visit with a confirmation of pregnancy, a due date, a calendar, prenatal and extra iron pills, and a chart that showed the baby's growth in terms of weeks. Anything from the doctor's office looked completely legit. There's no way Jack would have known she was lying. None of us did."

"She is really a piece of work, that girl," I breathed out.

Nora leaned over and tapped the magazine meaningfully. "All in all, the article paints an extremely unflattering picture of this Chrystle person and makes you and Jack out to be the victims, without looking stupid."

I nodded. "So, with Vanessa's interview, ours would sort of be redundant?"

"I believe so. My suggestion is that we wait and see how this plays out. I can't imagine there will be any more questions after people read this interview, but it might not hurt for the two of you to make a joint statement." She tapped two of her fingers along the side of her jaw. "Maybe we do a more upbeat article and photo spread on your new apartment, your lives, how happy you two are here in New York. More like a public image, life, and style piece. But there's no rush."

I smiled. "I like that. I think it's a good idea."

Jack barely smiled, possibly still in shock over everything Vanessa's article revealed. "I do have one question, if you don't mind, Nora?" Jack asked.

"Of course."

"How did you get in touch with Vanessa?"

My eyes grew wide as I realized I hadn't even thought about that. Nora smiled and looked at me. "This one's best friend."

I narrowed my gaze. "Melissa?"

"She's a little firecracker that one," she breathed out. "I think she got Vanessa's phone number from Jack."

Jack tilted his head back in recollection. "She did ask me for her number. But that was months ago. After the annulment."

"She did? That's weird," I said.

"I swear she told me she wanted to thank her. Knowing her, she probably did."

Nora spoke up. "Well, she passed along Vanessa's contact information to me and I was prepared to reach out to her when Melissa let me know I didn't need to. She said that she had spoken to Vanessa, and she was only too obliged to give us an interview for the magazine. Apparently the poor girl has been sick over Chrystle's publicity stunts and Melissa convinced her to talk to us."

"She's the only reason Chrystle signed the annulment papers. Otherwise, I'd probably still be technically married to her." Jack winced, giving my hand a quick squeeze.

"She's come through for us twice now," I said.

"So as I mentioned, there's no need for us to do the interview we had intended. We'll schedule the upbeat piece for later, and this article will run in both the online and print versions starting Wednesday." Nora smiled. "You can keep those copies. I'll see you in the office tomorrow, Cassie?"

"I'll be here. Thank you so much." I stood and walked over to her desk to give her a hug.

Nora straightened her jacket and skirt when I released her. "It's nothing. Just good business." She tried not to smile.

Jack reached across her desk to shake her hand. "We really appreciate everything you've done for us."

Her face softened. "You're welcome. Now, go win some games."

◇

I hated to admit that I was relieved about the tell-all interview being canceled. I would have gladly done it, but part of me was thankful we didn't have to. All the same information was going to come out, but it didn't come from me or Jack. I assumed there would be fewer accusations that way.

Once we were in the back of the taxi, Jack threw his arm around me and asked, "How do you feel?"

"I'm relieved we don't have to do that kind of interview. I'm angry at hearing all those things, and I'm sad that it all happened. But I'm happy that it's all going to be over soon." I leaned my head against his shoulder as he pulled me close against him. "How do you feel?"

"I'm pissed off at reading all that shit. I'm mad at her for being crazy. I'm mad at me for being stupid. I just want it all behind us once and for all."

"Soon," I promised.

While Jack paid the fare, I exited the cab and headed into the lobby of our apartment building. My legs almost folded on me when I saw a familiar petite brunette at the front desk talking to our concierge. I bolted through the revolving door, ignoring our doorman as my insides raged. She turned toward me, and I screamed,

"What the fuck are you doing in here? Antonio, she's not allowed in here. She's not welcome."

"Oh look," Chrystle said in her honeyed accent. "It's Cassie, the home wrecker."

"Why don't you go back to Whore Island already? What are you doing here?" I screeched at the last person on earth I wanted to see.

She placed her hand on her hip and leaned toward me. "Did you know that people will pay thousands of dollars for a juicy gossip story? They don't even really check their facts anymore."

My hands balled in and out of fists as she smiled at me triumphantly. "The truth will come out soon enough, and then everyone will know what a lying, psychotic bitch you are," I spat out.

"I don't think so. People love little ol' me. I'm just a victim in all of this and they feel so sorry for me."

"I think you overestimate your ability to deceive."

"It's gotten me this far, hasn't it? And it got your boyfriend to marry me. Remember that?" Her mouth twisted into a wicked grin as she pointed in Jack's direction.

I swallowed the lump in my throat and pulled my arm back. With as much forward motion as I could muster, I slapped her wretched, conniving, evil face. The sound echoed through the lobby as she gasped, a red handprint outlined across her cheek.

"You bitch!" She glanced outside, where I hadn't noticed a lone photographer standing before. Flashes of light bounced off the windowpanes.

She set this up.

I refused to be her victim any longer. "Next time it won't be a slap. Don't come near me again and stay the fuck away from Jack."

Adrenaline made my heartbeat thump in my ears as Jack suddenly appeared at my side. "What the hell are you doing here?" he shouted at the unwanted trash.

"Oh, Jack!" she whined. "Your girlfriend just hit me. Do something!"

He puffed out his chest, looking down at her. "I'll hold your ass in place if she wants to do it again. Now get the fuck out of my apartment building, you stupid bitch."

She gasped, her face scrunched in horror. "You'll regret that. Both of you. You just wait," she threatened as she shuffled in her high heels toward the door.

"Are you OK?" Jack's voice turned caring and concerned.

I released a quick breath, still shaking from my actions. My hand vibrated and pulsed from the impact. "I can't believe I did that."

He smiled. "I can't believe I missed it!"

"Oh, don't worry. Someone was taking pictures, so I'm sure you'll see it soon enough." I gestured toward the photographer trying to keep up with Chrystle, and Jack bolted out the door.

I watched him shout until the photographer slowed down. Jack pulled him aside and talked to him, while Chrystle looked on from a short distance away. Jack smiled and then jogged back in to our building.

"What did you say to him?"

Jack smiled. "I told him that it would be in his best interest to not publish those photos. Chrystle was a stalker, I was filing a restraining order against her today, and everything that comes out of her mouth is a lie. And I mentioned that if he published anything that further damaged your reputation, I'd hunt him down and shove that camera so far up his ass he'd need a doctor to remove it."

"Um, babe." I shook my head, knowing full well that threats don't work on paparazzi types.

"Then I bought the pictures from him and demanded exclusivity. If they show up anywhere, I'll sue him. Looks like I will get to see you hitting her after all." He kissed the top of my head and turned toward Antonio, who looked confused and unsure what to do. "That woman is a stalker. I'll be filing a restraining order against her this afternoon. Please see to it that she does not come in here again."

"Yes, sir," Antonio responded.

Jack joined me at the waiting elevator, and I whispered, "Are you really getting a restraining order?"

"She's stalking me, she threatened us, and I think she's unstable," he said with a smile.

"She's definitely something, alright." I leaned up to plant a kiss on his cheek before pulling out my phone.

I typed out a quick text to Melissa:

Thank you for getting Vanessa to do the story. It's unbelievable. You're unbelievable! :) PS. Chrystle was just here. In our building. And I slapped her! LOL

Melissa responded immediately.

You did? THAT FUCKING ROCKS! HAHA I heard she was in NY trying to shop around a potential book idea. As soon as the article hits, she'll be dead in the water. No one will touch her. And you're welcome. Vanessa was scared at first, but she really pulled through.

I quickly typed back:

Yeah, she did. If you talk to her again, which I'm sure you will because you're like that . . . please tell her I said thank you.

"Are you texting Melissa?"

I looked up at Jack. "Yeah."

"Tell her I said thank you."

"I will."

A Proposal

Cassie

T hings changed once the article came out with all of Vanessa's revelations. The public's desire to know everything didn't ease up, but at least Jack and I were no longer viewed as the bad guys. Melissa told me that the online message boards were filled with comments about how much I must have loved Jack to forgive him for everything, and how strong we must be as a couple to have endured it all and still be together. True to my word, I hadn't been online to read any of it since the night I broke down. And Melissa had been right, I did feel better. I guess sometimes ignorance is bliss.

I also attended Jack's games without the fear of being ridiculed or mocked . . . unless he lost, then the fans were still unforgiving. Even a few of the mean wives commented about the article and what a horrible thing happened to me and Jack. They still didn't go out of their way to talk to me, but at least they acknowledged my existence. Which I'll admit was hard at times, considering I knew what some of their husbands were doing behind their backs.

Work got busier for me, and I was assigned to my first on-location shoot after a tornado practically destroyed an entire town in the Midwest. It was harder than I imagined, shooting the devastation and witnessing people's pain up close and in person. My heart literally ached with each shot I captured.

Sometimes I questioned if what I was doing held true value. And I wondered how I was any better than the paparazzi, invading people's personal space for the sake of a photograph.

But when one of my photos was chosen to solicit donations and another was used to focus on rebuilding the town, my fears were eased. I convinced myself that my pictures did good and helped bring to light the true devastation, so others could see it and be called to help.

◇

I walked the short distance from the subway station to our apartment, excited to see Jack. His team had an afternoon playoff game that day and I didn't attend partly because I knew Jack wouldn't be pitching and I was also under a deadline at work. It was embarrassing how excited I got at the idea of coming home to Jack. He wasn't normally home before I was, and I liked walking through the door and into his waiting arms. I looked up at our apartment building, the shadow casting halfway across the street, and grinned. I allowed myself to get lost in the sounds of the traffic rushing past me, finding comfort in their constant accompaniment.

When I opened the front door, a familiar smell hit me, and I struggled to place it. "What are you cooking?" I shouted into the apartment with a smile.

Jack peered around the kitchen wall at me. "You won't believe what I got Gran to do," he said with a laugh.

"That's where I know that smell from! That's Gran's sauce!" I raced into the kitchen, reaching for a spoon before dipping it into the saucepan on the stove. I blew on it lightly before tasting it. "Oh my God. So good. Did you make it?"

Jack wrapped his arms around my waist. "I had her freeze some sauce and then overnight it to us. She's been freaking out the whole time."

"That is awesome." I dipped my spoon in again and Jack swatted my hand.

"Get outta there. Wait for dinner."

I turned to eye him. "What are you up to, mister?"

"Nothing." He let out a breath. "Can't a guy just cook dinner for his girlfriend?"

"Sure." I nodded. "Can I do anything?" I glanced around, noticing a vase of red roses on the table.

"Nope." He smiled and kissed me on the cheek.

◇

Jack

I wanted to do this right. That's why I reached out to her father and asked for his blessing days ago.

I knew I didn't have to do that. Cassie would have insisted it wasn't necessary, but Gran would probably have me killed if she found out I hadn't. I figured it was the right thing to do, which should have pointed me in the opposite direction given my past, but I followed my gut anyway.

The phone rang as my heart thumped in my ears. "Hello," a soft voice answered.

"Mrs. Andrews?"

"Yes."

"Hi, it's Jack Carter. I was wondering if your husband was home, and if I could speak to him," I asked as politely as I could.

"Oh hi, Jack. Is everything OK? Is Cassie alright?" she asked nervously.

"Cassie's fine. Everything is OK."

"Oh, OK. That's good to hear. Hold on a second and I'll grab her father."

"Thank you," I exhaled, wanting to get this over with as soon as possible.

The phone clanked on the other end and a male throat cleared. "Hello? Jack?"

"Hi, Mr. Andrews. How are you, sir?" I hated being respectful when he'd let Cassie down so many times over the years.

"I can't complain. What can I do for you?"

"Well, sir," I stalled, clearing my throat before continuing. "First of all, I want you to know how much I love your daughter. She's the most amazing person I've ever met in my life."

"Uh-huh," he said.

I knew I was supposed to ask for permission to marry his daughter, but I didn't want it. And I knew damn well I wouldn't need it. He couldn't stop me from marrying her if he tried. So I worded it a different way. "I just wanted you to know that I plan on asking her to marry me, and I wanted to ask for your blessing."

"Do you think she'll say yes?"

What the hell kind of question was that? I gripped my hair with my free hand. "Yes sir, I do."

"Well, alright then!" he said happily into the receiver. "You have my blessing."

"Thank you." I smiled, and hearing shouting in the background I asked, "May I speak to your wife again quickly?"

"Oh sure, sure. Congrats! And let us know what we can do. We'll pay for anything you need and handle anything you kids want."

I hesitated before realizing that he'd never follow through on those offers. Cassie was right about how easy it was to get sucked in by his charisma and enthusiasm.

"Jack? Tell me you asked him what I think you asked him!"

I laughed into the phone. "I did."

She squealed with delight. "When are you asking her?"

"I'm not sure, so please don't say anything to her if you two talk."

"I won't say a word. We'll wait for her to call us with the big news!"

I exhaled with relief. "Great, thanks. I'll talk to you later, OK?"

"Alright, Jack. And hey." She paused before continuing in a hushed tone. "Thank you for calling. I know you didn't have to, but it was nice that you did."

I smiled to myself, finally convinced that I'd actually done the right thing for once.

◇

Nerves rarely raced through my body, but they were having a field day as I waited to pop the question. I loved this girl more than anything in the world and we'd been through a lot.

I longed to make this girl my wife, and I hated sitting here at dinner, waiting to ask. Why couldn't I just ask her now, while her mouth was filled with pasta? Should I get down on one knee? I wondered if she sensed what was coming. I'd never cooked dinner for her before and here I just went all Gourmet Chef on her ass.

What if she says no?

She won't say no.
Fuck.
She'd better not say no.

◇

Cassie

After dinner, Jack carried all the dishes into the kitchen and loaded them into the washer. He refused to let me help at all. I stared out the window at the skyline. I really did love living in New York.

Suddenly, Jack was kneeling next to my chair. As he placed my hand in his and started speaking, my heart began to race. "I don't know any other couple who has been to hell and back more than the two of us. I feel like everything we've been through has only made us stronger. We've had to learn to work together. To be a team. To support each other and stand by each other."

I started to shake. Nervous energy consumed me, and I could barely hear half the words he said. My brain started to spin, and I couldn't concentrate on anything other than the fact that Jack was kneeling next to me.

◇

Jack

Her eyes glazed over, and knowing Cass the way I do, I wasn't sure she could even hear me anymore, but I kept talking. "I promise to stand by you, to hold you up when you're about to fall, and to always keep you safe. I never believed there was a girl out there for me. Until I met you. You changed everything. And I never want to live without you. I love you more than I ever thought possible."

I closed my eyes before taking a deep breath. All my confidence wavered in this moment as I realized Cassie held my future in the palm of her hands.

"Kitten. Be my wife. Marry me." I opened the black velvet Tiffany's ring box.

◇

Cassie

Seeing the diamond inside caused me to gasp. It sparkled and danced in the light. The center diamond was huge and was surrounded by smaller diamonds. It looked too pretty to touch.

"Kitten?" Jack's voice cut through my sparkle coma as I realized I hadn't answered him yet.

My gaze moved to meet his. "Yes. Of course I'll marry you. Who the hell else would I marry?" I smiled, still not reaching for the gorgeous ring.

He grinned and his dimples appeared as he reached inside the box and pulled out the ring. I held out my left hand, and he pushed that gorgeous piece of jewelry into place. My eyes were transfixed on the diamonds lighting up my finger. "It's huge," I said breathlessly.

"You don't like it? We can take it back."

I pulled my hand away from his, clutching it against my chest. "No way. It's amazing."

"We're going to be very happy."

"I already am."

Epilogue

Jack

I stood at the end of a makeshift aisle in Gran and Gramps's lush backyard. It had been transformed into a light-filled wonderland. Every tree, bush, and branch was covered with tiny bright white lights. I waited underneath the large tree where lanterns flickering with candlelight hung from the branches. Oversized Mason jars were lined up in two rows, forming the aisle, and each jar was filled with a few inches of quarters to hold up the white candle burning inside. I glanced at the few round tables decorated all in white and smiled. My eyes grazed past my old teammates from Fullton State, Melissa's parents, Cassie's parents, Gran, Nora, and, finally, Matteo and Trina, who started dating pretty soon after Trina and Kyle broke up. I found myself smiling at our group of friends and family filling the small space, excited to share our intimate moment with us.

I loved the fact that Kitten and I shared the same views when it came to today. Thankfully, neither one of us needed a large formal wedding to mark the special occasion. Although in all honesty, I would have given her anything she wanted, we both craved the privacy and security that only our close friends and family could provide. So we opted for a more casual setting and dress code. I looked down at my charcoal gray suit and adjusted my black tie.

Where the hell is Dean?

I smiled at Gran, who was already holding a tissue to her eyes, as I stepped away from the altar. She dropped her hand and asked, "Jack? Where are you going?"

"I'm going to find Dean."

I stormed into the house, trying not to accidentally see Cassie while I looked for my brother, who just happened to disappear minutes before I was supposed to get married. I peered into the empty kitchen. Glancing in the front yard and the living room and finding them empty, I made my way back toward our bedrooms.

Both of our bedroom doors were closed. I knew Cassie was in my room, so I knocked on Dean's before turning the handle. I didn't wait for a response before I opened the door and barged inside.

"Shit. Really?" I eyed my brother, lying on top of a partially clothed Melissa, his tongue down her throat and his hands who knows where.

"Get out, Jack. Jesus," Dean shouted, covering Melissa's body protectively.

"Do you think you two could figure your shit out after the vows? I'd like to get married sometime today," I shouted, my patience wavering.

I slammed the door and knocked on the door to my old bedroom. "Kitten?"

"Don't come in here, Jack!" she yelled, and I laughed.

"I'm not. I just wanted to say I can't wait to see you. Make sure those two actually leave the bedroom, please. Tell them they can fuck after the vows."

"Oh my God," she called out through the door. "Is that where Melissa is? I've been waiting for her to come back for like half an hour!"

"Well you're going to be waiting forever if you don't go drag her out of there. I'll see you soon," I said, leaning my cheek against the door.

With another hasty knock on Dean's door, I yelled, "Today little brother! Let's go!" Since he obviously couldn't be trusted alone with Melissa, I waited for him to come out of his room before I walked back outside. I nudged him as we headed down the aisle toward the tree. "Really couldn't wait until later?" I whispered.

"You kidding me? With her, later might mean never. I gotta take what I can get."

I shook my head. "I do not envy you, brother."

"Yeah?" He gave me a look. "Well, I sure as shit envy you."

"You should," I told him and I meant it.

If I weren't me, I'd envy me. I shifted my weight between my legs as I waited for the best day of my life to begin. People always talk about being nervous on their wedding day, but I wasn't. If any emotion surged through my body, it was excitement. I couldn't wait to make this girl my wife and spend the rest of my life making her smile.

The processional music started and everyone rose to their feet. I stared at the back door as if my life depended on it. Melissa walked out first, a huge smile on her face. I noticed that she locked eyes with Dean and never stopped looking at him her entire walk down the aisle. She wasn't fooling anyone.

All my thoughts disappeared, my mind going blank, the moment I saw Cass in the shadows. When she stepped out of the darkness and into the backyard, my heart jumped from my chest and flew into her hands. She looked so fucking beautiful walking toward me in that strapless white dress. I grinned like an idiot. I know because my cheeks burned, and I couldn't stop the feeling if I tried. Not that I wanted to try.

Her hair was pulled back, revealing her delicate neckline, and my mind raced with dirty thoughts. All the blood rushed from my body and into one place the second I started thinking about all the things I wanted to do to her. Shit, I couldn't get married with a fucking hard-on. Think about something else; think about anything else. Think about baseball.

Fuck.

When she finally arrived at my side, I reached for her hand, caressing it with my thumb as she gave me a subtle squeeze. "You look beautiful," I whispered as I leaned toward her.

"You look hot," she whispered and gave me a little wink.

Gramps cleared his throat, and I glanced up at him. He stood before us with a businesslike expression on his face. After he'd gotten ordained online with Dean's help, Gran told me he took his role in the wedding very seriously. "I have the most important job of all. I have to get it right!" She told me, he said.

Gramps swallowed once before asking, "Shall we begin?" He started reading the first few lines of the ceremony, and I struggled to keep my impatience in check.

I was standing before my family and friends, marrying the only person in the world I've ever wanted to marry. There would be no annulling this marriage. No end to this beginning. No trade for this team.

People spend their lives searching for their one true love, their other half. I found mine in college, dancing in a fraternity house driveway. Lucky for me, she found me right back.

I can't wait until she's knocked up.

Thank You

This will be short and sweet because the truth of the matter is this book was never supposed to exist in the first place. And it's only because of the fierce love that you, my dear readers, felt for Jack F'n Carter, and Cassie, that it does. You wanted! Demanded! Insisted! I write more to their story . . . and here we are. I truly hope you enjoyed it. I appreciate you all so much, and I always want to do right by you. Thank you for supporting me, believing in me, encouraging me, challenging me, and being the best readers a girl could ask for. Don't know what I'd do without you! :)

Thank you to my team: Pam Berehulke, Jane Dystel, Michelle Warren, Carmen Johnson, and Rebecca Friedman. Editing, agenting, and designing wouldn't be the same without any of you.

And to all my family and friends: Life has a funny way of showing you who has your back and who doesn't. Thanks for always having mine.

About the Author

Jenn Sterling is a Southern California native who grew up watching Dodger baseball and playing softball. She has her bachelor's degree in Radio/TV/Film and has worked in the entertainment industry the majority of her life. She loves hearing from her readers and can be found online at:

Blog & Website: http://www.j-sterling.com
Twitter: http://www.twitter.com/RealJSterling
Facebook: http://www.facebook.com/TheRealJSterling

The Mighty Storm and Jake Wethers are copyrights of Samantha Towle. To learn more about Jake and TMS, get a copy of *The Mighty Storm* on Amazon.